The Passenger

by

Joie Lesin

The Passenger

Cover Art by *Kristian Norris*

The Wild Rose Press, Inc.
PO Box 708
Adams Basin, NY 14410-0708
Visit us at www.thewildrosepress.com

Publishing History
First Edition, 2024
Trade Paperback ISBN 978-1-5092-5664-8
Digital ISBN 978-1-5092-5665-5

Previously Published, 2007
Published in the United States of America

Dedication

For my mother, Patricia, who believed in me and my
writing—always my biggest fan.
You embodied for me what it means to be a strong
woman. Whenever I encounter a challenge, I remind
myself whose daughter I am and face it head on.
And for my "brother" Glenn who left us much too soon.
You were my very first memory, my very first friend
and one of my most favorite people.
I miss you both every single day.

Chapter One

Cana, California, Late July 1945

The horn section of the Benny Goodman Orchestra blasted over the airwaves. Giovanni Clemente leaned forward, switched off the radio, and stretched out his stiff knee. The injury not only earned him a Purple Heart, but time recovering in England before his discharge from the army. The ache helped him predict the weather.

A change was certainly in the air.

His mother looked up from her knitting and frowned. "Turn the music back on, Gio," she said in Italian.

"No, listen."

"To what? You shut off the radio. I hear nothing."

"Exactly. The quiet." *No planes, no whistling bombs, no mortar fire, and no man snoring in the foxhole next to me.* He leaned his head back on the leather rim of the armchair. "Did I tell you how glad I am to be home?"

"Only one hundred times." She smiled and set the half-knit blanket in a basket at her feet. "Your Uncle Michael telephoned today while you were out."

He closed his eyes and settled deeper into the chair. "What did he have to say?"

"He invited you to stay in San Francisco while he and your aunt are in Minnesota," she said. "They are traveling to visit your cousin Angela and meet the new

1

baby."

Gio opened his eyes and sat straight.

"After harvest, of course." She nodded. "You'll deserve a holiday. Miriam thinks the ocean view will do you wonders."

"Outside that wall," he said, pointing, "is all I care to see when I wake up in the morning."

She cleared her throat. "There is more than the view."

"Hmm. More than the view," he said under his breath. He knew what she meant. There was always more than the view with his aunt and every other busybody woman who arranged some unwed young woman for him to meet.

Content with his life, he'd make no time for their matchmaking *ever*.

Gio stood, pressing his bare foot into the rug, and braced himself. His anticipation of the painful knee cramp sometimes overshadowed the actual spasm.

"Your Aunt Miriam's niece," his mother said. "The one from San Diego. She will be staying with them. Michael asked if you might escort her about the city while they are away."

"Don't they have a daughter-in-law or two who can entertain this niece?"

"Yes, and I told him asking someone else would be his only course of action. But Gio—"

Sighing, he headed toward the door. "No, *Madre*, I've been away from here for four years. The only thing I need right now, and in the months to come, is work."

He paused before exiting through the doorway, peering over his shoulder at his mother. The hair she'd bound in a tight chignon at the nape of her neck accentuated her youthful, thin face. At fifty-four, she continued to turn men's heads. Adriana Clemente could have picked between any number of husbands, but instead she chose to fill her time with the vineyard and being his mother. She'd done fine without a man to occupy her time and he'd done as well without a father.

With those life lessons firmly ingrained, he'd decided early in life marriage would wait until he was a matured, gray-haired man, and only to produce an heir to the vineyard. All his adulthood, he'd worked hard to avoid anything more than superficial associations with women. Love, or any similar emotion, was not a complication he wanted.

****

The same day in East Boston, twenty-five-year-old Elizabeth Reilly climbed the streetcar steps and deposited her dime. Holding onto the seat handles, she strode to the middle of the car where her sister, Anna, already sat sideways with her legs folded beneath her. Sketchpad open, Anna peered at a new subject.

"Sit back there." Anna pointed over her shoulder to the seat behind her and swept a loose auburn curl behind her ear.

"Fine," Elizabeth said, amused at the nineteen-year-old's authoritative tone, and slumped into the seat. "Don't get too comfortable," Elizabeth said. "We don't have far to go."

Leaning back against the cool metal seat, she let her heavy lids close to the clink of the streetcar gliding over the rail. An image of a vine-filled forest fluttered into place in her mind's eye. Stepping forward, she walked deeper into the maze.

All around Elizabeth, dark green vines climbed an

invisible wall, cutting off the sun's light. Plump, burgundy fruit hung in clusters from the branches. She plucked a single grape and smashed the juicy fruit between her fingers as she brought the berry to her lips.

Shaking her head clear, Elizabeth opened her eyes. The flavor of the sour-sweet fruit was like a lingering phantom on her tongue. The vision struck her sporadically over the last few months and was part of her gift. The ability she'd fought hard to block out at fourteen years old. She opened herself fully again only to receive the spirit of her dead husband, Patrick, four months earlier.

When her husband was on his way to her to say goodbye, she'd sweated through the cries of soldiers falling into the mud around her and the deafening noise of battle.

Don't go there, Elizabeth. You couldn't help him.

She'd known the only help she could provide was to help him pass on in peace.

Elizabeth had expected Patrick's ghost to visit her. For weeks, she braved the early spring chill to await his arrival. Bundled in layers, she waited on the beach for him. Their special place. When he finally came, he met her there. Patrick sat next to her on the blanket he'd given her as a birthday present when they were younger. The one with the purple daffodils. When she thought of his final goodbye, she thought of the daffodils she'd stared down at while he talked—as if the color of the flowers were the most important detail of the day.

Yet the broken dead man who sat beside her was.

Patrick's once handsome face wore sadness like a caul. He'd wished she would remember him as the whole and healthy man who she clung to and kissed before he shipped off to war. When she pictured the delicate purple flowers imprinted on the fabric, she overlooked the bloodied gash in his side where he'd taken the bullet. She no longer saw the torn trousers revealing his damaged skin and jagged, exposed bone. She forgot the matted dirt covering his cheeks like rouge. Instead, she remembered his way of smiling that made her laugh and how he always placed his hand on the small of her back as they walked.

After four years of missing him, she only wished her chance to say farewell to her most precious friend had helped her settle back into her life. Yet she couldn't because she'd outgrown her existence.

Unsettled by her thoughts, Elizabeth shook her head to clear away the memories and locked eyes with a woman. The familiar woman walked down the aisle toward her and quickly looked away. Elizabeth resisted the urge to say, *"Excuse me. Don't we know one another?"* as the woman passed her by.

Instead, Elizabeth frowned to herself and recalled opening the door to the middle-aged, well-dressed blonde who smelled of expensive perfume. She hadn't introduced herself but came seeking help from Dora O'Brien, Elizabeth's mother.

Elizabeth longed to be somewhere where people didn't pretend to not know her. She longed to find a new life where she wasn't the odd woman from the strange family.

Elizabeth secretly hoped the blonde never found the money her late sister had hidden from the family. The ghost refused to give up the information to Elizabeth's mother but spoke of other things Dora refused to repeat.

The smell of onions and sage from a roadside stand

carried in on the still August air through the trolley's windows—attracting Elizabeth's attention. The aroma reminded her of the five-cent frankfurter she'd shared earlier with her sister. Like most things she ate nowadays, the food sat like a rock in the pit of her stomach.

She leaned forward to see what Anna was working on. The girl always left the house prepared with pencil and paper. Elizabeth envied how her sister found the beauty in ordinary things.

With adroit, delicate gestures of charcoal, Anna transformed the white paper into the outline of a face. Enthralled, Elizabeth watched her sister sketch a crooked nose she vaguely recognized.

She looked to the seat across the aisle, and Elizabeth's breath caught. Anna's subject was the man who stood by Elizabeth on the beach the day of Patrick's visit.

The man had been kind to her, standing silently beside Elizabeth on the beach all those months ago as she cried after Patrick had gone. The man hadn't asked questions. He didn't know why she cried but offered his hand and helped her to her feet.

Shifting her attention back to Anna's drawing, she now saw a wrinkled, weathered face, unshaven and sad. Yet the eyes were kind, seeming on the edge of a smile.

Yes, this was the man who kept her company while she dried her tears, but he'd said little. He continued to stand looking out at the horizon as if also watching for someone to arrive. They were kindred spirits and Elizabeth thought of him often, though she'd not seen him again.

A man of Italian descent in his late thirties and

dressed in a light blue seersucker suit passed between them. He stopped, adjusting the newspaper he held tucked under his arm, and turned toward Elizabeth's friend.

"*Buongiorno*, Paolo," the man said. "Are you feeling okay, *signore*?"

"*Si*," Paolo said. "It is this heat."

"Well, take yourself home and sit in front of the fan. Carbone cannot make his elder work in this."

"Ah." Paolo managed to laugh. "Carbone is a good one and would allow me rest," he said. "Still, this is a day of holiday for me. I will take your advice once I reach my room."

The man smiled and nodded but hesitated a moment before he continued down the aisle.

A steady stream of stifling, hot air blew in through the open windows and whipped through Paolo's hair. The dull gray locks, peppered throughout with streaks of blue-black, fluttered in a mess around his head. He gave a low, wheezing breath and mopped his sweaty brow with the back of a black, tattered coat sleeve.

A bizarre chill hovered around Elizabeth. She gathered her arms close to her chest, fighting the freezing energy that seemed to pour from Paolo's body and into hers.

Reacting to this living, breathing man in this way didn't make sense.

Her heartbeat quickened as she leaned forward to look at Anna's drawing again. If Paolo were deceased, no one else would have noticed him—not Anna nor the man who stopped to talk with him.

Paolo wasn't a ghost, but why did she feel as if he were?

She bit her lower lip and slumped back against the seat.

Lord, but how odd.

All the signs were there signaling to her a ghost lingered nearby. Her pensive mood, sitting still was outright painful, and the hairs spiking on her arms and back. All as if this man needed her help to pass from this world to the next. Of course, she'd ignored the dead for so long, letting eleven years pass before lowering her guard and opening herself to her husband.

Eleven years of ignoring those tickles at the back of her mind warning of a dead person's whispers and their pleas for help. Ignoring the brush of a hand as someone walked by her unseen. Wrinkling her nose at the scent of a cigarette when no one near was smoking. Knowing if she let down her guard, she'd open herself to someone she didn't want in.

She shook her head and rubbed her arms. Was she misinterpreting what her senses were communicating to her? Surely, she wasn't feeling Paolo. Perhaps someone else was nearby.

Still, I should speak to him.

Elizabeth wondered if she spoke to him, would he recognize her? She'd changed over the months. Each time she caught a glimpse of herself in the mirror, a thin face and tired eyes stared back at her instead of her once round face and bright eyes. She appeared gaunt, as if a ghost stood behind the glass.

Not wanting to stare, she glanced above his head at the advertisement for brandy. The ad reminded her to drink conservatively just as he gave a sputtered, wheezing breath.

"Excuse me, sir?" Elizabeth leaned into the aisle

toward him. "Are you all right?"

Turning slowly in his seat, he offered her a weak smile. His face looked fatigued, with dark shadows beneath each eye. "*Si. Si*," he answered and exhaled. "I am fine."

"Beth, I didn't realize you knew him," Anna said.

Elizabeth jumped, startled by her sister's voice, and inclined her head slightly toward Paolo. She whispered, "I don't—not really."

Minutes later, the streetcar screeched to a stop. Several passengers exited. Paolo stood on tenuous legs, grabbed the seat in front of him, and stumbled forward.

The poor man. She hated to see him struggling and doubted he'd travel far on his own. Elizabeth rose from her seat.

"Anna, I'm getting off here." She rushed to aid him and asked, "Do you need help?"

"This is kind of you, *Signorina*, but I do not want to put you to trouble."

"It's no trouble." She gently took his elbow. Numbing electricity shot into her fingers, and biting back a gasp, she snatched them away. *Easy, Elizabeth. He's a sick man. Nothing to be frightened of.*

"I'd be happy to escort you." She peeked over her shoulder at Anna. Her sister had collected her belongings and stood waiting to follow behind them.

Elizabeth touched his elbow again.

"*Grazie, Bella, grazie*," the man said and patted her hand with his clammy fingers.

Despite their mismatched heights, Elizabeth being only five-foot-four, Paolo leaned heavily into her. He weighed less than she anticipated, but she hoped her own trembling legs would hold out as they walked down the aisle and descended the three steps off the trolley. She bowed her head and noticed his swollen ankles.

How in the world can he walk?

Together, they climbed down onto the cobblestone sidewalk with Anna at their heels. The metal hinges on the door squeaked as it closed. Behind them, the trolley's wheels engaged, and Elizabeth looked over her shoulder to see the car hustle toward the Court Street Station.

"Beth, where are we taking him?" Anna asked as she reined up beside them.

Elizabeth shrugged and asked, "Sir, is there somewhere we can escort you to?"

"I was on my way to the beach, but I do not think I can make the walk now." He slowed to a halt. "I am so tired."

A businessman dressed in a crisp seersucker suit passed by and stared curiously from her to Paolo. Out of the corner of her eye, Elizabeth saw Anna approach the man and talk with him quietly. He nodded and hurried away.

Elizabeth considered what they looked like, the two of them standing there together. On observation, they didn't match. Paolo was a sight in his tattered jacket, threadbare at the elbows and sleeves. She wore the latest, a petticoat-ruffle dress from the department store on Washington Street. For her and Anna, appearance was important when so many people in their neighborhood considered them pariahs.

Elizabeth guided him toward a large stoop leading up to an office building. "Would you like to sit?"

"*Si.* Yes." He lowered himself to the cement step. Elizabeth settled beside him and smoothed the hem of her dress over her knees. Anna remained standing, nodding warily to the pedestrians, and eyeing the hub-nosed automobiles rolling by unhindered on the busy street.

Elizabeth smiled. "I'm Beth. Elizabeth," she said and gestured to her sister. "And this is Anna."

He smiled, and his crooked nose twitched. "My name is Paolo Clemente." He coughed, grabbing a dingy handkerchief from his breast pocket to cover his mouth. He sighed and rested against the step behind him. "I am an old man, and I am not faring so well."

"Do you have somewhere to go?" Elizabeth timidly touched his arm. "We can take you." She glanced at Anna, who nodded in agreement.

"I will be fine. After a rest, I should be able to find my way home on my own."

Elizabeth doubted he'd be able to walk another foot let alone a block. His face paled to an eerie gray, and his lips settled into a dirty-violet blue.

Her heart sped. Paolo was gravely ill. He struggled more with each breath. They needed to get him away from the busy street, where people stood, watching. "We can contact someone to come and get you, if you'd like." Or the hospital. But she avoided those words, not wanting to frighten him.

"N-no, I live alone. I have a room in the north end. Above the restaurant." He leaned forward and rested his elbows on his knees. "The restaurant Carbone's."

Anna bent toward them, concern spread across her charcoal-smudged face. "Do you have any family?"

"I shall see them soon, I suspect." He clutched at a tarnished locket hanging from a golden chain around his neck.

"Where are they?" Elizabeth asked.

"They are dead. My youngest brother, my wife, my son." He swallowed. "They all died on their way from *Italia* to me." His gaze drifted over Elizabeth, next Anna, his eyes a dull brown beneath unshed tears. "Their ship sank into the ocean."

"My condolences," Elizabeth murmured. How sad to be all alone in the world.

Worry lines furrowed deep in his brow. "It was long ago. I have lived many years without them."

How did one go from having a person who was a constant in their life to the individual being forever gone? When Patrick left for the war in Europe, she held onto the belief he would return home. Would she have been content for Patrick to haunt her? With the loss of her best friend so fresh, Elizabeth didn't understand how her broken heart would heal with the passage of time. What she did recognize was the numbness with which she coped.

"I have missed them," Paolo said, drawing Elizabeth away from her own thoughts.

"It's hard to lose loved ones," she responded.

"*Si.*" He nodded in agreement. "My life was no longer bright after I lost my beautiful Adriana. She was a spitfire. This means a willful woman in English, yes?"

"Yes," Elizabeth said in agreement.

"And my son, Giovanni," he said before giving in to a fit of coughing. When the cough quieted, he drank in a deep breath before he continued. "Giovanni." Frowning, Paolo shook his head. "He was a *bambino*, a baby, when I left *Italia*. So small. He never knew his papa."

"Oh, Paolo." Without thinking, she caressed his wrinkled cheek.

"You are too kind, *Bella*. Few would aid a man such

as me. You would never guess I was once a man of wealth, would you?" His breath caught and released. "I once purchased a vineyard of my own in California." He closed his eyes and slowly opened them. "I was a foolish man. I left everything behind."

He started to rise but let loose an eerie groan. Elizabeth's heart skipped a beat as he slid to the cement.

Anna gave a startled gasp as his body met the ground. Elizabeth lunged beside him and drew his head into her lap.

"What's taking them so long?" Anna asked, frustration clear in the tone of her voice. "Beth," she said. "I'll be back."

Elizabeth looked up as Anna hurried away. The drawing pad grasped tight against her side, she walked with determination.

"I'll stay with you," Elizabeth whispered, turning her attention back to Paolo. "Just hold on. Anna will bring someone back if she has to drag them the whole way."

A small crowd of people gathered to watch Paolo die. People who'd have given him a wide berth if he'd passed them on the street, or ignored him, now invaded his life in this very private moment. She ignored them all, turning her attention back to him.

Elizabeth caressed his rough, whiskered cheek, ashamed she too might have walked past this man without acknowledging him. With a bit of apprehension, she'd have dismissed him as a vagabond, a hobo, but the man once had a family and a life.

He may have once been like her.

Paolo's breath weakened, and his eyes glazed over. "*Grazie*," he whispered, his voice hoarse, before his breathing stopped. His chest stilled, and though his lips did not move, Elizabeth heard him whisper, "Help me, *Bella*. Help me return to my *famiglia*."

She closed her eyes and knew she'd help him—no matter what she needed to do.

Chapter Two

Cana, California, Late August 1945

Elizabeth paced the gravel walkway in front of the Lowell Inn.

Of course, she'd come out too early, but sitting in the room waiting for someone from the Clemente Vineyard to pick her up almost drove her mad. She didn't expect this visit to be any easier for the ghost's family. No, she'd taken Paolo's cousin quite by shock the night before. She'd arrived in Cana without an announcement. From the telephone in her rented room at the inn, she called and asked for Marco Clemente. Relieved when the man answered, she'd let herself relax. The ghost had told her his cousin, Marco, would still be there running the vineyard. Paolo was right. Elizabeth wasn't surprised, however, when the man dropped the receiver after only a few words from her and took several minutes to return.

Am I doing the right thing? Would any normal person travel across the country at a dead man's bidding?

"Normal people don't see ghosts, Elizabeth," she whispered to herself.

"Ah, but the special ones do, *Bella*."

Elizabeth jumped, placing her hand over her heart at the sound of Paolo's voice beside her. From the corner of her eye she watched him materialize. He walked beside her. She glanced at him and smiled in response to her friend's crooked smile and wink. She couldn't be cross with him for startling her. Elizabeth should be accustomed to Paolo appearing the way he did. If she'd not been so anxious, she'd have sensed him there before he appeared.

"You think too much for a young *donna*," Paolo chided.

Elizabeth resisted the urge to respond to him. Trying to pretend there wasn't a dead man standing next to her on the street talking was as hard as when he entertained her on the train with his stories.

After making sure no one else was near enough to see or hear her, Elizabeth said, "Oh?" She smiled. "Do I have to be an old man like you to contemplate my life?"

"You, *cara mia*, will never be an old man like me." He pinched her cheek. "Much too obstinate."

"You're insufferable, Paolo."

"Ah, *Bella*, so I have been told by many a *signorina* in my day."

My, how she'd miss him when his soul finally passed on. "I don't know, Paolo," Elizabeth said. "I should have contacted Marco from home to tell him the news instead of showing up on the doorstep this way."

He shook his head.

"Or better yet," she said. "I should have sent a telegram."

"It is too late for such doubts now," he said.

He was right. A bothersome voice in the back of her mind told her the chances were better for people to believe news of this magnitude if given face-to-face. With Paolo's soul being uncertain, she didn't want this done halfway.

She smiled at the ghost. He showed such complete faith and confidence in her, she almost believed she would succeed in helping his soul find peace.

Elizabeth studied Paolo's features as she'd done so often over the past weeks as they'd gotten acquainted with one another. This man, with deep wrinkles framing his eyes and mouth, and a nose positioned at an angle on his weathered face, was so dear to her. After his death, he'd told her so many things about himself. Paolo told her how his nose, once broken, healed on its own and how he'd come to live in America.

Back home as they were becoming friends and he was convincing her to travel to California for him, he also described his enduring love for his lost wife and son. He smiled and told her Adriana was the only woman capable of turning him from a frivolous bachelor to a faithfully married man.

Elizabeth glanced up at the autumn California sun and found comfort in its warmth on her face. The air was crisp, and each breath soothed her frayed nerves.

An automobile door slammed, and she jumped, thinking her ride had arrived. Elizabeth relaxed her shoulders with relief as she noted the vehicle stood parked in front of the General Cana Store. The driver entered the store without a thought for her.

Deciding a little diversion might quiet her overwrought nerves, she looked both ways to ensure the road was free of traffic. She nodded to Paolo, and they crossed the cobblestone street together.

"This was not here when I left, *Bella*," Paolo said. "Much has changed."

Arriving in front of the store's plate glass window, she cupped her hand over her eyes and peered in. This wasn't a neighborhood market because they sold clothes, groceries, and even housed a post office scale. A young, dark-haired, vivacious woman leaned behind the counter talking to a customer. The woman smiled in Elizabeth's direction and waved.

"Oh." Elizabeth backpedaled and turned to face the street.

"She frightens you, *Bella*?" Paolo said with amusement lacing his voice. "The woman looks harmless. Entertaining? *Si*, perhaps, but not frightening."

"Must you speak constantly?" Elizabeth eyed him.

Without a doubt, the residents here knew she was a stranger. She'd never be able to live in such a small town where the downtown spanned one city block. A person with her ability wouldn't be able to hide here so easily. Not that she'd expected to live there, but this wasn't her place. She needed a big city where no one knew her history.

To pass more time, she continued to walk and passed a restaurant, The Vines. The morning clerk at the inn had told her this restaurant was one of two in Cana. Stopping, she yawned and tugged at a stray curl resting over her face.

"Your pacing is making us both nervous," Paolo said. "You should sit. Rest. I will be with you. I promise."

Elizabeth narrowed her eyes at the man. Of course, he was calm. He wasn't a stranger to whoever was coming to meet her—especially if it was Marco.

She grasped the handle of her brown leather bag, wishing the drawing of Paolo inside—the one her sister Anna illustrated—would be enough to convince the Clementes she knew the man. But what would the man in the charcoal sketch mean to a family who hadn't seen him in three decades?

His stories would serve her better in proving Paolo was her friend. She'd share his secrets, what set him on his journey, and who he truly was. She'd do anything to help the ghost return home. He'd worked his charm and persuaded her to come. In such a brief time, he'd won her friendship and few claimed such a feat.

In companionable silence, the two of them crossed to the inn together. While Paolo turned in a slow circle, taking in the town, Elizabeth sat on a stone bench amid a small marigold garden. Arranging her bag in her lap, she tried to ignore the ghost who now settled beside her.

Elizabeth inhaled the scent of late-blooming begonias flourishing in the Town Square. She glanced down the street toward the courthouse where the clerk had told her the mayor's office and jail were located. Hopefully, his relatives wouldn't think she was ready for the insane asylum, showing up unexpectedly with the stories of Paolo, and have her sent there. She'd be left to stew in a cell until her siblings showed up to defend her. She crossed her legs under her black skirt and looked up at the hazy blue sky.

"You know my mother and father didn't want me to come here in the first place," she said, looking askance at the ghost.

"*Si*, I was a fly on the wall during the conversation," he said. "I was of a mind to agree with your *padre*. I would not want my daughter to travel the rails alone."

"I'm a grown woman, Paolo. I was married, lived on my own," she said. What neither her father nor the ghost appeared to remember was the year. In 1945, women worked jobs previously held by men. She'd lived on her own for a time after Patrick left, until the apartment's empty rooms saddened her too much. Still, she was responsible enough to travel without an escort, which was what she told both of her parents. "And besides, I'm not alone," she told Paolo now. "You're with me."

"Ah, *Bella*, but I am a ghost, am I not?"

"Ugh," she said, throwing her hand in the air. "You wanted me to come." She'd journeyed all this way for this impossible man. Why was he trying to talk her out of the trip now?

"Did I not suggest you invite your sister to accompany you?"

"Yes," was all the response she was willing to give. She'd wanted to make the trip on her own but now she'd give anything to have her sister with her. The girl understood how to manage people. Anna would have waved back to the woman in the store instead of hurrying away like a bashful child.

Upon lowering her gaze, she saw a black pickup truck pull up on the street in front of her. A tall, suntanned man exited and slammed the door shut. A long wisp of straight, black hair fell out of the strap that held it back.

When he faced her, her heart quivered.

Paolo shot to his feet and shuddered where he stood.

The man must have been six-feet tall and lean, much like Paolo.

The stranger approached, walking with a slight falter.

Elizabeth's limbs grew numb, and she mustered all her strength to keep from sliding off the bench into the dirt or from taking Paolo's hand. She uncrossed her legs, planted her black shoes on the ground, and rose to stand beside the trembling ghost. She tightened her grip on the leather handle of her bag.

"Elizabeth Reilly?" The man's voice, though attractive, lacked the charm of Paolo's accent. He'd either been born in America or immigrated at an early age.

"Yes, I'm her." Trying not to glance at Paolo, she held out her unsteady hand to the man.

Ignoring it, he asked, "So you're a friend of Paolo Clemente?"

"Yes," she said. "We met each other in Boston. B-before he died." She fisted her hand at her side. Lying would not be so easy.

Elizabeth wished Paolo would mention who this man might be. She could sense the panic rolling off him and her own heart threatened to beat from her chest. She didn't dare risk a look at her friend. Of all the times to be quiet, why did the ghost pick now?

The stranger raised his eyebrow and asked, "Did you tell Marco he died recently?"

She nodded, slowly. Did he not trust Marco? "Yes. I'm sorry to deliver such sad news."

"I see." He glanced at her single bag.

Elizabeth peeked at Paolo out of the corner of her eye. He didn't move and appeared frozen in place.

"Do you have any other bags?" the other man asked.

She turned her attention back to him and looked down to hide her heat-flushed cheeks. "What do you mean?"

"Do all your things fit in one small bag?"

Were all the Clementes so condescending? No wonder Paolo agreed to leave Italy. She gazed up into the stranger's striking coffee-colored eyes. "No. My things

21

are unpacked in my room."

He turned and motioned to the inn's door. "Let's get them."

"Excuse me?" she asked.

"Shall we get your clothes? Pack them in your suitcase?" he asked. "Since you're coming to the vineyard, you might as well stay there. We have guest rooms."

"Well, I didn't plan—"

He walked away from her before she finished. "Planned or not, let's go. My father's been missing for over thirty years. I don't intend to drive back and forth into town so you can tell me where the hell he's been."

Elizabeth turned toward Paolo. His face blanched stark white. "Paolo?" she mouthed and reached for him. He backed away, shaking his head, and releasing a hoarse groan, he vanished.

Elizabeth stared at the empty space where Paolo should have been standing. *Come back*, she wanted to scream, but instead she turned and hurried after the stranger. She needed answers. With his height and long legs, he walked fast, and she scrambled to catch up to him.

"Excuse me, please wait. Did you say your father?" Elizabeth asked. All warmth left her face as she reined up beside him. "I'm sorry. Who are you?"

He froze. "Giovanni Clemente," he pronounced with exaggeration.

Elizabeth's heart stopped. Giovanni? *My Lord, Paolo, you told me your son died.* Why did Paolo vanish? She needed him by her side whispering words of explanation. Instead, the ghost abandoned her to deal with this stranger and the impossible situation on her own.

Panic churned in her stomach as the man claiming to bear the same name as Paolo's son glared at her with an expectancy clear in the set of his jaw. His eyes narrowed.

"No, you can't be Giovanni," she finally said.

"Well, I am." His face was blank. "Why would I lie?"

This wasn't possible. She stumbled into him and dropped her bag to the ground.

"Miss Reilly, are you okay?" He caught her elbow and steadied her, glanced down at his hand, and snatched it away.

Elizabeth backed away from him in two swift steps, trying to make sense of this turn in events. Her heartbeat returned to a rapid thumping. Uncertainty and anxiety warmed her cheeks. "I need to sit, I think."

"You'll have some time to sit once we get your things," he said and cleared his throat. "The ride to the vineyard will take us half an hour."

****

Elizabeth shoved her clothing into her portmanteau while Giovanni waited below. With shaking hands, she closed and snapped the case shut. Taking one last look around the room, she wondered why she was checking out. She should stay put and make him come to her if he wanted to know *what the hell* happened to his father. She'd come here to help his family, not to take orders from anyone. Turning back to the bed, she hauled the hard-sided case off with a thud.

"I should tell him I'm not going."

She dragged her belongings to the door.

She grabbed the doorknob and closed her eyes.

Lord, there's no turning back now.

"*Bella*." Paolo's voice carried to her on a breathless whisper.

Her eyes shot open, and she leaned forward, bumping her head on the solid, oak door. Paolo squeezed her shoulder and rested against the wall. Tears swam in his eyes and drifted down his weathered cheek.

"How can he be Giovanni? H-how can he be?" he asked.

His anguish erupted through her, fisting her heart and turning her legs to liquid. Paolo's despair overwhelmed her with the confounding urge to rush down and gather Giovanni Clemente into her embrace.

She'd like to see how the man would respond if she did.

Elizabeth pried her mind away from the son and focused on the devastated father. Lifting her unsteady hand, she caressed his lifeless cheek. "I don't know, Paolo," she said. "But we'll find out."

****

After Paolo faded, leaving her alone, Elizabeth returned to the foyer and found his son pacing. Giovanni's long legs afforded him only a few strides across the floor before he spun and returned the way he'd come. She stood in the open doorway and watched him. From the side, she saw his dark eyes were troubled. Her heart plummeted.

He walked to an immense window. The large panes ornamented the small room. With his back to her, he stood looking out at the courtyard. His shoulders slumped forward, and Elizabeth suspected—no, she realized her arrival was not easy for him.

She cleared her throat, not certain if the words "I'm

here" would be suitable, and he turned to face her.

"How long have you been standing there?" he asked.

"Not long." She swayed on her feet.

He took one step forward. "Do you often sneak up on people?"

"No, I don't…" Air caught in her dry throat. "I mean, I didn't."

He approached her, holding her still with his gaze until he stood looking down at her. Elizabeth's breath hitched as he took the bag from her hand and maneuvered around her. She turned to watch him walk to the front doors. A subtle limp in his right leg marred his otherwise smooth exit. Sudden warmth radiated up from her abdomen, humbling her. The man unnerved her.

Giovanni spoke over his shoulder without looking at her. "I took your other bag out already."

"Only for you, Paolo," she mumbled under her breath, and followed his son outside.

Gio tossed her suitcase into the bed of the truck. She waited by the passenger door, expecting him to be a gentleman and open it for her. Instead, he continued to his side of the vehicle. He paused at the door before climbing in.

He frowned at Elizabeth and closed the door. "How gallant," she said under her breath, climbed into the seat and tugged the heavy door shut.

"So, this man," he said, not bothering to look at her as he spoke. "Did he ever tell you he had a son?"

"Yes. Yes, he did. Your father spoke of you often. He thought—" She bit her lip, wishing Paolo were beside her now.

Giovanni planted both hands on the wheel and, with

the look of a wounded man, stared ahead. "What did he think?"

"He thought you were dead."

Chapter Three

Elizabeth's stomach churned in nervous knots. She squirmed on the cloth seat, and her foot twitched. If he heard her erratic heartbeat, he'd realize how frantic she was—and hot. Perspiration built up on her forehead. Grabbing the metal handle, she rolled down the squeaking window, and inhaled the pure air. The fragrances of the forest filled her senses—the resinous scent of pine, the earthiness of soil, and damp detritus of fallen branches and decaying leaves. The surrounding land was alive, vibrant, and something more she couldn't quite identify. Somehow, the vehicle they drove in and the path it traveled seemed out of place.

Gravel on the uneven road crunched and ground under the truck's tires. Elizabeth sat straight in her seat and stole stiff, awkward glimpses at Giovanni. A frown marked his lips. His lean, well-defined face held soulful eyes bringing to her mind images of the sad little boy he must have been.

A thin red scar stretched down his right cheek and she itched to run a finger along the faded edges. She'd caress his stubble-shadowed chin and tell him how terribly his father missed him. Instead, she stared out the truck window.

Enormous ancient trees shrouded the road and hid the valley from the rest of the world. Elizabeth closed her eyes to the beauty. She was here, on the way to Paolo's vineyard with his son, aching to tell Giovanni everything. If she did, he'd send her away, and she'd never be able to help his father.

"When we reach my house," he said, breaking the silence, "please don't tell my mother why you're here."

She opened her eyes. "What should I say?"

"We'll speak about my father in private," he said with an undertone of superiority. "As far as my mother's concerned, I'll tell her you're an acquaintance of mine here for a visit."

"Are you telling me you want me to lie to her?" She frowned. Elizabeth already needed to lie about how she and Paolo really became friends, but she wasn't prepared to make up false pretenses about just being there.

"I don't want you to lie to my mother," he grumbled back.

"I'd be misleading her about why I'm here." Did he think her dishonest? "Then I would be lying."

"I'll tell her. You don't need to say anything," he snapped.

"You'll be the one who's lying." She crossed her arms over her chest.

"Listen," he said, his voice rising with impatience. "As far as we know, my father has been dead for a very long time. Her heart will break if there's any possibility he was in Boston and deserted us."

"He didn't desert you," she said. "I told you. He—"

"If he didn't, he would've come back here. To his vineyard." His knuckles grew white as he clung to the steering wheel. "To sell the land or close the estate down—something—and return to Italy. To his family there. Wouldn't that have made sense?" Gio asked. "He'd have found us here alive and well."

Elizabeth rested her hand on his arm. "Please try and understand." Her breath caught as nervous energy shot through her fingers. She snatched her hand away. "Your father died a very sad, lonely man. He didn't intend to spend his life without you or your mother. You were his world."

"I don't care about this man's intentions," he said. "If he is my father, my mother doesn't need to mourn him all over again."

"He is your father. However, I understand. I'll leave it up to you to tell your mother." She bit her lip. "I have one question, though."

"Yes?"

"Since you don't trust me, why are you bringing me to your home?"

"Well, if there's even a remote chance your friend was my father, I need to know."

"I've no reason to make this up." How in the world was she going to convince him?

"How would I know?" he asked. "I have no idea who you are and what reasons you'd have. And until I do, we handle this my way."

"I'm here to help your father."

"My father is dead," he said. "How can you help him?"

"I simply can." She stared straight ahead out the windshield. *How am I ever going to do this?* Paolo wouldn't be of much help, she feared. Not now when his grief was so fresh. He'd been distraught when he left her. The raw emotions ripped through him, surged into Elizabeth, and still echoed in her blood. He'd asked, "*Why didn't I go home?*"

Yes, Paolo, why didn't you go home?

29

Joie Lesin

Gio veered the truck down a dirt road. "What do you do in Boston?"

His voice was nice, almost soothing to her emotional state, when he wasn't so accusatory or threatening.

"What do I do?" she asked.

"Yes," he said, condescension clear in his voice with the one word. He was impatient with her again. "How do you make a living?"

"Well, I don't at the moment. I live with my family." She rubbed her arms to smooth the hairs standing on end. Utter panic swept her body. The sudden sensation of flight assaulted her. Someone chased her, and she ran for her life.

A woman ran into the middle of the road, glancing over her shoulder at something behind her. She wore a long, tattered dress with rips at the hem revealing dirty, scuffed black boots.

"Hobby then," Gio said. His voice reminded her where she was—in the truck with him.

Pain shot through her head.

"Gio!" she screamed and grabbed his arm at the same moment the woman ran into the truck's path.

"What the hell are you doing?" He twisted the wheel abruptly. The truck spun to the left and passed through the woman.

"No-no-no," Elizabeth chanted on the edge of a sob. Her body grew ice-cold as a shiver climbed her spine.

The woman ran past the passenger side window. Her crushed skull exposed jagged, bloody bone. Dried blood covered one side of her dress.

"You hit—" Elizabeth groaned as the woman fled down the empty road and vanished out of sight.

"I didn't hit anything." Gio punched the brakes and

30

swung his door open. After a quick peek over his shoulder at her, he hopped down from the truck. He walked around the vehicle until he ducked down to inspect the underside.

Leaning forward into the dashboard, Elizabeth closed her eyes to ride out the nausea churning in her belly and the fading fog of pain clouding her mind. Gio was right. He didn't hit a thing. The truck hadn't collided with the woman but passed right through her. The visions of the dead grew stronger. The emotions, the fear, the sorrow, the despair were back.

Those emotions prompted the frightened young girl she'd been to beg her mother to stop the gift. Such feelings would cripple most adults. Together, they'd worked so hard to close her mind. Lord, she hadn't considered the repercussions of reaching out to the spirit world. Yet she would face those consequences repeatedly if they meant an end to her husband's suffering. She would sacrifice herself again and again to help him move on in peace.

If she hadn't opened herself up for Patrick, she wouldn't have been able to aid Paolo now.

Elizabeth didn't open her eyes when she heard Gio climb into the truck or feel the weight of him settling in his seat. "There's nothing there," he said. "Whatever it was, the lucky bugger crossed the road unharmed." He touched her shoulder. "I promise. I didn't hit a thing. It's all right."

Taking a deep breath, she opened her eyes and, still trembling, leaned back into the seat. "I'm sorry," she whispered.

****

Gio clung to the steering wheel and scanned the

trees every few minutes, watching for other animals, making sure none darted in front of them. The pure fright he'd witnessed from his passenger was enough for one day. His emotions were already shaky. He'd be better off sparing the life of any gopher or coyote. At the entrance to the vineyard, he swung the truck left.

Clearing his throat, he said, "You can see the house ahead."

He glanced at the woman. Elizabeth Reilly was pale and still visibly shaken. Why did an animal running into the road frighten her so much?

"It's so beautiful, Giovanni," she said, awe in her voice.

He shifted his attention back to the view in front of him. Gio looked with pride at the vineyard's three-story main house, crafted of stone and brick. He agreed. His abode was beautiful, composed of deep reds and browns. The porch extended across the front of the house and wound along the left side. Vines climbed the pillars and stretched to the rooftop. The warmth emanating the structure enveloped him. He was glad to be home. Here, and only here, would he have the strength to deal with Miss Reilly.

He loved this house, this vineyard, and it was not his father's—not the man who left without deference for what he held.

"My mother's pride and joy," he said. "When she's not bossing me about in the vineyard, she's out here." He nodded toward the garden. "Where she tends to her plants and flowers."

Two potted hibiscus plants with large orange petals stood on the porch, and multiple varieties of ivy and a rather large fern stretched their leaves to the railing.

Giovanni swung the truck into a spot along the right side of the house, shutting off the engine. Facing Elizabeth, he hesitated. When he left the vineyard to meet her, he'd not intended to bring her back with him. He'd planned to confront her, find out her story, and ask her to leave. Once he saw her, he'd let all his plans go awry.

Sucker for a pretty face, Gio?

No, her attractive face hadn't persuaded him. Something in those brown, almond-shaped eyes did. They whispered honesty and, perchance, compassion.

He was falling right into her trap.

Damn.

He resisted the urge to throw his hands in the air. "Now, remember, my mother has no idea why you're really here."

"Yes," she said with a sigh.

"And," he said, hating to switch gears on her after she'd suffered such a fright, "I want you here so I can keep an eye on you." He needed to keep the upper hand. If she got control, she might take advantage of him and his mother. This Elizabeth Reilly was a grifter, a criminal planning to con funds, claiming the money was for a tombstone or some fictitious unpaid expense his father owed. Now here he was taking her to his home, so she'd see her potential bounty.

"Why would you want to watch me like that?" she asked.

"I don't know, but I'd rather be safe." He avoided her gaze.

"Do I appear dangerous to you?" she asked with a frown.

This woman was going to be a challenge. "I don't

think you're dangerous."

"I want you to realize I'm not here to cause problems for you or your family. I'm here to bring your father home."

"If this man is dead, how can you bring him home?"

"You need to know what happened to him." She opened the truck door, exited, and swung the heavy door shut.

Gio sat for several seconds, focused on the empty space where she'd sat. No matter how he handled this, things wouldn't be easy. He took one long, steady breath before exiting through the driver's door.

He met the woman at the back of the truck. Gio collected her bags, placing her smaller valise under his arm, and holding the other by the handle. He watched her while she did anything to pretend she didn't sense the weight of his eyes on her. She side-eyed the valise and looked away.

Finally, when she opened her mouth to speak, he cut her off.

He asked, "Shall we go in?"

She pressed her lips into a tense smile and nodded. Together they walked around to the front of the house and into a garden of rock, varied shades of green shrubbery, and spots of poppies adding a touch of red. Odd-sized weathered stepping-stones guided them to the porch steps. Reaching two massive oak doors, Elizabeth stepped in front of him and pushed the doors wide open. She stood examining the interior of the house while Gio adjusted the weight of the luggage in his hand. His knee was aching. He cleared his throat, and she turned to him. Her gaze sought his.

Now he saw kindness, and unless he was mistaken,

longing shimmering in her eyes.

What was she expecting?

She offered him a shy, hesitant smile and cleared the way for him to enter.

Chapter Four

Elizabeth followed Giovanni into a sun-filled room.

He set her bags by the front door and avoided looking at her. "I need to tell my *madre* we have a guest." He walked toward the back of the house, paused, and spoke over his shoulder to her. "Don't touch anything while I'm gone."

"Well." Elizabeth wrinkled her nose at Giovanni's back as he walked away. She whispered to herself, "I'll open my bags and start shoving things in. Give Mr. Sunshine something to find when he searches them."

With her hands on her hips, she examined the room. The furnishings were a mixture of antique and art deco. Two curved, cream-colored sofas faced each other across a low table made of dark walnut. While sparsely decorated, the room's walls were hung with painted Mediterranean landscapes and flower-filled vases sat atop various tables. A long, thin table lined the south wall.

Elizabeth's heels clicked on the gray-tiled floor as she crossed the room to study the photographs displayed on the table. One featured a couple on their wedding day. Beneath a trellis covered with vines, the woman sat on an ornate stone bench, carved with nude baby-faced cherubs. The man stood behind the woman, his hand resting on her shoulder. Plump grapes hung in clusters above their heads and more fruit traveled down the lattice sides.

Without a doubt, this was Paolo, and the person with him was his wife. He adored the woman. When he spoke her name, Adriana, it sounded as if he prayed.

In the photograph, Adriana wore a delicate lace dress and the happiest smile. The youthful and handsome Paolo wore a matching one, giving the appearance of an aristocrat in a tailored black suit.

"Do you see something of interest?" Giovanni asked.

Startled, Elizabeth stepped forward, bumping her hip on the table as he stood beside her. She counted to five in her mind to steady herself and picked up the picture of Paolo and Adriana. "This picture of your father and mother. You look so much like him." She bit her lip.

"How can you be sure he's my father?" he asked. "The man could be any one of many of my relatives."

He was right, wasn't he? But this was Paolo.

"Because the man in this picture resembles my friend Paolo." While in Anna's sketch, Paolo appeared the ravaged, aged man, his eyes remained the same. Giovanni wouldn't see the resemblance, though. "I know your father. I recognize the man in this picture."

He raised an eyebrow. "Isn't it you *knew* him?"

"Yes." Her cheeks heated. The man was tenacious, weighing her every word. She set the frame down. "I'm right though, aren't I? It's your parent's wedding picture, isn't it?"

"Yes," he hissed in response.

What Giovanni Clemente didn't comprehend was just how tenacious she could be.

Running her finger over the gilded frame, she murmured, "Adriana's so beautiful. I can see why your father never let go of her."

"You mean my mother. Yes, and she is. You might want to call her *Signora* or Mrs. Clemente. Adriana is far too personal for someone you've never met, don't you think?"

"I feel as if I know your mother." She winced, knowing she wasn't saying the right things to him. "Your father shared a great deal with me."

"He may have." He scowled. "But to us you're nothing but a stranger."

Elizabeth took a deep breath. "I'll do my best to avoid your mother, if that's what you prefer."

"No," he said. "Now that my mother knows we have a guest, there's no way I can keep her away from you."

"Fine, whatever you wish of me. As long as I'm here, I'll follow your rules." Sarcasm charged her voice. Her hands shook with the effort of holding onto her fragile self-control.

"You can't possibly feel so familiar with me since my father wasn't. I was a baby when he saw me last." He picked up the picture of his parents. "I have no recollection of my father. Or didn't he tell you he left before I could form any memories of him?" Giovanni placed the photograph down with a thud and it tipped backwards, toppling several others in the path. He threw his arms into the air in frustration.

"Yes, Giovanni." She picked up one of the framed portraits and placed the black-and-white picture back in place. "Or am I required to call you *Signore* Clemente? I'm not sure what's expected of me. Your father told me I'd be welcomed." She continued rearranging the frames.

"When did he tell you that?" He snatched the two photographs she held and placed them face down on the table. "Did my father come back from the dead and tell you?"

She turned away to hide the trepidation she was sure showed on her face. Why would he say such a thing? Should she call his bluff and say, "*Yes, Mister, as a matter of fact, he did*?"

She flexed her hands and spun to face him. "I really don't appreciate you speaking to me this way. Is there somewhere you'd like me to wait until," she said, her voice rising as she fought back tears, "until you find another reason to belittle me? Please point me in the direction."

She wouldn't let this man see her cry. This man was Paolo's son? She left the table, walked towards the front door but stopped and turned to face him. "I don't think it's a good idea for me to stay here. Please take me back to town. Or should I walk?"

A tear slid down her cheek. *Blasted tears*! She feared this impossible man would see her emotions as a sign of weakness, but she had two choices. She either allow herself a few tears *or not* restrain herself from smashing one of the delicate, embossed framed pictures over his head.

Lord help her, she wasn't a violent woman.

"Giovanni, what is happening here?" a tall woman asked from where she stood in the doorway. Her voice favored a melodic Italian accent. Soft wisps of gray-streaked hair hung around her lean face.

"*Madre*," Giovanni responded in surprise and fell silent. He fidgeted in place, keeping his eyes on his mother.

"Gio, why is our guest crying?" Adriana crossed the room to stand beside Elizabeth and placed an arm around her shoulder. "You must pardon my son, *cara mia*. He sometimes has the sensitivity of an ox. Unfortunately, his father was not here to show him the courteous ways. I tried but fear I did not do a good job."

Elizabeth managed a meager smile despite her ebbing tears. She studied the mother and son. Gio shared Adriana's deep brown eyes, but the shape of his face he inherited from Paolo. He was the perfect combination of his striking parents.

"Come, let us sit." Adriana took Elizabeth's hand. She led Elizabeth a few steps forward and stopped in front of her son. "You should be ashamed," she said. "You bring such a beautiful young lady to our home and treat her so disrespectfully."

"You didn't hear, did you?" he asked.

"No, I did not. However, I am well acquainted with your expressions, Giovanni. When you were a *bambino*, you wore this one often. When I caught you doing something you should not. Perhaps a walk will suit until you calm yourself."

He stood stock-still for a moment, crossing his arms over his chest. "If I didn't know better, I'd say you're trying to get rid of me."

"Why, I am, Gio." Adriana smiled. "I am thinking some space between you and our guest would be wise at the moment."

Giovanni eyed Elizabeth. "Maybe you're right." He turned toward the door, pausing to say to Elizabeth, "I expect Miss Reilly to remember her promise."

Elizabeth nodded, careful to not look at either of the people in front of her.

Giovanni sighed, exited the house, and slammed the front doors behind him.

Adriana led Elizabeth to the back of the house to an oversized, beautiful kitchen. One entire wall was a window overlooking the rows of thick healthy vines. Elizabeth saw Gio limp into a vineyard aisle.

"Sit, *per favore*." Adriana motioned to a high-backed, ladder chair fashioned of oak.

Smiling, Elizabeth nodded and sat.

"I hope you will not hold his behavior against us. Sometimes," Adriana said, "my Giovanni is too stubborn." Smiling, the woman took a seat. "Sofia, would you be kind to bring the *signorina* a cup of tea and freshen mine, *per favore*?" Smiling, Adriana toyed with the handle of the teacup already set in front of her. "We were not properly introduced. I am Adriana Clemente. Please, call me Adriana."

Elizabeth smiled as a young Italian woman, fresh out of girlhood, placed a cup on the table in front of her and filled it with steaming tea. She refilled Adriana's before setting the porcelain teapot on a delicate, crocheted cozy in between the two of them.

"And this is Sofia." Adriana motioned to the girl. "She is employed to help me around the house, but I consider her a member of the family."

"Thank you, Sofia. Nice to meet you."

Elizabeth nodded to the young woman who curtsied and returned to a wood block table where she'd stood shelling peas.

"And thank you for your kindness, Adriana," Elizabeth said to her hostess. Giovanni said calling his mother by her first name was too personal. *Ha.* "I'm Elizabeth Reilly."

"What a lovely name," she said in response. "Do you prefer Elizabeth?"

"Actually, I do," she said and smiled wider. "My family calls me Beth. But I'm partial to Elizabeth."

"This is what I will call you. Elizabeth." Adriana raised her teacup to her lips, blew the steam away, and placed the cup back on the table without drinking. "Gio tells me you are from Boston. This is on the other side of this country. How have you come to know my son?"

She hated lying to this kind woman, so she stayed silent.

"I'm sorry, it is not necessary to tell me all this. Not when you and Gio have had an argument." Adriana picked up her teacup, finally taking a sip. "My son is so secretive. To have known a woman long enough to have such a quarrel and not tell his *madre*. He did not even mention you were coming to stay until you stood in our home."

Her face held curiosity as she lowered her voice. "You must be very special to cause him such emotion. My son has become so stoic and reacts to so little. This is sometimes a worry to me." She frowned. "Tell me, how long have you known him?"

Elizabeth opened her mouth to answer, though she didn't know what she was about to say. Relief flooded her when Gio entered through the back kitchen door. Adriana glanced at him.

After studying both women, he asked, "Am I interrupting something?"

"Of course, you are," Adriana answered. "Elizabeth was about to tell me how long you two have known one another."

Gio glared at Elizabeth. "Was she?"

Adriana placed her cup on its saucer with care. Smiling, she cocked an eyebrow at Elizabeth, but addressed her son. "Yes, she was, but your walk gave us too little time. Are you sure you took long enough to calm yourself? Hmm? Perhaps you would show Elizabeth where she may freshen up. There will be time for talk later." Rising from her seat, she faced Elizabeth. "You are staying for a time, I should hope?"

"Yes." Elizabeth stood. "Thank you."

"*Eccellente*!" She smiled, keeping her attention on Elizabeth. "This should give the two of you time to settle your earlier *disputa*, *si*?"

"*Madre*, this isn't what you think." Gio shot Elizabeth a warning glare.

"Perhaps. But shoo." She gestured at him. "Take Elizabeth and her things up to the east bedroom." She offered Elizabeth a hand. "It has such a beautiful view of the vineyard. Once you see it, you will not be quick to leave us."

Chapter Five

Gio closed the door behind him, leaving Miss Elizabeth Reilly alone in the guest room. Who was this woman? Did she expect him to take her word alone?

She looked at him in the pickup as if they were long lost friends. The worst part of the entire ordeal was her touch hadn't felt like an invasion when she laid her hand on his arm. The contact comforted him as if she'd cared enough to lessen the confounding pain. As if she could dampen the ache he experienced at the idea that his father truly did desert them.

For a fleeting second, he wondered, hoping, if she'd take his hand. The hope and his reaction were as irrational as *everything* related to her.

He descended the stairs and crossed through the parlor to the front entrance, which he used on rare occasions. His work in the vineyard was a dusty, sometimes downright dirty job, so he usually entered and exited through the back. Now, however, his mother stood in his path. The more he avoided her, the easier it was to keep perpetuating the story he'd told to explain Elizabeth's presence.

He hurried down the porch steps and crossed to the left side of the house, where Sebastian, or Seb as most affectionately called the man, readied more rodent traps. They battled a constant problem with critters burrowing holes under the vines.

"Seb, have you seen Marco?"

"He is in the wine house," he answered without breaking from his work.

"Ah." Gio paused. "Has he gotten into the brandy?"

"*Si*." Seb nodded. "He has been in there since you left this morning."

"Things will be a little strange here for a while."

"Is it the *signorina* you brought home?" Seb asked.

"It is not what you think," Gio answered.

"Of course not," Seb said and turned away but not soon enough to hide his broadening smile.

Gio couldn't fault the man for taking interest in their visitor. Sebastian was a fixture on the vineyard and witnessed as Gio grew up amongst the vines. The man was more family to him than his father.

Sighing, Gio headed toward the stone wine house. He'd never brought a woman home to the vineyard to meet his mother. Why was everyone thinking he'd do so now?

Of course, he *did* bring a woman home and *did* introduce her to his mother.

What's more, now that Marco had downed the brandy, Gio would have no hope of discussing Miss Reilly's arrival with the man. First, Gio would have to sober up his father's cousin, and then they'd talk about how to deal with their houseguest. Gio needed help. His difficulty controlling his emotions around her surprised him.

Miss Reilly was young and uncommonly pretty and not at all what Gio had expected when he set out for town. No, a worn out, shifty-eyed person with obvious designs on stealing from them would have been easier to turn away.

45

Yes, Gio, you are a sucker for a pretty face.

She carried herself with class. The clothes she wore were expensive and by appearance, the woman came from an affluent background.

Gio shook his head at his thoughts. Who was this woman?

Her face was hard to place. Was she Greek? Italian, maybe? With a name like Reilly, she must be at least part Irish.

He stopped outside of the building and rested his hand on the outer wall. The feel of the cool stone and sturdy foundation grounded him and calmed his shaky nerves.

The wine house was older than the house they lived in, and he often suspected it might have been a long, single-story home at one point in the estate's history. The structure encompassed the heart of the winemaking operation. Gio stored the oak barrels with fermenting grapes in various rooms above ground depending on the grape, the stage in the process, and his mood. The bottled wines remained below ground, shelved in the cellars until sold or adopted into his small yet refined personal collection.

Entering the workroom, Gio inhaled the scent of earth, dust, and ripened grapes. This was his favorite room on the whole vineyard.

In the dimly lit corner, he found Marco asleep in a chair with his legs stretched out in front of him under the table. He rested his head on the back of the chair. His thinning gray hair looked as if he'd run his hands through it more than a dozen times. A half-empty bottle of brandy sat uncapped next to a drained Mason jar.

Gio lifted the gaunt man from the chair.

"I am so sorry," Marco slurred.

"It's fine. You can't handle your brandy the way you used to, *signore*."

"*Signorina* Reilly. Is she here?" Marco staggered away from Gio and fell into the table.

"Yes, she is." Gio helped the man to his feet, held him up, and walked him towards the back of the structure to a small cot. "Sleep this off. We can talk about it later."

"Your *padre*? What about your *padre*?" Marco pushed up against Gio as he tried to guide him down.

"We'll talk later."

Marco lay back, closed his eyes, and snored.

Gio shook his head and crossed back to the table. He picked up the brandy bottle and hesitated before lifting the bottle to his lips.

His mother would be upset if he smelled of brandy so early in the day. Of course, he was still his own man, but there was no woman he wished to impress more than Adriana Clemente. If she only understood what he was going through. If Elizabeth Reilly knew his father, how would he explain this to his mother? Sitting in Marco's chair, he took another sip before he extended his stiff knee.

Of all the people in the world, Adriana Clemente didn't deserve to be hurt again by anyone. Gio lost himself in his memories. *Again, he was five years old, and his mother was drawing him onto her lap. Her perfume enveloped him in a cloud of chamomile and summer air.*

"Gio, your father was a good man and so handsome." Gio stared down into her lap, knowing she'd cry. She always cried when she talked of his poppa. He concentrated on the front panel of her blue-checkered dress.

"You are going to look like him, I can tell," she said, her voice breaking. "You will be a good man like him." Two tears dropped to her bosom, darkening the light blue material.

"I hate him, Momma." He bunched his small fist. A good poppa would not leave a momma and little boy all alone.

"Oh, my *bambino*." She wrapped her arms around him, gathering him in. "It is hard for someone so small to understand. But when you are a man—when you are a man, you will."

He wouldn't. He'd never understand why a man would make his mother cry.

Even when he'd grown up, he'd still catch his mother lost in her memories. She'd sit on the front porch, staring at the vineyard's entrance as if watching for his father to walk down the road. After all this time, she still loved him, but Gio didn't love Paolo Clemente at all. The man was a stranger.

He set the bottle on the table harder than he intended.

He was only beginning to settle back into his life and put the war behind him. Now this visitor shows up, invading his home.

Capping the bottle, he rose from the chair. Getting drunk wouldn't help. He needed to keep his wits and figure this out.

He checked to make sure Marco slept peacefully before heading to the house. He paused in the back doorway, watching his mother fuss about, setting up a guest tray. To her, Elizabeth Reilly's visit was a happy diversion.

If she only knew.

"*Madre*," he said as he stepped further into the room. "There's no reason to fuss over *Signorina* Reilly."

His mother forced a smile. She wasn't pleased with him. "No? Is she not a guest in this house?"

"Yes." He sighed. "Yes, she is, but I'm not sure if we want her to get too comfortable."

"Oh?" She froze. "And why would this be? Because you argued with the young woman?" She headed to the large kitchen bureau. "Or, if she is some bad person, I would wonder why you would bring her into our home. Is she a bad person, Giovanni?"

He ran his hands over his tied-back hair.

Dammit. I don't know.

He hoped bringing her to the vineyard wasn't a mistake. When he headed out to pick her up, he hadn't planned to have her stay at the house. "No, *Madre*, she isn't, but—" Gio stopped short, unsure what to say next.

"But?" she asked over her shoulder as she retrieved a bowl from the bureau shelf.

Tell her something, anything, you fool. "But she may have come here expecting more from me." His throat tightened.

Adriana walked to the stove to ladle soup into the bowl. Gio inhaled the heavenly smell of rosemary, garlic, and tomatoes. His stomach growled with hunger from lack of food, but his mind was too troubled to consider eating.

"Either you tell me, or you do not," she said. "Do not give me crumbs to go on, *per favore*, and expect me to treat the woman with less than my usual hospitality."

"Fine." He tossed his hands into the air. "She's here hoping," he said. "She's hoping for more to our relationship."

"You have a relationship?" she asked.

"A correspondence, really."

Liar.

"We met while I was serving," Gio said. "When I was on furlough." There, he'd lied to his own mother. He was lower than low. "So I wouldn't want her to get the impression it's more than it really is."

"And tell me, *per favore*, why would it not be?" She finished setting the tray. "You are not growing younger, Giovanni. I have yet to see you pay more than cursory interest in any woman except Zola." She glared. "Did I tell you her *padre* made Sebastian pay our account in full on Monday?"

"Why?" He sighed and sank into a chair.

Idiotic question.

Zola's family ran the Cana General Store. Her father didn't like him because he and Zola spent time together before the war, and she'd happily resume their association again now he'd returned. Her father said she was closing off her chances with a reputable man by cavorting with him. He did not come bearing a marriage proposal.

"Because, Giovanni, you think I do not realize what you do? Or *Signore* Kavouras does not know what you spend your time with his daughter doing?" Her cheeks reddened, she looked away and sighed. "Enough of this sermon. You are an adult, but it pains me to see you wasting your life. So set against marriage and a *famiglia* of your own. Always looking in from the outside." She faced him again. "I want you to be happy."

She picked up the tray, approached the door to the hall, and paused. "If there comes a time when you can tell me the real reason Elizabeth is here, do so, *per favore*. Until then I will treat her like a welcomed guest."

She exited through the swinging wooden door.

"*This* is my family," he whispered to himself.

Gio rested his elbows on the table, cradling his face in his hands. Elizabeth Reilly brought chaos in her wake. The sooner he sent her away, life would return to its routine.

****

Elizabeth stood at the window, looking out at the vineyard. In awe, she delighted in the beauty of the rolling hills covered with vines and the aisles dipping and curving throughout. The breathtaking view of the vines' leaves, and the trees bordering them, changing to burnt ocher and honey yellow, buoyed her soul.

She breathed in the sweet, crisp, flowery scent of the land. Beneath the traces of life in all its stages, Elizabeth sensed something ancient and otherworldly. Something she couldn't put a name to and wasn't willing to focus on. Her visit there was for Paolo and nothing else.

She turned her attention beyond the Clemente vines, to the southwest. There stood a cluster of brick cottages. Paolo told her about the bungalows he refurbished when he took over the vineyard. The former owner, a widow, had left much of the grounds in disrepair, with the vines sick and unkempt. Paolo's year without his wife and son was a busy one. He prepared the estate for its mistress and nursed the vines, not able to keep the fruit they produced. The idea of his family living there kept him going.

When Paolo falsely learned his brother Michael, Adriana and Gio had perished, he'd been devastated. Paolo's purpose for living evaporated. This was the key to making Gio see. She needed Paolo by her side, though, giving her the words. So she'd stay for her friend, Paolo, no matter how difficult Gio made the task.

Turning from the window, she studied the four-poster bed. Once she laid her head down on those pillows, she'd dream of finding herself walking amongst the vines outside. How many times did she lose herself in them before coming here?

"Elizabeth?" Adriana called and knocked from the other side of the closed door.

Startled, Elizabeth responded, "Yes?" She crossed the room and opened the door.

"It is past lunch time. You must be hungry, yes?" Smiling, the woman entered, carrying a sterling silver tray. The scent of rich, spicy tomatoes filtered into the room smelling too delicious for even a person of minimal appetite to pass up.

"Yes." Elizabeth smiled back. "Thank you."

Adriana walked to a table positioned before a pair of large, paned windows. "Is this not a lovely spot to dine?" She set the tray down. "My husband chose this house wonderfully."

"Please let me help." Elizabeth joined her and picked up a teapot and two teacups, placing them on the table. "I was admiring the view. It's as beautiful as you said."

"It is true, Elizabeth. I cannot imagine anywhere else for me to live." Once the tray was empty, Adriana deposited it on the floor and gestured for Elizabeth to take a chair.

"Thank you." Elizabeth sat and glanced up at her hostess. "Would you like to join me?"

"Yes, I would like that." Adriana took a seat across

the table. "So, Gio tells me you are friends."

Avoiding eye contact, she nodded and spooned the sweet tomato-based soup into her mouth. She couldn't lie if she were eating.

"You met while he was away at war?" Adriana picked up the teapot and cups and poured tea for them both. "Are you still upset with my Gio?"

"Well," she set the spoon down and leaned back in her chair, briefly closing her eyes. How am I supposed to respond? "It was a misunderstanding. I showed up without a word."

At least something she said was truthful.

"I see," she said. "But you were right not to wait for an invitation." Adriana's eyes met hers. "A man like my Giovanni needs to be steered with a firm yet loving hand. Like his *padre*."

"Gio and I—" She stopped, exhaled, and spoke again. "I have no interest in steering your son anywhere, Adriana."

"No? He tells me the two of you have a correspondence."

"Well—" Elizabeth shifted in her chair. She wished Gio would have filled her in about this correspondence ahead of time.

"My son does not give his heart freely. Losing his *padre* when he was a baby has made him cautious."

"Oh?" No longer hungry, Elizabeth pushed the bowl away.

"Do not be embarrassed. Gio told me because I insisted he tell me."

"So, he told you—"

Adriana interrupted. "Do not be upset, *per favore*, please. He was drinking brandy. In the middle of the day and this is not like him. You, *cara mia*, are affecting him more than you realize."

"I'm sorry."

"Do not apologize." Adriana leaned in, placing her elbows on the table. "I feel there should be no secrets between us, yes?"

Elizabeth averted her eyes and nodded.

Adriana lowered her voice. "Giovanni mentioned the two of you met while he was on a furlough," she said, smiling. "He told me he thinks you are hoping to build more than a friendship."

Oh, the idiot! So, he's so sure of himself. "I'm afraid he's mistaken. I traveled here to visit the vineyard. I've never been to one." Seems the man wasn't uncomfortable lying to his own mother. Well, she'd avoid helping him as much as possible.

"I am afraid he does not place much value in relationships. He thinks to love someone will bring hurt. Gio was too young to see the good his *padre* and I shared. He only saw how much losing him hurt me. I loved the man and would not have given up a minute with him. Even if I knew hurt would follow."

"And he loved you, Adriana—" Elizabeth bit her lip. "What do you think happened to Paolo?"

Adriana placed her face in her hands for a moment and leaned back in her chair.

Elizabeth shook her head at herself. She needed to remember what Gio told her. They didn't know her. She had no right to ask these personal questions so soon. "I'm sorry. I shouldn't ask such things."

"No, no, it is fine. Much time has passed since I spoke of this." She inched forward, resting against the table. "Gio does not speak of his *padre,* but he told you his *padre's* name. Hmmm, interesting." She paused and took a deep breath. "We were never sure what really happened to him. To my Paolo. When we arrived in Boston from *Italia*, we were three days late. Our ship traveled out of the way to avoid a storm at sea. When the ship docked, Paolo was not there. At the time, I did not speak very good English and I was young. So young."

She glanced into the air and back at Elizabeth with a sad smile. "It was very confusing to me. Thank goodness Michael, Paolo's youngest brother, accompanied Gio and me to America. He was able to take control. He contacted Marco and found out Paolo set out to meet us. He told us which hotel Paolo planned for us to stay."

Adriana fiddled with the delicate handle of her teacup. "When we arrived there, they told us he never checked out and did not return to ask for his key after his first night's stay. We waited for a week. People, the authorities, were not as eager to help us as we expected. We were immigrants. When there was still no sign of him, Michael said it would be best for Giovanni to be settled in California. So, we left." She rose from her seat and stepped to the window. She looked out for what seemed like a long time. Finally, she spun around and leaned back against the glass.

"Once we were settled here on the vineyard, Michael returned to Boston to look for Paolo but found no traces of him."

Elizabeth ached to tell her about Paolo but remembered her vow to Gio. If she were to break the promise, he would never accept the truth from her and make everything exceedingly difficult. "I'm sorry."

"Do not be sorry, Elizabeth. I mourned for a very

long time. For many years, I expected to see Paolo running down the road to draw me into his arms. He would tell me how he ached for his exceptional beauty…the only *signorina*." She sighed, cutting off her words.

"Able to turn a frivolous bachelor into a faithfully married man," Elizabeth murmured more to herself.

"*Si*!" She laughed and jumped up from the window. "How would it be you know this?" Her smile faded.

Elizabeth shifted in her seat. Where was her mind? The only way she'd possibly be aware is by Paolo telling her. She needed to think before she spoke, or she'd never last another hour without Gio tossing her out on her posterior. "It's just…Gio told me."

Lord, she was not a born liar and keeping up this pretense was going to be darn near impossible.

Adriana frowned. "My memory must be failing me. I did not think I told my son."

Much too close. Elizabeth stood and bent to pick the tray up from the floor where Adriana had set it earlier.

"What are you ladies doing here?"

Elizabeth jumped up, hitting her head on the table as she heard Gio's voice in the doorway. "Ouch!"

"Goodness, are you hurt?" Adriana rushed to Elizabeth's side as she stood up holding the back of her head.

"Of course, she is, *Madre*," Gio said, now beside them. He grabbed the tray from Elizabeth's hand. "She should be more careful." He shot her a warning look.

"I was," she said and continued to rub the smarting bump on her head.

"And you should be more polite, Giovanni." His mother took the tray, placed it on the table, and cleared the dishes.

"*Si, Madre*." Gio aimed a look of annoyance at his mother.

"Perhaps you would show our guest around the vineyard?" Adriana said, showing him an equal amount of annoyance.

"Sebastian, our groundskeeper, can show you around," he said to Elizabeth.

She nodded in relief. She wasn't up to another round with *Signore* Clemente.

"Nonsense," Adriana piped in. "Seb is an elderly man and not much entertainment for a young lady. You will take her, *si*?"

"*Si, Madre*," he grumbled under his breath.

Adriana spun with the full tray in her hands and winked at Elizabeth. "They are never too big to listen to their *madri*."

"Shall we go, Miss Reilly?" He held his hand toward the door.

"She does have a first name, Giovanni." Adriana walked to the door in front of Elizabeth.

"Fine," he said and sighed in resignation.

"Your son wants me to call him Mr. Clemente." Elizabeth said, sure the comment irritated Gio.

Adriana paused at the door and peered over her shoulder at the two of them. Smiling, she said, "Such nonsense. Why do you insist she be so formal? You were corresponding after all, were you not?" She winked at Elizabeth. "My son does prefer to be called Gio." She walked out the door.

Gio walked past Elizabeth and without looking back, uttered hotly, "Shall we go, Elizabeth?"

"Why I'd love to, Gio."

Chapter Six

"In this section, the vines' original roots were brought over from Italy by my father." Gio grabbed a light purple berry from the vine, crushed the grape between his fingers, and tasted it. He shook his head.

"What are they called?" Elizabeth took in the sight of the blue-black fruit. A single stake at each individual trunk supported the vines. "The grapes?"

"We call them *Primitivo*. These were the mainstay of the homeland vineyard." He plucked another berry. "Here, taste this."

She took the grape from his hand and bit into it, swirling the moist, bittersweet berry over her tongue—just like in her vision. Unsettled, she silently counted to five before asking, "Are they ready for picking?"

"No, not ripe enough yet but soon. These are early ripening grapes, though," he said. "I'm judging I have two more weeks." He grabbed a handkerchief out of his pocket and offered her the crisp, white cloth. "Soon, the whole vineyard will be teeming with people."

"From where?" She accepted the handkerchief, wiping the grape's juice from her fingers.

"We invite people from town. My Uncle Michael will come with his wife and usually his sons. This year his youngest son Paolo for sure." He took the handkerchief back.

Rubbing her hands together, still feeling the

stickiness of the grape, she concluded now wasn't the best time to comment on his cousin's name.

Gio walked down the aisle. "This whole area is *Primitivo*, but beyond this hill is my favorite."

Elizabeth followed behind, enjoying the companionship and the late afternoon sun filtering into the aisle. Gio guided her through the vineyard, and he appeared to forget why she was there. No lines creased his brow. He held his shoulders erect but not like those of a burdened man trying to keep his troubles at bay. He was a man who was sure of himself, of his surroundings, and liked who he was when he was amid them.

She could like this man, too. They walked down a slight incline. "Here we are," Gio said and stopped, waving his hand in a broad sweep to the vines around them. "These are *Cabernet Sauvignon*."

With curiosity, Elizabeth gazed at the deep purple grapes. "Did Paolo bring these over, too?"

"No, definitely not. These vines originated from France and were here when my father purchased the vineyard." He smiled. "My uncle was dead set against keeping a French vine, but with my mother's insistence, they stayed."

"My father has your *Cabernet Sauvignon*. He says it's wonderful." Her father considered himself a wine aficionado.

"He does? From when?" Gio asked.

"Two—weeks ago," she answered, unsure of the importance of when her father had the bottle.

He laughed. "No," he said. "The vintage. What year was listed on the bottle?"

"Oh," she said, her cheeks hot with embarrassment. "I don't know."

She didn't. When her father came up from the cellar with a bottle of Clemente wine cradled in his arm, she noticed the vineyard and the place. She'd almost jumped out of her own skin at the realization that Paolo's vineyard had survived without him. In that moment, she'd known what she needed to do.

"It was probably 1938," he said with a nod. "So, your father?" he asked with interest in his voice. "What does he do?"

"He's a businessman. He runs two pubs and a small brewery where he produces lager for his pubs."

"Ah, another family business."

"Yes. All passed down through the family. My father benefited from several of them," she said. "My grandfather used to run cargo ships out of the East Boston shipyards."

"What were the ships used for?" Gio bent and yanked out a tall weed.

"Well, there was a time they did a good business importing wines. The trade slowed and died completely with prohibition."

"With a name like Reilly, your father must be Irish." He walked forward again with Elizabeth falling beside him.

"Yes, my father is Irish through and through." She frowned to herself, not bothering to point out O'Brien was her family name.

"Your mother, is she Italian?"

"My mother?" She shook her head. "No, I don't think so."

"Don't think so?"

"My mother was orphaned as a baby. We have no idea who her parents were." She stopped and hesitated before reaching out to stop Gio as well. "The children at the orphanage used to tease my mother," she said. "Taking guesses at what she might be."

The other children called Dora a witch, but Elizabeth decided not to mention this part.

"We think she may have Narragansett blood, but it's hard to tell by looking at her. I resemble her. We're like chameleons, really."

"Does it bother you, Elizabeth?" His eyes met hers. "Not to know where her people are from?"

Her cheeks heated with the intensity of his gaze. She suspected where he came from meant everything to this man.

"No, not really." She looked away.

Her mother's unknown heritage didn't bother Elizabeth, but the gift she'd inherited from the woman did. She continued, "My mother is very comfortable with who she is. My father loves her. And me?" She shrugged. "I feel like Elizabeth, not one thing or the other. However, I must admit, growing up in an Italian neighborhood I sometimes pretended I was Italian."

An Italian girl who didn't get visits from dead people.

"Ah, so you are familiar with us Italians."

"Somewhat." She frowned. "The neighbors kept their distance for the most part."

"They did?"

"Yes, there aren't many families like ours. Half-Irish, the other half a mystery." Not to mention many in the neighborhood also considered Dora O'Brien a witch and held suspicions about Elizabeth as well.

She shivered. She'd taken a chance to tell Gio her mother's orphanage story. She wanted to see if he'd turn her away. If he did, he wouldn't be worth helping.

Ready to get on to the next subject, she asked the first question entering her mind. "Gio, what did your family do during prohibition?"

"Well, my father left us to tend to the vineyard as you are well aware." He jogged to catch up with her. "My mother, Marco, and Uncle Michael made a good start to establishing the Clementes as wine makers in California. But five years after they started, when prohibition hit, the harvest was a loss."

"Do you remember any of it?" she asked as they strolled at a comfortable pace.

"No, not the early years. As I grew up, I remember my mother selling the grapes by the bushel to men who drove in from the city. She knew they'd be used for moonshine, and the grapes would never see their full potential. But the endeavor kept the vineyard going. She and my uncle also petitioned the government for permission to make wines for churches and pharmacies."

"Was it hard for them?" Elizabeth asked.

"It was. Especially for my uncle. This wasn't his dream in the first place. He accompanied us in order to help his brother." A sardonic laugh escaped him. "He moved to San Francisco the spring of nineteen-twenty and opened his own grocery. He met my Aunt Miriam the following year and left my mother to manage the vineyard. With Marco and Sebastian to help her, she ran the show." His eyes sparkled with admiration. "Most of the men who bought the grapes were contacts Michael made from the city."

"Adriana ran the vineyard then." Elizabeth smiled, sharing in Gio's admiration for the woman.

"Yes, my mother is a very strong woman. Between

her hard work and Michael supplying the customers, they were able to keep the vineyard going when most others folded up and left. Without any help from my father."

"Paolo could not have predicted the prohibition."

"I suppose not, but, nonetheless, he brought his family from Italy to become grape farmers."

Elizabeth was glad she didn't sense Paolo. To see how much Gio hurt because of the cataclysmic choice he'd made would devastate the ghost. She took a deep cleansing breath and said, "It wasn't your father's intention. Besides, you're much more than grape farmers now."

"Yes, again with no help from him."

With a muffled sigh, she stopped walking and regarded him. "You know, it's obvious my being here isn't a pleasure for you."

"Your point?"

Of all the arrogant men! If Adriana hadn't admitted as much, Elizabeth would wonder if Gio was Paolo's son at all. "My point is your mother isn't a child. She deserves to hear the truth, and I don't appreciate you asking me to deceive her."

Gio narrowed his eyes in her direction. "You're right. What good is having you here doing, really? I mean, let's gather your things. I'll personally see you to San Francisco and put you on the train myself. I'd relieve you of any responsibility and be free to tell my mother when I feel it's time."

"What if you didn't tell her?" She bunched her fist. If she were a man, she'd punch him one and knock the half-smile off his patronizing face.

"That would be my choice, now, wouldn't it? You

63

have no stake in my mother or me. You're free to leave whenever you wish." Gio stepped past her. "Think about what I said. In a matter of hours, you'd be on your way home."

Chapter Seven

The next morning Adriana stood at the bay window in the dimly lit kitchen. Her coffee cooled on the table behind her. She could neither drink nor eat because her stomach had danced a nervous ballet all through the night. She'd cook once Gio, Marco, or Elizabeth showed their faces or Sebastian if he lumbered in from the cottages to breakfast with them. He'd been a frequent visitor at the main house since his wife passed away two years before. Seb often laughed and said his daughter and her family needed a break from his constant presence. Adriana suspected *he* needed to escape the cottage where he'd spent his life with his late Esmerelda.

Adriana sympathized with her friend. She experienced, every day, what it meant to miss someone—body, and soul.

Outside the window, the waking sun sliced beams through the mist large enough for a man to walk through. She shivered. *Foolish woman, do not even think it.* Paolo died or else he would have come home three decades earlier.

She wasn't nervous nor was she agitated. Rather, excitement hummed in her blood. Why?

Whatever the reason, Elizabeth Reilly brought it with her. Did Gio have a future with this woman?

She was not a fool. Lord knew Gio was not telling her the truth about what was passing between him and their houseguest. He'd tell her in his own time. Pushing him would not bring results. She'd raised him to be a strong man but playing both mother and father had never been easy. Of course, she hadn't accomplished his upbringing alone. Still, no matter what she, Marco, or Sebastian did, it never equaled what Paolo would have given their son.

She braced her hands on the cool glass and closed her eyes. Her heart pulsed with the eagerness of youth.

She was eighteen again, unmarried, and back in Italy.

****

The searing sun flamed bright on the Clemente vineyard. She watched the married women as they laughed and stomped barefoot in the season's first harvested grapes. They held their long skirts up to their thighs, while the men, children, and unwed women stood around and cheered them on.

Lorenzo Clemente stood to the side watching her.

Their elders did not allow them to speak in private and she was always under the guard of her aunt's hawk-like eyes. Adriana stole a sideways glance at him and smiled. He was a gallant and comely man. His dark features rested well on his heavy frame. She could be content married to him. Any woman would do well to catch one of the Clemente heirs. If her father and his got their way, she'd be married to him within the year.

If her aunt were correct, she'd learn to love him.

She inched away from her chaperone. If only the prude joined in the crush, she would have been set free.

"Where is she, little brother?" A man locked his arms around Lorenzo's waist and lifted him off the ground.

"Put me down, Paolo," Lorenzo said between his teeth. He laughed and broke from his brother's grip when his feet hit the ground. "You're the last person I would tell." He grinned, yanking his buttoned-down shirt straight. "A man would heed well to lock his woman in when you're around."

"Ah, this is why I use the element of surprise."

Adriana edged closer. This new arrival interested her. This was the eldest of the three brothers. The one her aunt warned her to avoid. He was one to ruin a woman's virtue. Was this why neither his *padre* nor *madre* had sought a bride out for him?

Just look at him. He was not a small man by any means, but he was built of lean lines and sinewy muscle. He was not at all like Lorenzo or the youngest brother, Michael. Paolo's features were sharper. He was an aristocrat made for Roman society, not to be the don of a country vineyard. What woman would not beat down the door for a chance at him?

"Adriana, come back here," her aunt ordered.

Never one to do as she was told, she approached the men, taking several sideway steps, stopping to catch sight of *Signora* Clemente marching like a young girl in the grapes. All other times Adriana met her, the petite woman was soft-spoken and reserved. To see this frivolous side to the mistress of the vineyard amazed her.

Adriana ran her hand along the table set with covered plates of food, a feast for the daylong harvest celebration. If she bided her time, waiting for refreshments, perhaps she'd be able to sneak away.

"Now this must be Adriana."

She turned toward the brothers, and her breath caught. Paolo leaned casually on Lorenzo's shoulder. He wore a mischievous, lopsided grin. No other man was as appealing.

"She is much too beautiful for you." Paolo's eyes didn't leave her face.

Too young to have the sense to blush, she smiled at him. "And you, *Signore*, are much too bold to pay such compliments to a woman. Especially when this woman is promised to your brother." Adriana always recognized what was meant to be hers. The first of the Clemente brothers had been born for her. She'd no longer be content to marry the middle brother.

"*Madre?*"

Her eyes shot open, and she spun from the window.

"Are you okay?" Gio stood in the doorway, his shadowed eyes wide with worry.

"Yes. I am fine." She cleared her throat and stepped to the stove, tightening the back straps of her apron. "I was enjoying the quiet."

Now beside her, with a stove rag in his hand, he poured himself a hot cup of coffee from the iron kettle. "I'm sorry I missed dinner last night. I was busy."

"Nonsense." She swatted his arm. "I have not been alone so long I do not see when a man is avoiding a woman."

He sipped his coffee. "I have work to do. There's no need to cook breakfast for me. I'll eat later." He set his mug on the table and left the house through the back door.

Yes, she knew when a son was avoiding his mother. She smiled and lit a fire underneath the cast iron frying pan.

****

Two hours later, Elizabeth threw back the hand-knit

blanket on the four-poster bed she'd lain awake in all night. She swung her feet over the side of the bed, onto the plush lamb's wool throw rug, and wiggled her toes. A feverish chill clawed at her bones. The vineyard teemed with disquieted spirits. When Paolo appeared again, she'd ask him if he'd seen them. Did any of them acknowledge him? Ghosts didn't see each other, her mother had taught her, unless they themselves acknowledged they were dead.

She looked around the room, letting her eyes focus in the early morning light. None of the vineyard's ghosts sought her out. Thank goodness. All she could handle was aiding the pained souls of both Paolo and his living son.

She rose from the bed, shuffled to the window, and slid the coral lace curtains to the side. Opening the hinged window, she welcomed the crisp valley air and invigorating sweet aroma it carried.

The orange sun still hung low in the eastern sky.

Normally, Elizabeth was a late sleeper and rarely woke before dawn except when she worked at the newspaper.

After receiving the telegram informing her Patrick was missing in action, she'd spent the last few years in a lazy haze. She did little that was worthwhile. Instead, she shopped with her sister and wallowed in self-pity. Closing her eyes, she took a deep breath to quiet the ache stirring inside. There was no time for regrets. When she returned to Boston, she'd make a new life, but until then, she'd pretend to be anyone she wanted.

She opened her eyes, and glancing below, noted the vineyard was already in full swing. Gio stood talking with an older man, Marco she presumed, next to the back of the truck. Since Gio never arrived to pack her suitcases for her, he must have accepted her choice to stay.

He jumped up onto the truck bed, landing firmly on one leg, and slid a barrel to the edge. Gio was handsome with those dark and brooding good looks. Elizabeth shook her head. Was she losing her mind? Gio was Paolo's son, nothing more. Still, spying on him this way, watching him unaware, stirred something inside her she'd never imagined possible. She could spend hours watching him. No doubt Anna would find him a worthy subject for one of her sketches. With charcoal, she'd draft his long legs, the lean hard muscles bunching under his sleeves.

Elizabeth shook her head again. She'd never looked at a man with such blatant interest. In fact, she was no different from the sailors back home who blew wolf whistles in her and Anna's direction when they walked by. To consider Giovanni Clemente in such a way was preposterous and not at all respectable.

Gio wiped sweat from his brow and glanced up towards the window where Elizabeth stood.

Their eyes met, and a breathless gasp escaped her. His lips turned into a crooked smile, and she backed away from the window, letting it swing shut.

The heat on her cheeks embarrassed her, though there was no one present to see it.

Get yourself together, Elizabeth.

Getting Gio to trust her was challenging enough. She needed to help Paolo, and any girlish attraction to his son would ruin everything. He'd avoided her after the tour of the vineyard. He'd left her alone to dine with Adriana. If he really believed her a threat, would he have given her so much time alone with his mother? Did he trust she wouldn't reveal her friendship with Paolo to Adriana?

Elizabeth grabbed undergarments, a white eyelet summer dress, and left the room for the washroom. She needed to get an early start at convincing Giovanni Clemente she was only there to help his father. The stubborn man would listen to reason before the day was out.

She hoped.

****

After Elizabeth stepped away from the window, Gio leapt down from the truck bed, careful not to place weight on his right leg, and gestured to the guest room window. What a shame she was so pleasant to look at. *Damn.* This was not the time, nor the woman, for such notions. *Well, at least she isn't some spoiled city girl who sleeps in late.*

"She's awake," he said to Marco in Italian.

"Ah, is she?" Marco glanced up at the cloudless sky.

"Yes," Gio responded. "Do you think you can stay sober long enough to meet her? I need your opinion of her."

"Yes." Marco scowled. "Do you think this old man is a drunk?"

"Well, you didn't do much yesterday to make me think otherwise." He lifted a barrel down.

Out of the corner of his eye, Gio saw Sebastian's grandson exit the vines. Fortuitous timing, since his aching knee was slowing him down.

"Esteban, help me with these, would you?" he called in English to a scrawny young boy of six who carried a small broken hoe in one hand.

Esteban swaggered over to the truck and dropped the hoe to the ground.

"Looks like you hit some hard dirt there." Gio observed the discarded item.

"*Si*, my papa says I have to pay better attention." Esteban climbed up into the truck bed. The boy slid the empty barrel toward Gio before he was ready, and it skidded off the back and hit the ground with a thud.

"Esteban!" Gio scolded him and surveyed the wood for any damage.

"Sorry." The boy sulked and climbed down.

"Do not be so angry with the boy, Gio. It was an accident," Marco said and walked forward. "It is not like you."

"I know," he said and shook his head. He looked at Esteban, who avoided eye contact. "It's fine. No damage done." Gio stood straight and pushed the cask to the side with the others. "You should get back to helping your father."

Frowning, Esteban turned and walked silently back into the aisle with his head bowed forward.

"A few glasses of brandy this evening may do you some good, yes?" Marco asked. "No? This young woman, is she upsetting you?"

Gio nodded. "Yes, she is. She seems honest, but I'm not sure."

"She knew your *padre*?"

"So she says," he answered, and his throat tightened. With irritation, he couldn't shake the feeling Elizabeth told the truth. "How do I tell my mother any of this?" He let his shoulders slump forward.

"I am not sure, Gio. Adriana is a strong woman."

Gio threw his hand in the air. "I want this all to be a

lie. I'd know how to deal with her."

"Did *Signorina* Reilly say why your *padre* did not return?" Marco asked.

"He was told the ship never arrived here with us," he answered, "and we all died at sea."

"Ah, my poor man." Marco frowned and looked toward the sky. "That would be the reason the *signorina* asked for me." He looked at Gio compassionately. "She did not know you were here."

"That's what she says."

"Paolo loved you and your *madre*. He would have returned unless something terrible happened." Marco stepped closer and patted him on the back.

"So I've been told." Gio wrinkled his face in frustration. Marco was more of a father to him than Paolo Clemente.

Marco asked, "What are we to do now?"

"I'm not sure. I need to get to know her more, to find out what she knows about us. I need to trust her enough to have no doubts she's telling me the truth." Gio turned a drum onto its side, hoisted the heavy cask up, and headed toward the wine house.

Chapter Eight

Elizabeth made her way to the empty kitchen. Her stomach growled. She considered going to find Adriana or Sofia but, instead, made herself at home and found a large red apple on the icebox's bottom shelf.

"Making yourself at home?"

Startled, Elizabeth jumped up to the sound of Gio's voice and spun around.

"Ah, well. Yes, I was hungry, and no one was in the kitchen." She fidgeted.

"Did you find anything?" he asked and walked towards her.

"Well, there is an apple." She stepped aside and let the door swing closed.

He opened the icebox. "Do you like eggs?" He ducked his head behind the door.

Was he being polite? Friendly even? She wasn't sure she trusted a civil Giovanni Clemente. "Why?"

He sprang up with two eggs in each hand and pushed the door closed with his foot. "Take a seat. I'll make you some breakfast."

"You don't have to cook for me," she said but obediently sat at the kitchen table.

"Sure I do. You are a guest, and my mother will have my skin if I don't."

Smirking at the back of his head, she asked, "Do you always do what your mother wants?"

"When it suits me, yes." After setting down the eggs, he busied himself, first washing his hands in the kitchen sink. Then, he lit a fire on the stove. He set a sturdy cast iron frying pan on top of the flame. Elizabeth watched in amusement. She'd never see the day she'd catch her father or brother making breakfast.

Gio expertly maneuvered around the kitchen. He sliced four thick pieces of bread and scooped out the insides.

He popped the excess bread into his mouth and chewed, the muscle of his jaw working slowly. He set the hollow slices in the pan. Next, he broke the eggs, each with a quick tap, and emptied the contents into the pan.

When the cooking food sizzled, Elizabeth sensed the heat flicker from the fire beneath the pan and smelled the steam rising off the eggs. Gio turned to her and smiled. Like a flash of lightning, she realized how striking his smile truly was. Butterflies did a nervous dance in her stomach.

He resembled Paolo even more when he smiled.

"Would you like some coffee?" He turned back to the stove and lit another burner. "You haven't had coffee until you've tasted strong Italian brewed coffee."

"I've never tasted coffee, but sure."

He glanced back at her, strode to a shelf, and took down two large cups and two plates. "Never had coffee. What about wine? Do you drink wine?"

"Love it."

"Good answer." He set the dishes down beside the stove. "But I wouldn't recommend imbibing this early in the morning."

Elizabeth rose from the table. "Where are your

forks?"

"Over there," he said and pointed to the kitchen bureau. "The top left drawer."

At the bureau, she rested her hand on the drawer handle but froze when she noticed a picture of Gio as a boy. He stood in the vineyard aisle, holding a large empty straw basket. He wore a lopsided smile. The image of the boy, whose eyes held a look of sadness and wisdom beyond his years, tugged at her heartstrings. Overcome with an urge to hug the man he'd become, she sighed.

"See something interesting?" Gio asked from behind.

"Not at all," she murmured and bit her lip. "Well, somewhat interesting." She hitched her chin toward the picture.

"What?" He stood beside her. "You can't imagine I was such a good-looking boy?"

"Yes. I mean no. Of course, you are. Were." Looking down, she quickly opened the drawer, accidentally hitting Gio in the leg. Her cheeks grew hot. He was too close.

"Ouch." He backpedaled, rubbing his thigh. "Not the usual response I get from a woman."

"Oh, Gio, I'm sorry." She grew more flustered by the second and quickly made her way to the table and away from him. She slid into her chair, setting the utensils down in no particular place. Was there some love-starved spirit hovering somewhere near the vineyard? What other reason could there be for her odd reaction to Gio?

He is meant for me.

Elizabeth struggled not to choke. *He is meant for*

me?

What the hell?

Suddenly, an image of Paolo floated before her eyes. He leaned on another man's shoulder. The lopsided smile he wore was much like the younger Gio in the photograph.

She swallowed, blinking her eyes to clear the vision.

Gio set the food-filled plates on the table before retrieving the cups of steaming coffee. He stood looking down at her. "Elizabeth, are you ill? Your face looks white as a sheet."

She looked up and managed a meager smile. These reactions, whether to Gio or not—and now visions in front of people who wouldn't comprehend—was almost unbearable. "No, I'm fine. But the last two days have been difficult. For both of us, I suppose."

Sitting, he set the cups down and picked up the silverware. "Yes, it's been difficult, but I've been thinking we can figure it out together."

"Really?" she asked in surprise, still feeling unsettled.

"Really. So, tell me about my father." Gio took a bite of his food and swallowed it. "How did you meet him?"

She picked up her fork, but only pushed the food around the plate. "On the beach."

"The beach?"

"Yes," she answered, careful to avoid meeting his gaze.

"Yes? Is that all the answer I get for cooking you breakfast?"

Fine. She did owe him more of an answer. If only he'd look at his food and not so intently at her. "He used to go there to watch and wait." She met his eyes now. "He relived the day he'd lost you every day of his life." *And after.* "He and I were kindred spirits."

She bit her lip. How much should she tell him? Why she was there on the beach all those times when she saw him there? She'd been there to say goodbye to her husband, and she was a widow? How could she? She'd let both Gio and Adriana call her Miss Reilly without correcting either of them. If she said something now, he'd think her dishonest.

Besides, how far did she want to let any of the Clementes into her life? Her only purpose for being on the vineyard was to help Paolo pass from this world to the next. There was no need to think about how, once he did leave, she'd be friendless again.

Besides, her family waited for her. Shouldn't they be enough?

"Kindred spirits?" He set his fork down and leaned forward.

"I mean he was lonely. Like I am sometimes. And I helped him."

Lonely. *Like I am sometimes?* Why was she saying so much?

"Did he take advantage of you?" Gio asked.

"Absolutely not." Elizabeth continued to push the food around her plate. "Your father was a good man. He wouldn't have hurt a soul."

Scowling at her, he said, "Obviously, everything he did wasn't perfect. Take leaving his family alone in America for instance."

"If you're looking for more reasons to dislike your father, I can't help you." Her cheeks grew warm.

"I'm looking for the reason a man would abandon

his young wife and son."

Lord, poor Gio. The poor boy thought his father had abandoned him. "I told you. He didn't abandon you."

"Yes, I heard you. Well, that part of the story makes no sense. He was a Clemente." He glowered at her. "We have too much pride. He'd have returned, no matter what, to make his father proud."

The look in his eyes challenged her. Gio wasn't aware of the secret Paolo had shared with her. Did Adriana know? She dropped her fork to the plate with a clink.

"There's something you're holding back. I can see it in your eyes."

"Gio, I'm not sure." She pushed her breakfast away, the plate nearly full.

"You're realizing he wasn't so perfect, aren't you?"

She leaned back in her chair and hugged her arms over her chest. "That's not it."

"Elizabeth, there isn't anything he said about my family that I don't know," he said with an impatient voice. "What hold did he have over you? You're a beautiful young woman *with* apparent wealth. I really don't see why you'd spend so much time on this man. Unless you have something to gain."

She sensed the early hint of irritation building in him, and those sparks fed her rising temper. "I suppose I can't expect you to trust me. Your father told me to talk to Marco. He knows everything."

"What are you talking about?"

"I want to speak to Marco." She stood, knocking the chair backwards. Her hands shook. "I'm wasting my time with you."

"Wasting your time with me?" Anger flared in his

eyes. "Dammit, Elizabeth. You can't manipulate me like this. You figure if you can get some time alone with another old man, you can work your charm. Well, I won't allow it." He stood, slamming his fist down on the solid table as he did. The table's contents shifting and clinking together on the well-worn wooden surface.

Elizabeth jumped, startled by the action. She took a few steps away. She glared up at him as her pulse raced.

Gio stared impassively at his hand. "No matter what you can tell me—" he looked up, "I won't accept that this man, this Paolo Clemente, cared about anyone's interest except his own," he said, his voice, threaded with intensity.

"That's not true," she whispered.

"He had everything in Italy," he said. "He was the eldest son and would've been handed the family vineyard on a silver platter. He gave everything up to come to America. He tore my mother away from her family and left her here to bring up a son. He wasn't the good man you say he was."

Elizabeth's anger swelled. Of all the mule-brained men! She'd stand there speaking until she was blue in the face, and he still wouldn't have heard a word she said.

"Do you really want to know why your father didn't return to this vineyard?" she spat back. "Without your mother, and a sorry excuse for a son, this vineyard didn't matter. He didn't turn his back on the vineyard in Italy. Your *grandfather* refused him the inheritance. Your father wasn't a Clemente!" Her whole body seemed to vibrate with frustration. "You're not a Clemente!"

The minute the words were out, Elizabeth gasped, and her hands flew to her mouth. Why did she let him get to her so much? Her mother never let her own emotions interfere with helping a lost soul.

"What the hell are you talking about?" His words were still harsh, but his eyes betrayed him. She'd scared him.

"Oh, Gio. I'm sorry." She approached him and offered her hand in comfort him.

He quickly stepped away, avoiding her touch. "What right do you have to walk in here and tell *me* I'm not a Clemente?"

Fisting her fingers, Elizabeth let her hand drop to her side as she whispered, "I'm sorry. I shouldn't have told you. Not like I did."

"You're a liar." Running his hands through his hair, he paced the floor.

"I'm not a liar. Ask Marco. He can tell you."

"Fine, I'll ask him, and when I come back, I want your bags packed. I want you out of my house." Gio spun, bumping into the counter, and knocking an ornately painted vase to the floor. The embossed clay shattered. Broken pieces of gold-etched terracotta lay scattered among wildflowers on the blue kitchen tile.

Elizabeth watched him storm out of the kitchen through the back door. No one ever aroused such emotion in her. She needed to temper her reactions if she were to be of any help.

The kitchen door to the hallway swung open, and Adriana paused in place, holding the door with her hand to keep it from swinging back and hitting her. She muttered something in Italian and said, "Elizabeth, what in heaven happened here?"

Chapter Nine

"Why didn't someone tell me?"

Gio paced. His feet hadn't stilled since he'd fled the kitchen.

Marco stood with a solemn face by the vine he'd been tending. "I appreciate your frustration." The older man yanked a handkerchief from his shirt's breast pocket, snapped the cloth open, and wiped perspiration from his forehead. "But, Giovanni, you must understand. The family did not see the point in telling your mother. Adriana suffered far too much when your father disappeared."

Gio paced several more laps. He ran his hands through his hair, and his fingers snagged the leather strap he'd tied it back with. He flung the strap into the leveled weeds carpeting the aisle. Stopping in front of Marco, he fidgeted, his nerves raw. Standing still pained him, but pacing only fueled his temper.

Marco was not to blame for this. Why hadn't his father told his mother? His was a family of secrets and a life of lies. "He should have told her," Gio said.

Marco groaned and leaned back against the vine's thick trunk. "Paolo wanted to wait until he made a success of this vineyard. He was adamant he needed to prove himself, prove he did not need the name."

Anger swelled inside of Gio, and he flung his hand into the air. "That's absurd. Even a fool could have seen how much my mother loved him." He pointed back toward the main house. "She would've understood."

"Yes, so true." Marco turned back to the vines and plucked shriveled yellow leaves from the lower branches. "But Paolo was a stubborn man," he said. "Much like his son."

Gio glared at the back of the man's head. "You can't think I'm doing the same thing by waiting to tell her about any of this." *About Elizabeth.* "There's a difference of thirty years here." He circled Marco like a starving animal. Marco's shoulders tensed in response to Gio's misplaced irritation. Attempting to control himself, Gio stopped and unclenched his fist. "He should have told my mother."

Marco turned back to him. "I should have, or your Uncle Michael, but we chose not to. We made a bad choice, but you, you have the choice to make it right."

Gio hung his head. He wasn't born when Paolo first deceived his mother. "When did my father find out? Or did he always know?" He glanced up.

"No, he did not always know," Marco said. "He found out the morning of your Uncle Lorenzo's wedding. Your grandfather Robert—"

"He's not my grandfather."

Marco continued. "Roberto made the announcement three months before your parents were to wed."

"He announced what?" he asked, fighting the urge to run. "That my father was a bastard?"

"He told the *famiglia* Lorenzo would be groomed to take over the vineyard as the eldest Clemente son." Marco strode to him, lifted his hand, and gently patted Gio's shoulder. "Roberto might have used more care to tell Paolo he was not his son, but he did not."

The simple touch calmed Gio, and his muscles shuddered. "How do you have knowledge of all this?"

"Your father told me when he asked me to come to America with him," Marco said. "He swore me to secrecy. He said he would tell your *madre* when the time was right."

Gio cleared his sore throat. "I need a drink," he said. "Will you join me?"

He led Marco down the aisle, past the vineyard staff tending the vines in silence. They did not nod hello or greet him. The aisles were uncharacteristically quiet, missing the customary laughter and conversation. Those nearby heard the conversation, and the news would have already spread through the vines.

His shoulders slumped when he and Marco arrived at the clearing. "Who was my real grandfather?" he asked without looking at Marco.

They continued their walk to the wine house.

"A wealthy merchant from Rome," Marco said in hushed tones.

"What happened to him?" Gio stopped outside the door, turned, and scanned the vineyard. Why should he care? The man obviously hadn't cared about his father.

Marco stood beside him and answered, "He was a married man with eyes for the young ladies, and Isabella was a beauty. Fidelio did business with her father and made frequent trips to Foggia. He found time to be alone with her under her father's nose. When Isabella's father found out she was with child, he approached Roberto and asked him to marry her, promising a large dowry donated by the merchant. The condition was Roberto claimed the child as his own."

Unbelievable. They'd bought Roberto to be

Isabella's husband. "Did he accept because of the dowry?"

"No, it is because of the money you have this beautiful vineyard. He put the entire sum away for the child."

"But he did claim my father as his, and everyone obviously believed he was. Why didn't he pass the vineyard down to him?"

"Pride, Giovanni. Men of Clemente blood always controlled the vineyard. It was passed down to Roberto from his father. Each generation before passed it to a man of the line. Clemente blood always labored the land. Paolo was not blood. Not to Roberto." Marco wiped his brow as he leaned against the stone wall. "The day of Lorenzo's wedding, he gave your father the total sum of Isabella's dowry. He asked him to take the woman he stole from his brother and leave for America. To start his own vineyard.

"We planned to leave six months after your parents' wedding," he continued. "But your mother was with child, with you. We delayed the trip until after you were born. This broke your father's heart to leave you, but his pride would not let him stay and live in Rome. Away from Foggia and the vineyard he always believed would be his," he said. He leaned his head back and closed his eyes. "He started all of this for you." Marco opened his eyes, swept his hand toward the vines, and the main house. "Giovanni, he wanted a legacy to hand down to you."

Gio wasn't convinced his father truly did anything for him. While Paolo Clemente purchased the estate, the man's wife made it a success. Gio's mother nurtured the land and then passed the labor of love to Gio. His father did not. He lifted a shaking hand to his dry throat. He needed something strong to keep the panic locked away. After a brandy, he'd figure out what to do.

He'd search for feisty little Elizabeth.

Lonely Elizabeth.

Despite the day's chaos, sparks of anticipation simmered within him when Gio pictured her standing in front of him. She stood with her hands fisted and her chest rising with each ragged breath. He recalled how her big eyes were wild with anger when she broke his family's most guarded secret. He didn't understand how to handle her, but he wasn't ready to send her away.

****

Elizabeth didn't intend to return to the guest room and pack. She ran from the kitchen without a word to Adriana. Her anger carried her at great speed into the vineyard aisles.

Where was Paolo when she was making such a mess of everything? She needed him to steady her. She'd only been there two days, and those two days seemed like a month.

Paolo needed time to regain the emotional energy he'd spent after realizing his family lived.

Still, what about me? Shouldn't I be up in the room packing?

She should return home. If she left, Paolo wouldn't be able to stay. She'd tried to help him, but he'd never get his wish. Paolo would haunt her. They were stuck with each other.

Elizabeth ran without regard to the people working in the aisles. Her throat burned. She gasped for breath, and her muscles threatened to give out. She pushed on and didn't stop until she found the area Gio told her was his favorite. She collapsed to the weed-covered ground on her knees. With a moan, she lay back to stare through the vines at the cloudless, barren sky.

It would have been a good time for Paolo to show up, sit beside her, and ask, *"What is it you are looking at, Bella?"*

She closed her eyes. "Oh Paolo, I'm trying but I've made a fine mess of things." Keeping her eyes closed, she dared him to be beside her when she opened them. When she did, he wasn't there. She was empty, alone, and jeopardizing any hope of the man finding peace.

The midday sun slipped between the canopies of vines and warmed her face. The heat comforted her, and the vineyard smells, ripening fruit, and earth, surrounded her. She drifted off to sleep.

She ran through the green maze.

****

Out of breath, she paused and bent, hands resting firmly on her knees. Biting back a scream, she jumped to a standing position as oversized mustard-colored flowers grew around her. The stalks stretched above her head as they spread. She ran through them until her foot caught on a vine. The thick, twisting branch stretched across the ground. With a gasp, she fell to the ground on her hands and knees.

"Were you looking for me?"

She looked up to see the shadowed figure of a man standing above her. He offered her his hand.

"No. Not you." She shook her head and allowed Gio to guide her to her feet. He gathered her to him and wrapped his strong arms around her. She sighed and rested her face on his firm chest. "I wasn't looking for you," she whispered and looked up into his face.

His lips descended upon hers. Hers parted, and she allowed his tongue to explore her mouth. Heat swirled up from her thighs, and she threw her arms up, wrapped them around his neck and shoulders, pressing herself into him.

Propriety be damned.

He withdrew, brushing his lips over hers and traced kisses over her cheeks, along the line of her jaw, and whispered into her ear, "You don't have to be lonely, Elizabeth."

"Gio," she moaned.

"Bella."

Paolo's voice woke her. Clammy and confused, she wrapped her arms over her chest and moaned. This wasn't how she should think of Gio. Yet her lips still burned from the dream's kiss. What did her dream voice say? *Propriety be damned.* Perplexing warmth washed through her body.

"Bella," Paolo said again.

She sat up, but the ghost was not in sight. "Paolo?"

Inhaling, she caught only a bit of Paolo's clean scent and then it was gone.

"You should've gone to my mother because I'm messing this up."

Nothing.

Lord, she missed her sister. Elizabeth wished she could talk to Anna about the predicament she found herself in, but since the girl was nowhere near, Paolo would have to listen.

"I'm dreaming about him now."

Lying back on the ground, she ran her finger over her lips. "It's a disgrace. I'm a disgrace. Thinking of Gio in this way. I shouldn't be so eager—"

"Eager for what?" Gio asked. He stood, looking down at her.

Cheeks burning, Elizabeth bit her lip and scrambled to her feet. "You misunderstood," she said hoarsely.

"I did?" he asked. "What do you think I misunderstood?" The lopsided smile he wore intimidated her.

"Nothing," was all she managed to say. Kicking at the weeds until they revealed naked dirt, she averted her eyes. She would refrain from saying another word.

He *couldn't* realize what she was talking about.

"My mother scolded me to Italy and back for whatever I did to make you run from the kitchen like you did."

"Of course, it was what *I* said." She spoke with a sigh, lifting her eyes to meet his. "I apologize."

"No, you only told me the truth. And I browbeat it out of you." Red rode high on his neck and cheeks. "You're really turning my world upside down, Elizabeth Reilly."

Her pulse quickened as Gio stepped forward, lifted his hand, and plucked a leaf from her hair.

"Oh," she said. Did she smell alcohol?

Gio beamed his crooked smile again and wavered on his feet.

She studied his movements. Giovanni Clemente was drunk. She drove the poor man to intoxication in the middle of the day. "I'm not ready to go back to your house yet."

"Not ready to face my mother?" he asked.

She nodded. "Exactly."

"So, what are you suggesting?"

"I'd like to sit here." She motioned with her hand to

the ground.

"That's sounds like a good idea. I think I'll join you." He plopped down and spread his legs out in front of him.

Elizabeth remained standing and fidgeted.

"You're a funny one." He patted the ground beside him. "Have a seat."

"Thank you." She smiled nervously and sat beside him at a comfortable distance. "Gio, I truly am sorry for coming here and dropping all this on you. I can only begin to imagine how it must feel to you."

"At this point, I can only imagine myself. I'm not sure what to feel." He plucked an overgrown weed from the ground. "But I did talk to Marco." He locked his eyes on hers. "He confirmed what you told me. I am not a Clemente after all."

"I wasn't sure if you were aware." She looked away. "I spoke without thinking."

"I was entitled to know, wasn't I?"

"Yes, of course you were." She leaned in closer to him and said softly, "But it wasn't necessarily my place."

"Someone owed me the truth." He lifted his hand and caressed her cheek. "My father obviously trusted you enough to tell you."

The air grew arid, and her heartbeat sped. His eyes bore into hers, showing something feral, and she wasn't ready for it.

"Gio." She scooted away from him. "I'm sorry."

He dropped his hand. "Don't be. You made me understand my father more than I did before."

"I'm glad," she said. "I should be, shouldn't I?"

"Yes, but I'd suggest gentler ways of getting your point across next time." He looked away. "Are you planning on leaving?"

"I'd like to stay," she answered and fell into an awkward silence.

Gio rose from the ground and offered her a hand. "We should get back now. My mother will assume I'm assaulting you again."

"It wouldn't look good to sit out here all night, would it?" She grinned and took his hand, letting him guide her up from the ground.

"Not at all." Gio turned and led the silent march back to the house.

When they entered the kitchen, Adriana and Sofia were preparing dinner. At the sound of the door shutting behind Elizabeth and Gio, Adriana turned to greet them. "Ah, there the two of you are. I was thinking I would need to send out a search party." She turned back to the stove.

"Adriana." Elizabeth cast her eyes downward. "I am sorry about earlier, the mess."

Facing them again, Adriana wiped her hands on her apron and approached. "Not to worry, *cara mia*, it cleaned up easily."

"But the vase." She glanced at the counter where it used to sit.

"Just a vase. What concerns me more is the fact my son has been in a relationship long enough to reach the point of an all-out battle. Yet I learned about you only yesterday." She tweaked her son's ear. "Ah, but this is between me and my Giovanni." Her words were playful, but her eyes said something else completely. She turned to Elizabeth. "I hope he did not scare you too much with his boorish behavior. He is not usually like this, but I see you have a way of heating his blood. This can be very healthy if channeled in the right way." She winked.

Elizabeth's face simmered.

Adriana took them both by the arm. "Out of my kitchen the two of you." She walked them to the doorway. "I see you need some cleaning up, Elizabeth." Releasing her grip on their arms, she plucked another leaf from Elizabeth's hair. "The two of you have been doing some healthy making up, no?" She pushed them both into the hallway. "Now go and clean up for dinner. Be down at five o'clock." The door closed on Adriana, and she called, "Gio, no more brandy. And do not break anything, *per favore*."

Elizabeth giggled. Gio glanced at her sideways and scowled. "So you find this all amusing?"

"Well, yes, your mother has a way about her."

He sighed. "She does. But it's not a good idea for her to think we're rolling on the ground together."

"And what would be bad about that?" *Ugh!* She'd never been one to speak without thinking. What was she doing? Once this was over, she'd take a vow of silence.

"I don't know. What *would* be?" Without hesitation, Gio gripped her shoulder, turned her to face him, and nudged her back against the wall below the stairwell.

She arched her face up towards his, meeting the crush of his lips. Her mind numb, she trembled and closed her eyes.

Don't think, Elizabeth. Don't think.

She moaned as his mouth covered hers, and his tongue caressed and explored, pushing its way through her parted lips. His kiss tasted of something warm and bittersweet. As she melted in a wave of shimmering heat, fluid warmth flooded her body. She wrapped her arms tightly around his waist and tugged his hard body to hers.

Gio withdrew from her embrace.

Elizabeth remained against the wall and pressed a nervous finger to her tingling lips.

Propriety be damned.

With a deep-throated voice, he asked, "Is that what you were eager for?"

Chapter Ten

Gio leaned against the wall of his room. He heard nothing except the hammering of his heart. He closed his eyes and waited until the beat slowed. Why were his emotions so hard to regulate around Elizabeth? First, he let his temper flare, now apparently his physical urges.

As a boy, he'd learned to take calculated, measured action. His mother spoke the truth. His current behavior was anything but normal.

He pressed his ear to the wall. The familiar creak of the last two steps on the staircase told him Elizabeth reached the top. A few seconds later, the door to the room across the hall opened and closed.

No time would be better for escape.

He pushed away from the wall, eased his door open, and slipped out on quiet feet. First, though, Gio stared at the carved oak door protecting him from her.

What possessed him? He'd kissed her as if he had a right to.

He alone was responsible for his body's reaction when he walked up on her in the vineyard, but he was *not* responsible for how she responded to his touch. The way she countered him, pushing her body against his. The memory of her reaction made him want to go to her.

Instead, he shook his head, opened the door, and rushed to the stairs, where he sprinted down them and from the house. He jumped into the truck, slamming the door.

He was not to blame for how enticing the kiss was. He was, however, responsible for the willpower it took to withdraw from her. A long drive would help him forget all about Miss Elizabeth Reilly's impact on him.

He needed to focus on the reason she was there.

Gio turned the ignition, punched the gas, and sped toward town. A half hour later, he parked in front of the Cana General Store.

As he entered, a young Greek woman bounded up from a seat hidden behind the cluttered store counter. "Wasn't I supposed to see you last night?" She pouted and scooted through an opening at the end of the long counter.

Now this was a woman he should enjoy looking at. She slid toward him, embraced him, and planted two kisses on either side of his face.

Zola's curves were everywhere, and even more delectable when bared. He'd caused those black eyes to cloud with pleasure on more than one occasion.

"How are you, Zola?" He cleared his throat, forced himself to smile, and stepped back out of her embrace.

"I am fine, but I have missed you, Giovanni." His name purred off her tongue. "I have not seen you at my door lately. Is there someone else possessing your heart?" She cocked her head. "Have you taken up again with the woman from San Francisco? Or is it the young woman from Boston you picked up from the inn?"

Cana was a small town. After Elizabeth checked out of the inn and left with him, there was no doubt Mina Chester, the hotel clerk, ran right over to the store and announced Elizabeth's departure to everyone.

Clearing his throat, he forced out the words.

"There's no one but you." His voice cracked, and her eyes widened.

Damn liar.

Before Elizabeth arrived, he'd been many things but never a liar.

Contrary to what his mother and Zola's father thought, he'd actually not visited her since returning home. The night before was to be their first date since before he'd left for the war.

"Zola!" A man's thickly Greek-accented voice called from a back room.

"*Oye*, Papa." She turned and yelled several more words in Greek. Facing Gio, she smiled defiantly. "My papa says I should stay away from you, Mr. Clemente. You'll only use me for your own fulfillment."

Her father scolded with his deep baritone voice, "Zola!"

Her cloaked suggestion left Gio flat. He begged his body for a twinge of need. He'd be satisfied with even the weakest response. Nothing. Not like what he sensed when he'd kissed Elizabeth. Not the breath-stealing desire he'd experienced when her body pressed against his.

Zola was a beautiful woman, but Elizabeth was *Elizabeth*. He suspected she wanted more than he was prepared to give. She'd want a man who was willing to offer a lifetime.

"Don't be so sad." Zola sauntered back behind the counter and rested her full bosom on the countertop. "Have I ever resisted you? I have forgiven you already for forgetting our plans. I'll leave the store's back door open tonight. Come by after Papa has gone home." She gave him a seductive grin, leaned back, and swung her thick, black braid to the side in a gesture of flirtatiousness.

In mid-nod, he stopped. Who was he fooling? As long as Elizabeth was at the vineyard, he wouldn't be able to think about another woman. There were too many things to think about, too many things to come to terms with where his father was concerned.

Zola raised her voice loud enough for her father in the back room to hear. "What can I help you with, Giovanni?"

"Can you help me find the number to the Boston Public Cemetery?"

****

Three hours later, Elizabeth stood outside the dining room entryway. She smoothed the front of her rayon crepe skirt, closed her eyes, and took a deep breath.

Is that what you were eager for?

Her stomach tensed. What an arrogant man! They had only kissed, and it would never happen again. She lifted her chin. She needed to face him and inform him frankly. She was *not* a charity girl. Besides, if Gio was man enough to dine at the same table, well she'd do so, too.

She turned the corner and found Marco. He rested his elbows on the table. Grim-faced, he stared straight ahead at the etched glass bureau.

His thin face showed the effects of a man who had lived a lifetime. The set of his frown exaggerated the lines around his eyes and the deeply imprinted crow's feet formed from years in the sun. His roughened cheeks dimpled with pockmarks. Paolo's descriptions of the man told her he hadn't been a saint, but he loved him all the same.

She cleared her throat. "Marco?" She took several steps into the room.

"Ah, Miss Reilly. Please come." He stood. "Sit."

She approached the table and smiled. "Aren't you forbidden to speak with me?"

"Yes, Giovanni has told me as much. He really is a good one and knows better than to give me orders. I do as I please." He pulled out a mahogany chair and patted the golden velvet-covered seat. "Your visit has brought him many surprises."

She sat. "Thank you."

He slid her chair in, took his own, and turned to her with a smile. "Adriana has gone to call Gio to dinner. We should have time to talk, no?"

"Yes, I think so." She hoped she wouldn't have to prove herself to him. There were no more deep hidden secrets to share to win him over.

He took her hand. "So, you were well acquainted with my Paolo?"

She looked down at their joined hands before meeting his eyes. "Yes. I was quite fond of Paolo. He was a wonderful man."

"So even as an old man, he possessed a way with the young ladies." He chuckled and released her hand.

"Yes, he charmed me, at least." She smiled at him with relief. Marco understood. "Your cousin can talk me into anything. Including coming all the way to California to find you."

"But you understand we are not truly cousins."

"Yes," she said. "Gio told me you confirmed my story. Thank you."

"No need to thank me, *Signorina*. It was a truth I should have told a long time ago," he said.

She let the smile fall from her face. Marco was so willing to accept her. She needed to be honest concerning anything she was able to speak the truth about. "I'm Mrs. Reilly."

"You are married?" He leaned straight-backed into his chair. "Gio did not tell me."

"I haven't told him, but I'm a widow." She looked down at the gold-rimmed plate set before her.

"Ah, I see." He shook his head. "You do not wear a ring."

"I couldn't wear my ring anymore. I was away from my husband for four years. I didn't feel married anymore. Not after a while." She picked up the fork beside her plate and set it back in place. "But you—Paolo told me he'd discussed everything with you."

"Yes, Paolo did. Like his son."

She looked sidelong at his trembling hands. This wasn't easy for any of them.

"What is it?" he asked and turned toward her in his seat.

"Paolo needs you to know what really happened to him."

"What did happen to Paolo, *Signora* Reilly?"

"Please, please call me Eliz—"

"Excuse me." Adriana stood in the doorway. "Have either of you seen Giovanni?"

"No," Marco replied. "Have you, Elizabeth?"

"No." She shook her head. Not since he kissed me. Her cheeks grew warm. "I haven't since earlier."

"Aye, Giovanni." Adriana turned, threw her hands in the air, and left the room muttering in Italian.

"He is not usually like this," he said, nodding to her. "Would you care for a glass of wine?" Marco stood and reached across the table to grab a crystal decanter filled with ruby-red wine.

"Yes, please." She lifted her glass.

After filling it, he placed the decanter onto the table and sat. "You did not realize you would be meeting his son?"

"No, Marco, I didn't. It was such a shock. My heart broke for all of you." She ran her finger along the edge of her glass. "Had Paolo *any* way of knowing they'd made it to America, Gio would have grown up with a father."

And where'd I be?

"Yes, but we cannot dwell on what did not happen. We need to learn from what has occurred."

"But I haven't come to learn anything," she said. "I've come to help a friend." Paolo was right about Marco. He was a good man with a caring heart.

"I am glad the two of you have met." Adriana entered the room with Gio in tow. "It appears my son left without a word." She turned, pinching her son's cheek, and he scowled. "My Gio is all work. Never have I caught him running from the vineyard in the middle of the day without a word to a soul."

Adriana patted his cheek and left him for a seat at the head of the table. "Giovanni, pour the wine, *per favore?*"

Still standing, Gio locked his eyes on Elizabeth, jerked on the chair across from her, and sat. "You're a wicked woman, *Madre*," he said without diverting his eyes.

"All women are wicked, my son. Some more than others." She winked at Elizabeth. "After you pour the wine, I will call Sofia to bring in our dinner."

He continued to stare at Elizabeth in silence. Not knowing what else to do, she leaned against the table and whispered, "Gio, your mother asked you to pour the wine."

He rose and did as Adriana asked, filling each glass before he settled across from Elizabeth again.

Dinner passed slowly.

Elizabeth shifted the rich risotto and clams around her plate and tore pieces from a slice of warm potato bread and popped them into her mouth, careful not to glance at Gio. He remained brooding and silent, but his gaze bore into her each time she spoke. Her stomach twisted in knots, and she yearned to kick him *hard* under the table.

Finally, he excused himself and stalked away.

She exhaled a breath of relief. She drained her wine, said her good nights, and escaped quickly to the solitude of her temporary room.

Chapter Eleven

Elizabeth sat bolt upright in bed. She gathered the hand-knit blanket up around her shoulders to fend off the cold hovering around her. "Is someone there?" she whispered. The hairs on her arms stood on end. "I-I know there is, but I can't help you."

A presence vibrated within the room as if the air contained a beating heart. While no sound met her ears, Elizabeth sensed one building, and she braced herself for a shriek.

She glanced around the room, letting her eyes adjust to the darkness. Nothing appeared and the room remained silent.

Throwing back the covers, she swung her feet to the floor. The softest touch brushed her shoulder, sending chills scoring up her spine. Elizabeth bit back her own cry. She stood up and fumbled at the foot of the bed until she found what she was looking for. She grabbed her soft, cotton robe and threw it over her shoulders.

"I can't help you." Her voice trembled.

This wasn't Paolo. He didn't terrify her. She'd known from the start he wouldn't bring her harm. He was her friend. This apparition frightened her down to her core. "I can't help you," she said again and edged toward the door. "So leave me in peace and don't come to me again."

The air grew arid, and electricity sizzled through

her. Visits like these terrified her as a child. They weren't all like Paolo. While her mother's skill included a tenacity to calm the enraged, reckless spirit down, Elizabeth's fear overtook any diplomacy she might possess.

"Rrrruuu." The unearthly sound echoed around her.

"Oh, God," she moaned with a threaded voice. "Leave me in peace."

She dashed out the door.

****

"Whoa." Gio rounded the last step and held his arms out to keep Elizabeth from falling down the stairs. She'd come at him in the dark with her head down.

"Wait." He grabbed her by her ice-cold shoulders, knocking her robe to the floor. "My Lord, Elizabeth, you'd think someone was chasing you."

Gasping, she rested against his shoulder without saying a word. She trembled against him, and silent tears wet his shirt.

Hesitating, he wrapped his arm around her, drawing her closer. With his hand firmly on the small of Elizabeth's back, he pressed his palm against the thin, smooth material of her nightdress. His throat grew dry at the feel of her petite, lean body pressing into his.

"Can—" He gulped. "Can you tell me what's wrong?"

Elizabeth shook her head against his chest.

"Should I take you back to your room?"

"No," she whispered.

"Well." He glanced around in the dark. "Downstairs? Should we go downstairs?"

She pulled away from him. "Please," she murmured and wiped the tears from her eyes with the back of her hand. "If you wouldn't mind." Sniffling, she bent and picked up her robe. He took her trembling hand and led her down the stairs.

"Did you have a bad dream?" he asked over his shoulder.

"Yes," she said softly. "A nightmare."

Why did a dream leave her so shaken?

Elizabeth's secrets no longer concerned his father. If she wanted his trust, she'd have to trust him in return. Earlier, her response to his kiss proved there was more to the woman and more to him.

The drive he'd taken earlier in the day hadn't helped cleanse his system of the desire. He gazed over his shoulder at her. She held her robe in her hand. In the dark, the nightgown covered her well, but in the light, he'd be able to see the curves of her body through the sheer material. His blood stirred, and his treacherous body succumbed to its pressure. The woman's purpose must be to drive him mad.

Was Elizabeth a test or a punishment?

****

Tying her night coat securely around her, Elizabeth followed Gio out onto the porch. What was she going to tell him? The truth wasn't going to work. Who in their right mind would believe she'd been chased from the room by a spirit? This house wasn't haunted. No, she unwillingly lured that angered ghost to her like a lighthouse in the dark. There was *nowhere* to hide from the dead for someone like her.

She exhaled and took a seat on the front stoop, away from where he sat on the wooden bench. She lifted her face toward the haloed moon, letting the chilled breeze dry her tears.

Gio cleared his throat. "What happened up there, Mrs. Reilly?"

Without looking at him, she asked, "Marco told you?"

"Yes," he said. "We tell each other most things."

"Funny." She glanced over her shoulder at him. His curved lips and the stubborn yet appealing jut of his jaw glowed in the moonlight. "He said you tell each other everything."

"Why didn't you tell me you were married?"

"I'm not married anymore," she said. "I'm a widow." She stood and proceeded to lean against a stone pillar. The column stretched from the cool floor beneath her bare feet to the porch roof. "Besides, how does a person bring the subject up?"

"I'm not sure, but it seems an important thing to mention."

Wrapping her arms across her chest, she hoped to still her quivering heart. "Why, Gio?" she asked. "My husband's been gone a long time, and I don't see any point—"

He stood. "Yet, you come here telling me I have to understand what happened to a father I didn't know. Why?"

She straightened to her full five-foot-four. "That's different."

He approached her, and she shrank back against the pillar. The rough stone pressed into her back.

"What's the difference?" he asked. "What's the difference if my father died only weeks or thirty years ago? He's dead." Now directly in front of her. "He's dead to me. Like he's always been. You have changed nothing by coming here."

"Y-you," she stammered and struggled to catch her breath. "You need to forgive your father. Then come to Boston. To say goodbye." She clung to the sides of the pillar behind her with unsteady fingers. He shouldn't be so close. After being awakened from sleep and frightened to tears, she wanted nothing more than to sink into him and, possibly, lose herself in pure physical sensation.

No, she wasn't there to give in to improper urges, no matter the reason, nor to forget who she was. She wasn't there for Gio to stand so near to her. His eyes seemed to suggest they were perhaps something more than friends.

They weren't friends or anything more. She was there for Paolo.

Paolo needed a chance to make amends for his mistake. "You, Marco, Michael, your mother," she whispered with a tremor in her voice. "You all need to come to Boston for a service. To say goodbye."

Gio ran a finger down the side of her face and along the length of her jaw. She fought to fend off the dizzy, warm jolt shooting through her body. He'd found a new way to torment her.

He dropped his hand. "I can't."

"Why?" She wished he hadn't withdrawn. "You have to."

Holding her gaze, he stood silent before finally saying, "I need sleep. Come." He turned toward the front door. "I'll walk you up to your room."

"Bella." Paolo's ragged voice whispered in her ear.

Her heartbeat quickened. This is Paolo, she reminded herself.

"No. I'll be fine." She walked over to the porch steps. "I think I'll stay out here until I get sleepy."

Gio hesitated. "Are you sure?"

"I'll be fine."

He considered her for a moment, nodded and entered the house.

Elizabeth listened until she was sure he was gone and spun. "Okay, Paolo, show yourself. You've left me to do this all on my own." She sank to the stairs. "And I'm not sure it was a good idea."

Dirt rose in a plume of dry powder, settling in Elizabeth's eyes, and she wiped it away with the heel of her hand and shivered.

Cold electricity shot through her veins, and a single word rang in her mind, "*Why?*"

Paolo was angry. He'd never been angry in her presence before. She hugged herself. "Did you come to me earlier?"

He materialized several feet in front of her. "No," he said and reached toward her with a trembling hand. "Have I frightened you, *Bella*?" Concern laced his voice.

Elizabeth shook her head. "No, not you," she said. "Someone else tried to contact me. Something did scare me and, to be honest, that's nothing new. I suppose, I'd be livid too if I was stuck somewhere between life and death, and didn't understand what was happening to me," she said and studied the ghost in front of her now. His anger dissipated, leaving behind an aching grief. "Just now, though, I've just never felt *you* so angry, Paolo."

"I forget," he said, "that you feel what I do, and I forget that there are others like me. I am sorry that you experience this."

"Thank you," she whispered. For him to understand brought comfort. "Tell me now," she said, shifting the focus to him. She had time enough to consider her predicament. "How are you coping with all of this?"

"I was such a fool." His face was pale with anguish and his voice tinged with weariness. "Why did I not come back?" His shoulders slumped forward.

"You didn't have a choice, Paolo. To you, they were dead."

He paced away from her and back. "So I told myself."

Elizabeth stood. "You can't punish yourself, Paolo. Your actions can't be undone."

He stopped in front of her. "I cannot punish myself?" His eyes flared, and the color settled back into his face. "No." He shook his head. "I do not need to punish myself. My son hates me. This is punishment enough."

"He doesn't hate you," she said, but didn't feel confident in the statement. What did Gio truly feel?

He confused her.

"He does not?" Paolo asked. "He cannot even see me buried."

She caressed his cool cheek. "He's afraid is all. He's afraid to love you." Giovanni Clemente hid a scared child in his grown body. Afraid his father wouldn't want him.

He threw his hands into the air. "How do you know, *Bella*?"

Biting her lip, she turned away from him and climbed the porch steps. "I guess I can't be sure. But sometimes, sometimes I think I see fear in his eyes." She sat on the bench. "Maybe Gio is a lonely soul like you and me, but he doesn't realize it." She patted the seat. "Sit with me."

As he strode up onto the porch, she studied his tired

face. She saw the crooked nose, weather-beaten face, and sad, sad eyes. "I've missed you. Where have you been?"

"Nowhere. In the gray place where nothing exists. I could not come back. No matter how I tried. Nor am I sure I wanted to." He sank down beside her. "They are alive."

"Have you seen her?" She'd expected he would've sought Adriana out before anyone else on the vineyard.

"No." He leaned his head back against the solid house. "How is she?"

"She's a bright and charming woman, and a beautiful one, who has never stopped loving you."

He smiled. "She always was a stubborn woman. She would continue to love me. Out of spite, if for nothing else."

"It's out of more than spite. Compared to you and your son, Adriana is not mule headed."

"Ah, she has mellowed with age. The love of my life possessed a mighty arm when she was young, and a very good aim." The sparkle came back into his eyes. "I learned to duck quickly." He laughed. "If I did not, I would risk being knocked unconscious."

"No." She laughed. "Not the woman I've met. She keeps Gio in line with words only."

His smile faded from his face. "Did she ever remarry?"

"Never. She's waiting for you," Elizabeth said.

"See?" He smiled. "She is a damn stubborn woman. I should have left her to Lorenzo."

"Lorenzo? Your brother?" she asked.

"*Si*." He wrapped his arm around her shoulder. "Yes. She was betrothed to my brother."

"What?" Elizabeth sat straight and turned to look at

him. "You never told me that."

"I did not want you to think me the heel."

"Anything else you haven't told me?" She sat back and glanced sidelong at him. No matter how much she and Paolo talked, there were still things neither ever mentioned.

He smirked. "If I left her to Lorenzo, she would have never left *Italia*. She did not want to. I gave her no choice."

"You didn't have a choice."

"You are wrong there," Paolo said. "I should have stayed in Rome, where her family lived. I might have claimed I did not want the responsibility of the family vineyard. I did want it, and I let my pride decide for us all."

"You wouldn't have been happy."

"Did I die a happy man?"

She sighed. "No."

"You are right. I did not. I did not, and I ruined so many lives." The sparks of ferocity shimmered around him again.

"You're hurting now." She patted his arm. "I understand, but I'm here to help. I'll convince Gio to forgive you. We'll tell Adriana and then you can leave this place."

"Why?" he asked. "Why? So I can exist again without them?"

"What are you saying?"

"Go, *Bella*. I will stay here and wait for them."

"Do you realize what you're saying? It's impossible. You're tied to me. If I leave, you come with me," she said. "If not for me, you'd haunt the street where you died. Maybe the streetcar." She didn't realize for sure where he would end up, but she was a beacon. Paolo and those like him were drawn to her and her mother like moths to a flame.

"I can't leave them again." He shook his head, and his shoulders slumped.

"I can't stay here. I have a family and a life back in Boston." *Well, I'll make a life.*

He leaned back against the wall. "What are we to do?"

Elizabeth rested her head on his shoulder and stretched her legs out. Lord, she wanted to be angry with him. He'd spent decades without his family. She couldn't blame him for not wanting to leave them again, but where did that leave her? There was no end to her challenges. What if Paolo refused to leave this earth?

"I have no idea."

Chapter Twelve

With her watering can grasped in her right hand, Adriana stepped out onto the front porch. Humming, she glanced at her wilting fern as Gio drove the truck to a halt beside the house. He rolled down the window.

"I'm making a delivery in town. Be back later," he called.

Smiling, she approached the steps. "Giovanni, may I ask you something before you go?"

He swung the door open and jumped down. "Sure."

"When is the shipment due in San Francisco?"

"In three days."

"I can make the delivery," she said. "I will bring Elizabeth with me."

"Why?" He narrowed his eyes.

"For a day of shopping and sightseeing. I think it would be nice to get her out for a day of amusement."

"Ah." He shook his head. "Marco told you and you're feeling sorry for her."

"Nonsense. I am not feeling sorry for her. However, losing a husband is not easy. I have firsthand knowledge of what a woman experiences, Giovanni. Perhaps she needs to talk about it."

He frowned. "Mrs. Reilly doesn't talk a lot about herself. So good luck."

Adriana knew Gio didn't like the idea of her reliving those memories. "Well," she said. "I am much nicer to the woman than you are."

"What is—" Gio looked over her shoulder. "What the hell?"

Adriana turned to see Elizabeth stretched out on the thin wooden bench, fast asleep. How did she miss the young woman when she walked out onto the porch? Was she so oblivious? Rushing forward, she set her watering can on the floor. "My goodness." She guided the woman into a sitting position. "Elizabeth? Wake up."

The young woman stretched awake.

Adriana straightened and looked down at her. "Are you all right?"

Oh," Elizabeth said in surprise and glanced about. "I'm on the porch."

"Yes, I am aware." Adriana hid a smile behind her hand. "What are you doing here?"

"I—" She bit her lip.

"Did you sleep out here all night?" Gio asked.

Elizabeth sighed. "Yes, I fell asleep."

"Well, what an asinine thing to do," he said. He now stood beside Adriana.

"Giovanni," Adriana scolded with a sideways glance.

"No, *Madre*. Don't. Look at how she's dressed. It's fortunate for her the vineyard staff has too much respect for us. But what if a stranger happened along?"

Elizabeth jumped from the bench. Her robe fell open and revealed a thin ivory nightgown. "Well, you didn't worry over as much when you left me out here last night."

"You told me to." He crossed his arms over his chest.

"And you were more than happy to listen. So I'd

suggest you keep quiet about it now." She glared at him.

Gio's jaw clenched, and his eyes strayed to her revealing attire.

"Elizabeth." Adriana cleared her throat. "You must be getting a chill." She motioned to herself as if she were tying her own invisible robe.

Elizabeth looked at Gio and then down. "Oh God," she moaned, covered herself, and headed toward the door. "I think I'll go in and dress myself properly." The door swung closed behind her.

Adriana turned to Gio. "So, you brought her out here last night? Half dressed?" She raised her eyebrows and struggled to keep the smile from her face.

"She had a nightmare."

"And where were you when she woke from this nightmare?"

He shook his head. "It's not what you think. She ran into the hall, cold and shaking. I comforted her. Nothing more."

"I see. Very gallant of you, Giovanni."

"Don't." He spun on his heels.

"Don't what?" She smiled at his back as he walked away and clucked her tongue. "So irritable this morning. If you were four years old again, I would send you back to bed for a nap."

He jumped into the truck and skidded down the drive. Adriana sighed and sat on the bench. She liked Elizabeth. She was a strong-willed woman and what her son needed. A doting woman would become too much of a bore for him.

Gio was a great deal like his father.

Resting her head against the house's bricks, she inhaled deeply. The aromatic, earthy scent of the grapes hit her. Adriana loved the smell, and she loved this vineyard even more because Paolo had desired to pass this dream down to their son. She closed her eyes and wished to tell him so.

****

An hour later, Elizabeth pushed the door into the kitchen open and found Adriana staring into her tea. "Good morning," she said and took a seat at the table.

Adriana looked up and smiled, but it never reached her eyes. "Good morning to you. I wondered if you laid down in the bed for a proper rest."

"It was tempting." She twisted from side to side at the waist, stretching her still cramping back muscles. "But I might have slept all day and found myself wide awake after dark."

"Are you hungry, *Cara*?" Adriana rose. "I saved breakfast for you in the oven."

Elizabeth held out a hand and rose. "Please, let me. There's no reason for you to wait on me." She strode to the stove and retrieved a cheesecloth-covered plate. Peeking under the wrapper, she frowned. Eggs in a basket like Gio made.

At the bureau, she grabbed a fork and froze as a chill shimmered through her. The heady scent of soap wafted toward her.

Paolo.

Elizabeth turned to see him standing at Adriana's back. Tears streamed down his cheeks. She crossed to the table, fighting back her own emotions.

"The last time I saw her she was a woman of twenty," Paolo whispered.

With trembling hands, Elizabeth slid into her chair, and she uncovered her food only to stare at the meal

115

blankly.

"Are you not hungry?" Adriana asked.

"No." She looked at Paolo. "I haven't much of an appetite lately."

"Yes. It is understandable."

Elizabeth bit her lip. "Why is that?"

"When I lost my husband, I became as skinny as a child." She placed her hand over Elizabeth's.

"Who told you?"

"Marco did."

Of course, Marco. Gio wouldn't care. He wanted to prove her a fraud and send her packing. "I'm sorry, Adriana. Doesn't it hurt? Doesn't it bring back your memories of losing Paolo?"

"Did my son tell you I am so fragile and not to mention his *padre*?" She stood, crossing to the window. "Do you remember what I told you when you first arrived?" Adriana asked and nodded. "Yes?"

"Yes," Elizabeth answered. "It doesn't hurt for you to speak about Paolo."

"Yes, but I was wrong about one point. It does hurt, but it is not a reason to keep from speaking of him. He was part of my life, and I would never choose to forget."

Elizabeth wrapped her arms around her chest. "Do you think that's what I am doing?"

"I am not sure. Giovanni told me you do not speak about yourself."

She glanced from Paolo to Adriana. His emotions swept through her. Air caught in her throat. "Well, I am a private person. I always have been. Besides, I'm not here to talk about myself."

"No? I do not understand. Are you not here to become acquainted with us?"

She pushed her plate away. She should tell Adriana here and now. Giovanni Clemente would have to deal. He might never speak with her again, but she'd live with the consequences. "I haven't met many people in my life who truly want to know me, Adriana. So it's not as easy to talk about myself." She decided to give Gio a little more time. "I'm not as strong as you."

"Ah. You think I have always been this calm." She smiled now. "It is not true. I was a headstrong girl," she said. "I was a quivering mess when we arrived in Boston, and Paolo was not there. I planned to throw myself at his feet and apologize." She leaned against the window. "I planned to tell him I would follow him to hell and back if he wished to go there.

"After he told me we were to make our home in America, I made the poor man's life miserable with my tantrums. I told him I refused to leave our birthplace. He did not plan for me to follow so long after him, but he delayed the original trip when I became pregnant with Giovanni. I wanted to be home with my mother and sisters when I gave birth to my first child. So he waited." She turned to the window. "After Gio was born, we both agreed we did not want to risk our infant son's health on a trip over the sea. Paolo made the trip with Marco, and I stayed behind. I set sail with Michael, who only agreed to come to accompany me. Gio was two and a half."

Adriana shook her head. "I was a spoiled girl and I believed if I waited long enough, he would return to me."

Paolo crossed the room to Adriana. He touched his wife's cheek, but his hand passed through her. He frowned and looked down at the hand he fisted at his side.

"But the girl I was grew into a woman while he was

away. I decided my home was with him wherever we might have buried our roots. I have longed to tell him this. I would have turned my back on *Italia* if it meant living without him. I have. California is the only home for me and for Gio." She shook her head. "I will never have the chance to tell my Paolo this and it hurts. It hurts very much."

"Adriana," Elizabeth whispered. "I think he knows."

****

Later in the day, Elizabeth walked through the vineyard with Paolo's ghost beside her.

"It is so much different. These vines here." He pointed to the *Cabernet Sauvignon* she'd explored with Gio the first day. "These were almost lost. I cut them back to nothing. I discarded the first fruit."

She smiled. If she spoke back to him, the people on the vineyard would come to doubt her sanity. Gio would give her a one-way ticket to the insane asylum.

"So many hands are needed on a vineyard." His eyes sparkled.

You should have come back, Paolo. You belong here.

"See there." He pointed again at workers busy examining the vines. "The grapes are like babes. They require constant attention. The sun is like mother's milk, it nourishes them." He smiled and glanced at her sideways. "It is not fair of me, is it?"

She shrugged in question.

"To carry on this one-sided discussion. It is not often I would find you so speechless."

She covered her mouth and coughed. "You cad."

"Marco." Paolo stopped in his tracks. "How are you,

old friend?" He shook his head and turned toward Elizabeth. "I keep expecting to find time has stood still."

Marco looked up and around until his eyes settled on her. "Elizabeth," he said from the top of the step stool where he stood examining the berries and smiled. "Have you come to help this old man? Or are you looking for Giovanni?"

"No, I'm not looking for Giovanni," she said too quickly.

"Then it is too late," he said from the side of his mouth. "Ah, Giovanni. We have an extra set of hands today. Do you have an extra stool for *Signora* Reilly?"

Paolo's hand rested on her elbow. He leaned in and whispered in her ear. "He fancies you."

She snapped her head to face him. "Who?"

"Giovanni." Paolo beamed a crooked grin.

"Who what?" Giovanni stopped beside her.

Elizabeth let loose a labored breath. "Nothing. Who nothing."

Gio frowned at her. "Is this how it's going to be?"

She crossed her arms over her chest and shrugged off Paolo's grasp. He wasn't helping. "I have no idea what you're talking about." Standing there between them was making her hot. She'd wished for Paolo's aid, but now he was present he wasn't exactly helping.

"No?" Gio smiled, mirroring his father's crooked grin.

This is madness. "Correct. I have no idea what you're talking about." She locked her eyes on Gio's. "And I don't think I care. I'll leave you to your work."

"*Bella*," Paolo whispered in her ear.

"I'm going back to the house." She turned and edged away.

"Elizabeth," Gio said now. "We have to talk."

She stopped and looked at him over her shoulder. "Are you going to tell your mother why I'm here?"

"Excuse me," Marco said and cleared his throat. "I think the time has come for me to take a break." He climbed down from his stool, walked past them, and tugged a handkerchief from his pocket.

Gio stared after Marco before turning his attention back to Elizabeth. "I'm not ready to tell my mother."

"Then we have nothing to talk about." She glanced sideways at Paolo, who bowed and disappeared. "Coward," she muttered under her breath."

"Y—I'm not a coward, Elizabeth." Surprise rose in Gio's voice. "But this is my family, my mother. I know what's best."

"I wasn't calling you a coward. But maybe I should have. Your mother is not as fragile as you appear to think."

"You've been here three days. Three days doesn't make you an expert. And it gives you no right to call Marco a coward. It shows an extreme lack of respect." He frowned and shook his head in disproval.

This was falling to pieces, wasn't it? She needed to name someone the *coward*. She couldn't very well admit she'd called his father's ghost one.

"I was calling myself the coward, Giovanni." She spun to face him now. "Because I should have told your mother the truth my first day here. It's not as if I'm preserving any friendship between you and me. I'm wasting my time here. Waiting for something you may never see fit to do."

"I'll tell her."

"When?" Elizabetha asked.

"It's not your concern," Gio stated. "I'll tell her when I'm good and ready."

"Not my concern?" This was asinine. "You expect me to stay on this vineyard until you're *good* and *ready*? Then say it's no concern of mine? Well, I have a life, too, for your information."

"I trust you do." He nodded. "But I can't help but wonder why you're so concerned with mine."

"Because," she said without looking at him, "I care about your father. And I care about your mother, too."

Without waiting for his response, she spun and rushed away. Mayhap, she really was calling herself the coward.

Chapter Thirteen

Elizabeth stretched her bare feet down into the lambs' wool rug and gazed toward the open curtains. Twilight was setting in. After rushing away from Gio, she'd retreated to bed and napped.

The people of the vineyard must think of her as a sloth. While they worked, busy preparing for their impending harvest, she walked the vineyard, wanting to help but not sure how to ask. Or she slept the day away. She looked down and smoothed the wrinkles out of her skirt. Of course, she hadn't packed clothes for labor. She'd packed for a holiday.

She bit her lip. She imagined she'd breeze in, tell the Clementes about Paolo, and sadly bid the man goodbye. Once she'd accomplished her task, she'd set off for a whirlwind trip and miraculously find her elusive life. When had her world ever been so easy?

Not even when Patrick was with her.

When she was a girl, she and Patrick were inseparable. They'd always been best friends, able to talk about anything under the sky. Having him in her life grounded her and made her feel a little bit ordinary, because without him she'd have only her close-knit little world of family.

Though she loved Patrick and expected him to be her friend for life, she'd never planned to marry him. When he joined the war campaign, he'd asked her, and she'd said yes. She'd loved him, yes, but there'd been a part of herself she'd held back. He'd deserved more, and given time she would have grown to love him the way he deserved.

Now there was no Patrick, and she never got the chance.

Gio's question warranted an answer—at least she owed herself one. Why was she so concerned with him? If she were honest with herself, she'd admit Gio mattered very much.

Perhaps, she was more of a liar than she cared to admit. Like what life did she have to get back to? With a frown, she stood and left the room.

The hall was still, and the faint melody of a slow love song floated up from the first floor as she descended the stairs.

Recalling Paolo standing near Adriana earlier in the kitchen, Elizabeth imagined the two of them dancing to the tender song. Like her own parents, their love survived despite the obstacles. Adriana was strong enough to withstand the news she'd brought but Gio wouldn't realize until it toppled onto his insolent head.

And what about her? *What a chicken.* She'd missed her chance, once again, to tell Adriana the truth. *"Adriana. I think he knows. Don't you believe he's looking down on you right now? If he is, he knows,"* she'd told the woman in the kitchen earlier in the day. When she should have said, *"He knows because he's standing beside you."*

Yes, and Adriana would have screamed for someone to come and take the strange woman from her house.

She followed the music and stopped in front of the open door. Gio, Adriana, and Marco all sat in separate seats, listening intently to the music. Paolo stood in the corner, eyes closed, swaying to the melody.

Dancing with his wife.

The wrinkles in his face relaxed. The ghost was in paradise. He was with his family. Lord, he really wouldn't want to leave.

Gio looked up from the chair, his right leg stretched out on an ottoman. His eyes met hers, and he nodded.

"Elizabeth," Adriana glanced up from her knitting. "Come in, *per favore*. Gio's favorite radio program is about to start." She set the blanket in a basket at her feet and patted the sofa beside her. "I tried to wake you for dinner, but you were dead to the world." She winked. "No more sleeping on the front porch, perhaps?"

Elizabeth's stomach growled. "Oh," she said, reflexively covering her with belly with her hand. "I'm afraid I should eat something."

"I'll help her with dinner," Gio said quickly and pushed up from the chair with his hands. "You relax." He shot his mother a look, and she nodded.

Elizabeth backed out of the way as Gio met her at the door. He took her by the elbow and ushered her down the hall to the kitchen. When they were alone, behind the closed door, he said, "Sit."

"Sit?" She frowned at him. "Do you think I'm a dog?"

"No, I don't think you're a dog." His voice was gruff.

He walked to the stove, and she wrinkled her nose at his back. She slid into a chair as he retrieved her dinner and set it in front of her.

Gio sat in a chair across from her.

She lifted her fork. "Are you going to watch?"

"No, I'm going to keep you company." He propped his elbows on the table and hid his face behind his hands.

Some company. He wanted to say something to her but apparently was going to wait until she'd finished eating. Was whatever he planned to say going to ruin her appetite? She'd eat slowly.

It was delicious. Little pasta dumplings filled with meat and cheese. Asparagus smothered in a butter sauce. She'd fatten up nicely on this Italian cooking.

"Enjoying it?" She opened the eyes she hadn't realized she closed to see him sitting straight-backed against his chair. She swallowed and smiled. He looked away. *What's gotten into me tonight?* Whatever it was, she was enjoying toying with him. Setting her fork down, she asked, "So, what is it you want to talk to me about?"

He stood, clearing away her dishes from the table.

She waited, but he didn't answer. "Gio, it's obvious there's something." She rose. "Are you ready to tell your mother?"

"No."

"Well?"

"Let's take a walk." He headed for the door without looking to see if she was behind him. She followed him through the yard and into the dimly lit stone winehouse.

He pulled out a chair for her.

"Sit," she whispered and did.

From the wooden shelf beside him, he grabbed two mason jars and a half-full bottle of amber liquid. After setting the jars on the table, he uncapped the bottle and filled both. He took his seat and slid a glass over to her.

"Thanks." She smiled again and lifted the glass to drink. The strong alcohol puckered her lips and burned her throat on the way down. She coughed, hastily setting the glass on the table. "This isn't wine."

"No, it's brandy."

"Hmmm, do you think I'm some hardened drinker?"

"Not sure." He sipped from his glass without incident. "I'd like to think you're a lady from the city and everything you've told me is the absolute truth."

"Everything I've said is." *Well, almost.* "Have I done something recently to make you doubt me?" She took another sip. The liquor went down easier, and she enjoyed the warmth in her chest. She still wasn't sure about the taste.

"What did you say to my mother?"

She eyed him, suspicious of his question and said, "I haven't said anything to her."

"No?" He took the glass from her hand when she held it halfway up to her lips. "Well, with whatever you didn't say, she told me you came here for a reason. She said your being here has helped her put my father's disappearance into perspective." He set the glass on the table, hard. "She also thinks you're a special person, and I'd be a fool not to see it."

"Oh."

"Yes, *oh*," he said. "So what's that all about?"

"Nothing. I only—she hoped your father realized she was sorry."

"My mother? Sorry to him? For what?" His eyes flashed anger.

Elizabeth grabbed the glass, drank a long sip, and slowly set it down. "Your mother didn't want to come to America. Not at first. It was your father's decision."

"See."

"No, I see nothing. In the end, she did want to come. Your mother loved your father so much. The only important thing to her was to be where he was. She didn't want Italy anymore. She wanted America and Paolo." She waited for an off-hand remark from him, but all he did was stare into his empty glass.

"Your mother wished for the opportunity to tell your father. She was here because she wanted to be. I just said possibly he was aware. Our lives don't end after we die. I suggested he knows now."

"Do you know our lives don't end?" Gio asked.

"Yes," Elizabeth answered and resisted the urge to provide the proof as she saw it.

"Really?" A cynical grin lit his face. He filled his glass and topped off hers. "Where do we go?"

"To heaven or hell," she said, "and sometimes somewhere in between."

"You believe these places exist?" His voice, and his face, held such skepticism.

"Yes, I do," she answered, though she wondered if anything she said would convince him.

"And there's a God?"

"Yes," she said.

"You haven't been to war," he said. "You haven't seen how a man dies."

Oh, Gio, yes, I have.

"Nothing to say now?" He shook his head. "I didn't think so. So please don't fill my mother's head with such hogwash."

Her heart dropped. Gio would never be a man to accept her gift. She'd accepted, long ago, most people didn't understand. Why did it suddenly matter so much if he did or didn't?

"I'm not filling your mother's head with any such thing. But don't you want her to have peace?" The brandy was smooth now and almost comforting. "If she lives with any regret over your father, she'll never truly have it. I, for one, want *my* mother to have peace and no regrets."

"And you recognize what I want for mine?" He laughed. "You have no idea what I want in any way. You're a stranger here, Elizabeth."

"I—" She bit her lip. "I am a stranger everywhere, Gio." She rose from her seat but dropped back down as a wave of dizziness overtook her.

****

With her face pale, Elizabeth propped herself against the table. "So," she said. "Since I'm such a stranger here, tell me about the place."

Gio swirled the smooth brandy over his tongue before swallowing. Getting inebriated was not the answer to all his woes. Sharing this with Elizabeth was comical, not to mention, asinine, *and* even dangerous. This one woman might be his undoing. This stranger made him second guess the plans for his future he'd long stood by, but he was in no mood to think about the consequences.

"Like what? I could talk all night about the vineyard."

"Good," she said and drained half her glass. "I'm thinking I might need to sit here all night." She grinned. "Talk. Tell me about making wine." She poked at the brandy bottle with her index finger. "And this delectable drink."

She kept him talking. He topped off her glass a few times while he described, at her continued insistence, the brandy- and wine-making process. He was grateful to stop discussing what was right for his mother and father.

He was content to talk to *her*.

Just Elizabeth.

His throat itched from all the talk and the corner of his lips ached from all the uncharacteristic smiling. He hardly recognized himself.

Their conversation ground to a halt after her speech slurred. In a fit of laughter, she rested her arms on the table and cradled her head in them.

"Elizabeth," Gio said as he leaned forward and nudged her elbow. How much did she truly consume? "Are you okay?"

"Oh, I am filled with ginger." She lifted her unsteady head to wink at him and flashed him an idiotic grin.

"No, I think you're drunk."

He stood and helped her to her feet. "Damn," he muttered under his breath. What possessed him to pour her the brandy in the first place? He hadn't ever seen her drink more than one glass of wine at dinner.

"What do you think you're doing?" she asked with a giggle as he supported her weight.

"I'm going to get you to your bed." He tottered on his feet. The woman was a waif, but he'd taxed his knee too much for one day. He'd never be able to carry her to the house. If he did, his mother was sure to hear the commotion. Soft-spoken Elizabeth was anything but quiet after several glasses of brandy.

"To my bed?" She stood on her own two feet, but he held on to her waist. Leaning into him, she whispered, "I surely hope you aren't planning on joining me."

"Don't flatter yourself, doll. You're sleeping by yourself." He turned her toward the cot at the back of the room. The safer option was for her to sleep there for the night.

"And you don't flatter yourself, mister." She pulled away from him and jabbed a finger into his shoulder. "Because your kiss wasn't so great."

"No?" He laughed. The woman was sauced and, to be honest, he wasn't exactly sober himself. He couldn't let her by with this. He sure in hell wouldn't let her forget it, either. He grabbed her by the waist with both hands and drew her to him. "That's definitely not what your reaction told me." He leaned down, brushing his lips over hers and she pushed him away. He stumbled backwards onto his rump.

"You, you pig. You have no idea how to treat a woman, do you?" With hands on her hips, she spun and fell onto the table.

The glasses crashed to the floor, and the brandy bottle toppled to its side, spilling onto the dirty floor. "Gio," Elizabeth moaned. "I don't feel so good."

****

Her head pounded. Elizabeth didn't want to open her eyes for fear the spinning would begin again. The spinning led to nausea. She knew better than to drink brandy. She'd never partaken of anything stronger than wine.

She ran her fingers along the edge of the narrow cot she'd slept on. The sound of steady breathing carried up from the floor. Opening one eyelid, she pressed her head to the side. Gio lay on a blanket on the floor beside her.

Her mouth tasted of something rotten. Dead even. She'd been sick. What a disaster.

Sitting up, she nudged Gio with her foot. "Pssst. Wake up."

Lord, my head hurts. What she wouldn't do to sleep

for a while longer in a proper bed. "Gio," she pressed her stocking-clad foot into his arm again. "Don't you have work to do?"

He rolled on to his side, facing her. "It's Sunday," he said and opened his eyes. "What do you know about work?"

"I'm not a princess. Besides, you promised to give me work to do, remember?"

He sat up, flexing each arm behind his neck in turn. "I'm surprised you remember anything."

She winced. *I remember knocking you on your rear.* "I do. I plan to hold you to it." *And telling you the kiss wasn't so great.* Boy, lying was coming too easy.

"Not today. We don't work on Sunday. My mother goes into town to church if you'd like to join her. And tomorrow she wants to take you into San Francisco with her on a delivery."

"And you think that's safe?"

"Stay away from the brandy, and it should be." He stretched up from the floor and held his hand out to her. "I'm sorry. I'm not being nice, am I?"

Taking his hand, she let him pull her up. Giovanni Clemente apologizing? *Are we becoming friends?*

"Besides, if you tell her now," Gio said and flashed a rakish grin, "you'll never have a chance to show me what a great kiss does to you."

Chapter Fourteen

It took a brisk walk through the vineyard aisles to clear the fog from Elizabeth's head. She couldn't walk fast enough away from Gio. The man whistled along with the radio in the parlor, the leg he favored propped on the ottoman and a half-smile on his face. He appeared almost happy to see how sick the brandy made her. As long as she lived, she'd never ever drink such wicked Clemente liquor again. Of course, Mr. Sunshine was unscathed after drinking such vile stuff. How anyone found any pleasure in imbibing was beyond her. Of course, if everyone disliked alcohol, her father's pubs would be nothing but empty rooms.

Still, Gio didn't need to sit there with the crooked smile on his face.

"The ass is enjoying my pain."

She glanced around to see if anyone saw her talking to herself. No one had. Her only company were the vines and they bowed under the weight of the plump grape clusters.

If she weaved through the aisles long enough, she'd find someone on duty, but Gio was right. Almost no one worked on Sunday. He didn't, which surprised her. Though she'd known there was so much more to him from the moment she saw him in the inn's parlor. He'd stood with the weight of the world weighing him down as he stared out the picture window.

Something about him had touched her heart even then.

Ugh. Gio's welfare shouldn't be her chief concern. Paolo's should.

"Where are you, Paolo?" She stopped in her tracks.

The dry weeds cracked beneath her hard-soled shoes. With a deep breath, she closed her eyes and inhaled the aroma of ripened fruit and dry earth, with no trace of Paolo's clean, soapy scent anywhere.

Quieting her mind, she concentrated on the noises around her. The hum of insects. Laughter from children near to where she stood. The sluggish call of birds echoing from the sky, and the rustling of leaves when a light breeze tickled her cheeks.

She did not feel Paolo's presence. Instead, the warm autumn air played against her skin.

It was no use. The ghost lured her here and abandoned her. He said she had a good heart. Was this how he repaid the people who helped him? Leaving her defenseless against a man like his son?

She opened her eyes and continued toward the aisle opening. If only the threat of a kiss from Gio didn't leave butterflies in her empty, queasy stomach.

She exited into the sunshine-illuminated clearing. The stone cottages where the vineyard community lived stood yards in front of her. The men, women, and children—all the families and individuals who depended on the Clementes for their livelihood. The people here were happy and wore a look of complete faith in Giovanni and Adriana.

How many of them remembered Paolo?

A woman, who must have been in her early thirties, swept the front stoop of one of the cottages. As she looked up from her task, inky black hair fell into her eyes, and she smiled. "*Señora* Reilly. How are you today?"

"Fine, thank you." Elizabeth managed to smile back. Fine if a splitting headache meant fine. "And you?" She stopped in front of the woman and extended her hand. "I'm sorry. I don't think we've formally met."

"Oh, you are right. Everyone knows who you are. I forget we have not." The woman set her thrush broom against the house and wiped her hand on her cotton skirt before taking Elizabeth's hand. "I am Anita Sanchez. Sebastian's daughter and mother to Esteban and Lolly." She pointed to her twin son and daughter, and several other children approaching. Each held a straw basket filled with apples.

Elizabeth turned toward them and nodded. "Good afternoon," she said to the children. Esteban grinned and averted his gaze. His sister behind him giggled and taunted him in Spanish. He growled something back.

Anita clapped her hands sternly at the children. "Now stop, you two. Go sort those apples and bring two basketfuls up to *Señora* Clemente, the others to the barn. Now. *Lejos con usted.*"

They were not but a few feet away when Esteban glanced back over his shoulder at Elizabeth and tripped, scattering his basket of apples on the ground.

His mother turned and called, "Oh, Esteban. You'll bruise them all." She gave a command in Spanish and hurried to right the basket and order the other children to help collect them.

The boy, sulking and red-faced, avoided looking at Elizabeth again. Two apples rolled toward her. She scooped up the two-toned red and yellow fruit, dusted each off, and brought them to the basket.

"These look fine," she offered and bent to retrieve three others.

When the ground was clear, Anita sent Esteban and the children off to their task once again. Elizabeth excused herself and headed toward the grove. Now she understood the source for the apple tarts Adriana mentioned they'd have for dinner. The heady scent of the apples assaulted her, more overpowering than the mellow grapes but enjoyable, nevertheless.

"*Señora* Elizabeth," called a young male voice behind her. Startled, she spun. Young Esteban fidgeted before her and flashed a toothy grin before ducking his head. The smile lit up his face.

"Yes?" She smiled back, resigned to the fact there were too many people here to be alone.

Since her time on the vineyard, she'd conversed with more people than simply ever. They accepted her.

She liked it.

"You don't want to go in there." He motioned to the trees behind her. "Too many bees today."

"Hmm, I guess I don't suppose I do," she said as an insect buzzed past her nose. "Too bad, though, because I've never walked in an apple orchard before."

"I can show you a different place I go to be alone. I mean if you'd like." His cheeks pinkened.

She studied the odd boy. A gangly, aloof child with dark eyes too large for his face. The frown he wore looked somehow out of place. "What made you think I wanted to be alone?" she asked.

"Guessed." He toed the dirt ground without meeting her eyes.

"So, where is this place?"

He stood straight, tossed his shoulders back. Excitement radiated from his body. He fairly bounced with energy. "This way," he said. "Follow me."

Elizabeth followed him in the direction between the cottages and the arbor. She was only a little self-conscious as she followed him over the progressively rocky ground.

Ice trickled through Elizabeth's veins, and she stopped short. Something about the place set her heart racing. She watched Esteban head toward a small stand of rocks. Waist-high and flat. He climbed on one, sat, and looked at her expectantly.

She considered retracing her steps or even risking the bees and heading back through the apple trees. Being stung was preferable to moving any nearer to *those* rocks. Still, Elizabeth straightened her spine and approached Esteban. "This is where you come to be alone?" She heard the doubt in her own voice.

"Sometimes," he said, and avoided looking directly at her.

"Do you know what I think?" she said.

"No," he said. "What do you think, *Señora* Elizabeth?" He seemed to vibrate with excitement and in anticipation of her answer.

"I think you don't like to come here alone," she said. "And you wanted company."

He smiled shyly and gave a quick, hesitant nod.

"I thought so." Elizabeth couldn't help but smile despite the shivers climbing her spine. "But you should have been honest about that, don't you think?"

He nodded again, leaned toward her, and said, "People say *alcoholes de los muertos* come here." He looked around as if to see if anyone else heard him. Then he leaned in again, adding, "Ghosts."

Why in the world did he choose to tell her this? She wanted to say there was nothing here and what he'd heard were made-up stories by people who didn't understand.

She'd done enough lying and she wouldn't lie to this child.

Something strong lurked here. This was no place *she'd* come to relax or to be alone.

Elizabeth leaned against the rock. The stone vibrated, and a sound, a whispered hiss, whizzed through her head. She lurched away and hugged herself, clutching her upper arms.

"My grandmother called this *la Roca Susurrante*, the Whispering Rock."

"Did you feel that?" She struggled to catch her breath.

Esteban shook his head.

Elizabeth bit her lip and averted her eyes, unable to meet his gaze. "Do you ever—have you ever witnessed why this is called—" Unsettled, she looked at the object. "Whispering Rock?"

He shrugged. "Maybe," he said. "But my grandmother used to *all* the time. She said only those with a strong gift can feel *los muertos* all the time."

"Hmmm." She glanced around and faced the boy again. "Why did you bring me here?" she asked almost too quietly.

"I heard my mother say you have the look of my grandmother," he said. "She thinks you might speak with the dead."

Her heart thrummed. What did he mean about *the look*? "Esteban, is your grandmother back at the cottages? Can I speak with her?"

Elizabeth's mother struggled to handle the gift without anyone to help her. This woman may be able to help them understand where the ability originated.

The boy hopped down from the rock. "No, she is in heaven."

"Oh." Elizabeth blushed now. "I'm sorry."

He smiled shyly and asked, "Did you hear the whispering, *Señora* Elizabeth?"

She only shook her head. If she admitted her ability, would Gio get wind of it? She wasn't willing to take the risk. He admitted to her he held little faith in anything. He'd send her away without waiting for an explanation.

Chapter Fifteen

After a full and eventful day in San Francisco,
Elizabeth rested her head back on the passenger seat.
Adriana rolled the black truck into its spot beside the
Clemente home as the crimson sun edged its way off the
horizon. The sun gave way to an evening haze. The
luminous fog blew in from the far-off ocean, crept up
over the hills, and slid down into the valley.

Elizabeth sighed and swung her door open. She
stepped down, and her feet hit the gravel driveway with
a crunch. Pushing the car door closed, she took three
steps toward the aisle opening. The sun disappeared from
the valley behind a distant hill. Misty shadows danced
through the illuminated vines cast by its light.

She took a deep breath and filled her lungs with the
sweet scent of the ripening fruit. A light breeze passed
through the grapevines, sending a ripple traveling from
one vine to the other, and the leaves applauded a
beautiful day. Another breeze tugged at her hair.
Sighing, she ran her fingers through her now shortened
ends. They hung in a pageboy at her shoulders. Despite
remorse over her new hairstyle, the magic drew her in,
filling her with peace.

Not even the idea of the Whispering Rock deterred
her. The fact Esteban and his mother suspected what she
was, and it didn't scare them, comforted her. She'd come
close to asking Adriana about Esteban's grandmother but

held herself back. Perhaps, there would be time before she left. She hadn't spoken much to Sebastian, or Seb as Adriana and Gio referred to him, but if she had the chance, maybe Seb knew about his late wife's gift.

Investigating where the ability to communicate with the dead came from, however, would wait. Here in this sanctuary, she could almost be who she genuinely wanted to be and, maybe, something more. Here on the vineyard, there was beauty and friendship. Peace surrounded her, and she was not in any rush to return to her life. She turned to see Adriana close the driver's side door.

Elizabeth smiled. The woman was quite capable of hearing the truth. Even the whole truth. Adriana wasn't the fragile woman her stubborn son took her to be.

She and Adriana were building a friendship. The two spoke with such ease, at times she forgot the woman was Gio's mother. Adriana's spirit was young, but she was a wise, intelligent woman.

Elizabeth found herself stuck in a quandary. She could not continue to lie to her friend, nor could she betray Gio's trust.

"I was about to come looking for you," Gio called and dipped into the truck's bed, heaving out four of the shopping bags. "The two of you must have bought out every shop in San Francisco."

"Of course, my love, what else am I to do with the money you sweat to make?" Adriana grinned and playfully patted his cheek.

He sighed.

Elizabeth joined them at the back of the truck. "Gio, your mother helped me pick out a pair of overalls perfect for working on the vineyard."

"Really? You're still hell-bent on that?" He frowned. "What did you do to your hair?"

"I cut it." She wrapped a loose curl around her finger. "Why? Don't you like it?"

Gio wrinkled his nose. "I liked your long hair." He turned, escaping to the house, arms filled with shopping bags.

Adriana winked, removing two bags from the back. "Pay no mind to him, *Cara*. Gio really is an old-fashioned man. He will have to cut his own. He cannot have hair longer than his lady's, now, can he?"

"I like his hair long," Elizabeth said. She was not his lady. When did Gio plan to let them end this pretense?

"Yes, I see you do." Adriana retreated to the house after her son.

Elizabeth glanced into the back of the truck to find all the bags were gone. She hesitated and frowned before she turned to follow her hosts. *It doesn't matter if he likes my hair or not.*

Upon entering the house, she found Adriana already dipping into the bags. Gio sat on the curved, cream-colored sofa facing the front doors. He showed feigned interest in what his mother was so joyfully showing him.

He glanced towards her, rolling his eyes. "She's always wished I was a girl."

"Elizabeth," Adriana exclaimed. "Come here and show him what you have bought."

"I don't think he wants to see all those."

"Nonsense." Adriana grabbed her hand and tugged her over to stand before Gio. "My Giovanni likes nothing better than to look at all our female trappings. Especially," Adriana said and dipped into one of Elizabeth's bags. "When the trapping looks like this."

141

Laughing, she held up a black lace nightgown.

Cheeks hot, Elizabeth glanced at Gio without meeting his eyes. "I didn't choose this one," she said. "You mother bought it for me." Elizabeth grabbed the nightgown from Adriana's hands and tossed it back into its bag. "He doesn't need to see my things."

"If not my Gio, who?" Adriana pinched her cheek. "My, my, such a *puritano*."

"What?" Elizabeth struggled to keep from smiling.

Gio stood. "She means prude."

"I figured but I am not a prude." She collected her three bags while saying playfully in return, "I think I'll take my trappings upstairs and away from *you* nosy people."

As she raced up the stairs, she heard Gio say, "*Madre*, you shouldn't tease her."

"Elizabeth? Nonsense," the woman said with a laugh. "She loves the attention."

Adriana was right. She loved the attention.

Elizabeth rushed down the hall.

"He's not a bad boy."

She froze, mid-step, as she passed Marco's open bedroom door. Her heart stuttered in her chest, and she held her breath.

"No, he missed having you around."

Was Marco talking to Paolo? Did Marco see him? Her shock gave way to relief. If the ghost somehow connected with the man, she'd have someone to discuss the whole truth with. She cleared her throat, set her shopping bags on the floor next to the hallway wall, and knocked on the door jamb.

Alone in the room, Marco looked up from his seat on the bed. "Ah, *Signora* Reilly." He stood. "Come in."

He smiled and retrieved a ladder-back chair from against the wall next to the open window. "Have a seat, *per favore*."

Elizabeth wiped her damp hands on her skirt as she strode into the room and sat. "Thank you."

The room was welcoming, like the man who occupied it. The furniture was quality but plain. Multiple well-worn books filled a small corner shelf. Photographs decorated the walls, his sparsely covered bureau, and two sat on his bedside table. One of a young Paolo, and two boys she supposed were his brothers. The second was a breathtaking framed picture of Gio. He stood tall in an army uniform with his hair cut short, accentuating his lean face.

Snap out of it. Drooling over pictures of Giovanni Clemente is not the reason you came in here. She managed a shy smile. "Marco, can I ask you something?"

"*Si,* yes." He sat, dabbing his forehead with a clean handkerchief.

"Were you talking to someone a minute ago?" She resisted the urge to look around the room. Paolo was there, listening unseen, and a permanent fixture in the house.

"Me talking to someone?" He shook his head and stopped abruptly. "Oh," he said with a chuckle. "You must have heard me speaking to Paolo."

Her voice caught in her throat. "Yes, to Paolo."

"You must think I am a senile man." He chuckled. "*Si,* I was talking with him. I do so every so often. I discuss life. His son, his vineyard. I do so in hopes he might somehow bring me insight." He nodded. "I always have, you see. I believed him dead all these years and speaking to him was a comfort to me."

Elizabeth stared at him blankly. Dumbfounded.

"See, you do think me senile."

She sprung from the chair. "No, never. I just—" She bit her lip.

"What?" Marco asked.

"It's nothing." She turned and saw Paolo standing at the window, gazing out. "I think you're right though. Insight or not, I think he can at least hear you, wherever he is."

Smiling, she glanced back at Marco. If Paolo's family wasn't consciously aware he was there, they undoubtedly sensed him.

****

Gio rose from the table in the wine house, leaving Seb and three other men to their conversation. He passed through the doorway as the laughs from those with more than one brandy under their belts rambled out behind him.

A light breeze blew over his warm face, carrying the crisp scent of ripening fruit with it. He'd harvest soon and looked forward to Michael and his family all coming home. They'd pick the grapes, and then they'd celebrate. Before the war, Gio always kept from drinking until after he'd completed the autumn work. However, Elizabeth Reilly had arrived and made sure this time turned out to be unlike any other.

His jar of brandy hadn't done what he'd hoped. He still thought about her but not the reason why she'd come.

Despite the number of times he told her to leave, he found excuses to venture up to the main house's second floor late each morning to catch his first glimpse of her. Before she tidied herself up, while the sleep still clouded her mind. Elizabeth carried the heavy-lidded look he liked, proving to him her night was just as restless as his.

A more efficient and productive use of those sleepless hours would be to burn off enough energy with her to fall into dreamless sleep.

No. The brandy corrupted his mind. He should be planning how he was going to get her to return to her pampered city life where sleeping until nine in the morning was acceptable, not how he was going to get her into his bed.

She'd slip on the lace nightgown his mother bought her. With luck, the sheer material wouldn't conceal much. His body responded to the picture of Elizabeth. His blood warmed at the image of the woman standing in front of him with the moonlight caressing her full lips, swollen from his kisses.

He pictured the lace material hugging the sleek curves of her breasts and hips.

He flexed his hands, knowing they'd fit nicely around her small waist when he lifted her. He'd cradle her bottom as she wrapped her legs around his waist.

Yes, an enticing way to consider spending a night.

They needed a little sparring match, something to get her flexing those petite fists and the color rising in her cheeks. She was a zealous one. If he kept the momentum going, he'd only begin to imagine what she was capable of. He'd thoroughly enjoy making her large, cocoa-brown eyes darken with desire. Skittishly, he turned to the sound of feet crunching over the gravel ground.

****

"Gio? I'm sorry, I didn't mean to intrude," Elizabeth said as he spun to face her.

While she hadn't meant to intrude, she did half-hope to see him since she'd left him in the parlor with his mother. His unspoken promise the day before of another kiss had plagued her all night. Her blood hummed in anticipation, and her cheeks warmed.

"Intrude?" He cleared his throat. "You're not intruding. Would you like to join us?" He motioned back to the open door, the light of a lantern flickering inside of it.

She rocked on her feet. Drinking with a group of men was not a smart idea. In fact, she was never going to drink again. "Well, I'm—"

"Perhaps not." He grabbed her hand. "Should we take a walk?"

He led her into the vineyard aisle, looking down at their entwined hands.

Fires blazed in scattered steel drums, making light dance furtively on the vine leaves trembling in the autumn breeze. The cloying smell of the grapes overwhelmed her. The chirp of crickets played into the air. A howl traveled in from a distance, and Elizabeth edged closer to Gio, grabbing his arm with her free hand.

"What kind of animal makes that sound?" Her breath caught, and warmth flooded her, not from fright, rather from being so near him.

"Coyotes. They live in the hills. They come down occasionally for the chickens out by the bunk houses." Gio smiled. "Don't worry. The fire keeps them away."

She looked around. "Do they come in by the house?"

"Rarely. They're not large animals and run from people. You have nothing to worry about."

"I'm not worried. It's just their cry. It's so lonely."

Like a lost soul. She yanked her hand from his. A walk with him wasn't a bright idea. The man jumbled up everything inside of her. She hadn't any common sense where he was concerned.

"I'm used to it." He wore a look of pride as if the entire vineyard, each vine, and every grape, the soil nourishing it—everything—including the coyote cry was a part of him.

I could fall in love with the look alone. She sighed and let herself bask in the allure of it. "You liked growing up here, didn't you?"

"I loved it. And I look forward to growing gray here as well." He stopped to check the flame blazing in a nearby drum before turning back to her. "My mother told me the two of you enjoyed your trip."

"Yes." Her hand itched for Gio to hold it again.

"And you attended a secretarial school."

The firelight shimmered over his wily grin as they stood regarding each other. What was he thinking?

"Are you a secretary back in Boston, really?" he asked.

"Well, I was a clerk for the newspaper." She hoped he'd not ask any more questions. The last thing she wanted to do was talk about herself.

"Are you on holiday from there?"

She wrinkled her nose. "Actually, no. I quit after," she said, "after I found out my husband was missing." Elizabeth averted her gaze, watching wraithlike forms dance over the dark ground.

Gio stepped closer and distracted her from the eerie figures cast by the flames from the drum. A renegade curl lay on her forehead, and he toyed with it. "Did you like growing up in the city?"

Her skin heated. "Not especially. My world was small."

"That surprises me," he said. "I've been to Boston. There are people everywhere."

It shocked her to hear he'd been to Boston. Had he passed his father on the street and not even known he did? A shiver travelled up her otherwise warm tingling spine.

His finger danced slow circles on her chin. She stepped away. She couldn't enjoy his touch when he insisted on talking about her. "My parents kept my brother, sister, and me close. The kids in our neighborhood were a little fearful of us. We were different from them."

"There's no reason to fear you." His gaze bore into hers. "It's hard being different though, isn't it?" he asked.

His eyes seemed to see right through her as if he were penetrating her skin. She wasn't prepared to let him know her. "What do you understand about being different, Gio?"

"I grew up without a father, didn't I? I thought I had to be a man and protect my mother. So I acted older than my years." He nodded. "I was quite serious."

"You serious? No."

"Sarcasm doesn't suit you." He led her down the incline.

She meant the remark to irritate him, but he took it as a jest. "Hmmm. I'll keep that in mind," she said, crossing her arms over her chest.

Gio stopped amongst the vines he'd told her were his favorite, tugged at her hands, and steered her to him. Elizabeth resisted, but he held her in place.

Something about him changed. He was feeling what she was or at least starting to.

"Gio, what do you think you're doing?"

"Feeling close to you." He leaned down, brushing his lips over hers.

Her lips tingled, and heat resembling the fire in the barrels simmered deep within her. His teeth tugged at her lower lip. Lord, giving in would be so easy, but now was the time to use her head and not her nether parts. She wrenched free of his arms and stepped away.

"I don't think this is a good idea. I think the brandy on your breath is making you crazy."

What's my excuse?

"Come on, Elizabeth. We're both adults," he said with a husky voice. He strode closer.

She held out her arm to keep him at bay. "Please don't. This is already complicated enough." If he pushed, she'd let him, and it wouldn't help anyone—least of all her.

"Fine." Gio ran his hands over his tied-back hair.

"Fine," she responded, gathering her arms about her chest. "We should get back to the house." Trembling, she turned away.

"No, wait." Gio touched her arm, stopping her. "Does this have something to do with your husband?" He looked angry now, frustrated.

Stopping had nothing at all to do with Patrick. He'd wanted Elizabeth to move on with her life. She wanted the kiss from Gio. She stopped because the desire overwhelmed and frightened her. "I don't want to talk about him." She frowned. "I regret ever mentioning it to Marco."

"I figure he must be the reason you ran away."

Her heart sped at the intensity of his voice. "Ran away?" she asked. "What are you talking about?"

"I've been thinking about why you came here, and the reason doesn't make sense to me." He walked past her to examine a vine and its berries. "You traveled all the way here for a dead man."

"Please don't refer to your father as a dead man. And, yes, I'm here. I took the train and then the bus here for Paolo." She turned towards him, frowning at his back. "Besides, I didn't run away. My family is there. I love my family."

"Do they know why you're here?" He swiveled back, the nearest drum's firelight casting more eerie shadows over his face. "Did they meet my father?"

"No, they didn't," she whispered. "Well, just my sister—once, but not my brother or my parents."

"Why?" Gio asked.

"I didn't see the point in it. Only I can help him. Only I see—" She bit her lip. "I don't really want to talk about this."

"Come on now." He took a step toward her and took her hand again. "You seem well informed about me. I'd think you'd be willing to share a little bit about you."

"I'm here for y—" She bit her lip again almost to the point of drawing blood. This walk was a disastrous idea.

"For me?" He looked down at their joined hands and then up into her eyes, "Well, then, I'd like to get a sense of who you are before I accept your help." He walked forward.

She tugged at her hand again, but he held fast. "You can't expect to know who I am after a ten-minute conversation."

"I'll ask questions," he said.

"I don't have to answer," she replied. *I don't and I won't.*

"So how did you meet your husband?"

"Dammit, Giovanni." She stopped walking and grasped his arm to get him to look at her, but he didn't turn around. "Do you want to torment me?" Tears built up behind her eyes. Lord, was he being mean on purpose? "What sick crazed thing has you kissing and tugging at me and next asking about my dead husband?" His grip tightened on her hand. "Do you think I have no feelings?"

If he suspected such a thing, he was wrong. The trip to California only showed how much more capable of them she was.

He released her hand and spun on her. "Do you? You expect me to trust you. To travel across the country at your bidding. Yet I have no idea who you are." He turned and paced away from her and back again. "I only have pieces of information about you. Most not even given to me firsthand."

He stood in front of her now. Even in the firelight, she saw his flushed cheeks. She held her ground. "I asked you to come to Boston for your father. To say goodbye to him. It has nothing to do with me."

"The hell it doesn't. It has everything to do with you. And I refuse to tell my mother anything. Not until I discover who you are." He stalked past her.

Her body numbed. "Lord help me," she whispered. *This is not about me.*

Chapter Sixteen

The next morning, Elizabeth exited the Clementes' study not feeling any better than before she'd telephoned her mother. Her hands shook. She should have asked her mother how to shut out feelings for a man.

Caring for Gio was *not* wise. The look of longing he wore the night before unnerved her. If she let him any further into her heart, devastation was sure to follow when he rejected her. With his doubts about there being an afterlife, he'd never be a man capable of accepting her gift.

Heading for the front door, she ran past Sofia, who stood midway up the stairwell, sweeping.

Elizabeth swiped at a rogue curl hanging in front of her eyes and opened the door to blinding sunlight. She hurried out and glanced back to see if Sofia noticed her. When she didn't, Elizabeth inched the creaking door closed.

With a disgruntled whimper, she sat on the weathered bench and shifted on the wooden planks. She'd find no comfort in this forsaken vineyard. There'd be no peace if Gio dashed around every corner and watched her, waiting for her to bare her soul. The only way to complete her task was to forget about her own life and focus on helping Paolo.

The wind's tender fingers caressed her face and arms. She frowned and wiped them away. She'd fooled herself for a while, thinking she was there to help Gio. Even if he were part of her purpose, she'd have to put any concerns for him aside to protect herself.

Voices floated in from the side of the house.

Elizabeth jumped up from the bench and fled the porch. One by one, she crossed the stepping-stones in the front garden, cautious not to slip on the loose pebbles crunching beneath her wedged-heel shoes. She took off with a fast clip toward the estate entrance.

Raw, volatile energy throbbed through her. She needed to walk, stay ahead of the self-doubt about why she hadn't told her mother the whole story as she intended to when she'd telephoned her. When she'd heard the loving, familiar voice, she opted only to check in.

Silly. Dora was the only person who might have understood what she was doing. Except, her mother never traveled across the country to help a troubled soul.

She should have told the truth, but she might have told her mother about Gio. She might have gone on to talk about the budding feelings she wasn't ready for. Those feelings terrified Elizabeth more than any apparition's visit.

Her shoulders slumped forward. When her mother asked when she planned to come home, Elizabeth responded, "*After harvest, Mother. The Clementes have been so nice to let me stay here. Especially when I told them what a fanatic dad is about their wine. The least I can do is stay and lend two extra hands at harvest. Two weeks most likely.*"

Elizabeth committed herself to two more weeks. Her family wouldn't insist she return home. She'd let them think this time away was a much needed holiday. Both her mother and father worried she'd grown too withdrawn in the years since the war—and more so after Patrick's death.

Why hadn't she at least listened to Paolo's suggestion and asked Anna to come with her? She might have managed things so much better with her sister by her side.

"Elizabeth!" Gio shouted from behind.

Her steps faltered, but she kept walking. There was no way she was ready to face him. If he tried to kiss her, she'd slap him. If he tried to make her talk about herself, she'd scream.

"Elizabeth, wait—" His footfalls approached her from behind. "We need to talk."

With her heart battering her chest, she increased her pace. She wasn't ready to face him. Lord only knew what she'd say to him or what she might admit. Rushing away from him was juvenile but she needed space.

"I'm going for a walk," she called over her shoulder. "We can talk later."

A voice shouted from near the main house. "Giovanni!"

Elizabeth kept walking. With him no longer pursuing her, she was free. She left for a quiet, mind-clearing hike.

****

The truck's headlights illuminated the pitch-black road. Gio scanned the area for any sight of Elizabeth. If he found her—when he'd found her, he'd what?

What kept her away from the vineyard for so long? Still shaken from Marco's fall, worry slowed him down. With the broken hip, the doctor would make sure the elderly man's days of climbing ladders to tend the vines were over.

A dim figure loomed ahead, outside of the headlights' glow. He shifted in the cloth seat, leaned into the steering wheel, and tightened his grip.

Elizabeth limped in front of him but halted and edged her body closer to the trees beside the road. He brought the truck to a screeching halt and swung his door open. He jumped down from the truck, not bothering to turn off the ignition.

He bore down on her, with his throat constricting, and asked, "Where have you been?" He'd meant to sound angry, but his anger fell flat.

The light from the truck highlighted her dirt-smudged face. She shifted uncomfortably. "I was walking," she said softly.

"Walking?" he groaned. "For hours?"

"I didn't stay on the road. I got—" She averted her eyes. "Lost."

He firmly grasped both of her shoulders. "Lost?"

"What?" She fidgeted and blew a flyaway curl out of her eyes. "Can't you say more than one or two words at a time?"

"You're driving me mad." Closing his eyes, he drew her into his arms and brushed his lips over the top of her head. Her petite body pressed into his. Having her so near awakened a need in him he'd never experienced before. Even in the disheveled state she was in, she elicited feral yearnings from him.

He wanted to be angry. He'd meant to scold her like a child for staying away from the vineyard so long, but instead he wrapped his arms around her.

She rested her face against his chest and sighed. "That makes two of us," she whispered. "Can you take me back now?" She backed away from him, and he opened his eyes to see her looking up at him with weariness etched on her lovely face. "I don't think I can stand much longer."

He leaned down, brushing his lips over hers. He inhaled her scent of lavender and the dusty sweetness of grapes. She was quickly becoming a part of the scenery here and he feared she would remain so after she left.

He swung her into his arms.

She snuggled into the crook between his shoulder and neck and yawned. "I'm so tired."

He carried her to the truck, put her on the seat, and stood studying her. How much would he miss her gorgeous face when she left? Her eyes held so much feeling and he ached to learn what each nuanced expression meant.

Damn. Where did the emotions Elizabeth uncovered come from? He'd lived all his life without expecting more than physical pleasure from any one woman. Yet one week with this bizarre Bostonian seemed to be changing his outlook.

She sighed. "What are you staring at?"

You. His gut clenched with the want to hold her again, but he held himself back. "My mother's frantic with worry about you," he said. "What should I tell her about this?"

"I don't know, Gio. What should we tell her?" She looked away from him. "What lie can we think up to coddle your mother next?" She bunched her fists into her lap and shifted her gaze back to his with clouded, troubled eyes. "Or perhaps you'd like me to lie to you. Maybe." She cocked her head. "Should I say I'm here for you? And only you? But I'm not. I'm here for your father."

Heat rose in Gio's cheeks, and he looked away. Speechless, he closed the heavy door and walked around to the driver's side.

Exactly when did he start to want her to be there for him? When did *Elizabeth* become precisely what he wanted?

God help him because he wasn't sure he was ready for her.

Chapter Seventeen

Elizabeth rolled onto her stomach. She buried her swollen eyes in the plush feather pillow she'd punched and shaped throughout the night. Her comment agitated him. When they arrived back at the house, Gio slammed the door and left her sitting in the truck by herself. She'd stayed there until Adriana found her and asked her to come in out of the dark.

His mother didn't ask any questions. She'd prepared a bath for her, and when Elizabeth finished, tea and soup waited on the table by the windows.

Turning to rest her cheek on the pillow, Elizabeth glanced at the midday sun shining through the open window. She'd never been a malicious woman, but the way Gio held her dislodged her heart. She needed to give him a reason to withdraw from her. She wouldn't be able to keep herself from embracing him with her entire being much longer because she *was* in love with him.

She'd known Patrick her entire life and loved him. Only, she hadn't fallen *in* love with him. Yet, she'd fallen so deeply for a man she'd only known a matter of days. With her heart weighed down by revelation and regret, she dragged herself out of bed. Regardless of whether Gio decided now was time to tell Adriana about Paolo or not, she was prepared to do so herself.

She went to the closet, shed her sheer lace nightgown, and quickly dressed in a red berry print, short sleeve blouse and her new trim-fitting overalls. Standing in front of the bureau mirror, she fastened the back buttons and tucked her hair back in a mesh snood. "There," she said, half-smiling. Before she left, she'd show them she wasn't a spoiled princess. Perhaps, Adriana or Seb would put her to work, even if it meant mostly stationary work.

"Good morning, *Bella.*"

"Oh, now you show up." She turned to face Paolo who sat on the bed. Here she was falling to pieces, trying to help him, and he'd left her to aimlessly walk the desolate dirt roads. In her search, none of them led back to the vineyard.

"I am sorry. I've been preoccupied."

"To say the least." Slipping her tender feet into her saddle shoes, she bent to tie them.

"Are you angry with me?" He stood.

Was she angry with him? No. She sighed and leaned back against the bureau. "Paolo, it's time for me to return home."

"Ah, I expected as much. I cannot say I am happy to leave here, but I do understand." He smiled, sadly. "You have done more for me than I have ever expected."

"But was it enough?" Her heart dropped, wondering if she'd accomplished enough for any of them.

She grabbed her small toiletry case and exited the room, leaving the ghost staring into the air.

"Did you sleep well?"

Elizabeth spun at the sound of Gio's voice, almost tripping over her suddenly clumsy feet. "Did you have to sneak up on me?"

He approached the top stair. "I wouldn't call walking through my own house sneaking up on you." He stood in front of her. "Are you ready to apologize for your behavior yesterday?"

Fisting her empty hand, she cursed under her breath and glared up at him. "What makes you think you deserve an apology?"

"So, you're angry with me, are you?" Gio gently wrapped his hand around her upper arm. He gathered her closer and she let him. "I can't possibly understand why. I mean, I did not intentionally try to bait you. Did I?" he asked. "Perhaps your husband gave in to your whims much too easily. Most men wouldn't have been so kind to you after you ran like a fool from the vineyard. Lucky for you I'm a gentleman."

"You're a gentleman?" She laughed. "A gentleman would not call me a fool."

"I didn't call you a fool. I said you ran like a fool. There's a difference."

"You're a fool if you think so." Trembling with emotion, she dropped her case but didn't step away despite knowing she should.

He whispered, "I'm not letting you push me away."

Beleaguered, she gave up the inner struggle and looked up into his intense eyes. "Then we're in trouble." *Dreadfully in trouble.*

****

Gio's throat went dry, and heat slammed into the center of his gut. Elizabeth didn't comprehend the power she wielded. He drew her against him and lowered his lips to hers. She was fluid, pliable in his arms. *His.* He rolled one hand up along her spine, under the snood, and into her unruly shoulder-length hair.

Her hand cupped the back of his neck, her soft lips parted in a moan. Everything about the woman set his senses to flame. The raspy sound of her voice and her scent was akin to warmed honey. She pressed her petite form into him, and he imagined peeling the clothes off her body. She withdrew from the kiss and whispered breathlessly into his ear, "Is this what you really want?"

This was dangerous. He could lose himself in a kiss from her. A very tempting idea, but here and now wasn't the time or the place. He'd only meant to talk to her, not accost her in the hall. Slowly, he dropped his hands to the side and backed away. He opened his mouth to speak but stopped.

He shook his head. *Where the hell has my self-restraint gone?*

"Gio, there you are. You had a phone call." Adriana climbed the stairs and joined them in the hall. "It was Zola."

His cheeks burning, he turned from Elizabeth. "Zola?" His voice cracked.

"Yes, Zola from the store. She left a message about some important package that you were awaiting has arrived from Boston."

In a stupor, he turned and watched Elizabeth back away from him.

"Good morning, Adriana," she said before she snatched up her small carrier by its wooden handle and stalked off toward the washroom.

His gaze followed her cute bottom. Who'd have known snug-fitting work overalls could be so enticing?

His mother nudged him with an affectionate shove. "Since you are going into town, I have asked Zola to put aside a bag of groceries for me." She headed down the stairs, calling back to him in Italian, "If you hurry, perhaps Elizabeth will be in the same mood when you return."

****

When Gio entered the store, Zola, the shopkeeper's daughter, did not rise to greet him as she normally would.

"So, Giovanni, did you come for your package or to see me?" Zola asked from her seat behind the counter. She challenged him with a gaze.

"Zola," he said, stopping short. "I've been preoccupied."

"With the woman." Her gaze fell from his, and she planted her elbows on the scarred wooden surface.

"Yes." He couldn't continue to lie. Elizabeth constantly occupied his mind in one way or another.

"What is her name?" Her voice softened.

"Elizabeth." He met Zola at the store counter. "If I've hurt you, I'm sorry but—" He wanted to say Elizabeth had nothing to do with why he hadn't shown up for their date. He couldn't because he'd told too many lies over the past few days.

Her lips settled into a slow frown. "My papa was right. Our association has come to an end, Giovanni." She smiled and looked down hiding her blushing cheeks. She'd never been bashful with him. She continued, "I understood you only gave what you were able, and I expected no more."

Gio leaned in, brushing his lips over her forehead. "I am truly sorry."

"No, I'm fine." She laughed, quietly. "What we had ended when you left for the war. I've known that. I *do* hope you are happy with this woman. This Elizabeth," she said. "I saw her peeking in the window one morning last week. She is very pretty."

He sighed and leaned into the counter. "I didn't say

I was happy." No, he was half-afraid the desire wouldn't cease even after Elizabeth returned to Boston. He'd miss their talks and the sweet way she sometimes looked at him. When she did, he anticipated her hand rising to caress his cheek.

"Love is not always joyful." She tapped his cheek. "Now would you like your things?"

He frowned. "Yes, the package and whatever my mother ordered."

Once Elizabeth left, who'd challenge him the way she did?

Love is not always joyful. Was he falling in love?

Zola retreated to the back room and returned moments later, her arms filled with an overstuffed paper sack, several letters, and one small tan package. She handed over the mail first. "Here it is." She read the package. "Boston."

Writing on the top indicated the parcel originated from the Boston Public Cemetery.

He'd called the cemetery the day after Elizabeth arrived, requesting any information they might provide on Paolo Clemente. The woman he spoke with was unable to help. So, he'd left his name and address with her, saying he'd be inaccessible by telephone. He couldn't risk them calling the vineyard and speaking with his mother. The woman told him someone would get back to him, and he hadn't heard a word until now.

By its size, the package contained more than a letter. He was terrified to open it, but he needed the truth. "Giovanni, did you hear me? Do you want to charge it to your account?"

"Ah, *si*." He looked up absently. "On the account." He grabbed the bag containing his mother's order and sped out of the store, knocking a jar of raspberry preserves off an overcrowded merchandise shelf. The sound of breaking glass trailed behind him. He glanced over his shoulder at Zola and whispered, "Sorry."

Gio exited the store, hoping his whispered apology would make amends for the mess he left behind.

He rushed to the safety of his truck and tossed his mother's groceries into the cab before climbing up into his seat. With trembling hands, he laid the package and mail on the passenger seat and closed his eyes. He gripped the steering wheel until his knuckles stung.

In Italian, he whispered, "Lord, please help me through this." Slowly, he released his grip and opened his eyes. Taking a deep breath, he grabbed the coveted package and cautiously edged it open, fearing one wrong action would break its contents to pieces. Once done, he slid out a typed letter. A small item, wrapped in tissue paper held closed by a thin white ribbon, fell into his lap.

The paper rustled in his hand. Depending on what this letter said, he'd know without a doubt if Elizabeth told the truth or not. Marco was convinced, but if she weren't who she said she was, Gio would have one last hope of not irrevocably losing his heart.

He skimmed the letter's introduction without comprehension. The words were illegible scratches on the page. The phrase *I took particular interest in your call to the cemetery* finally caught his attention. *I had the pleasure of knowing your father.*

Panic rose in Gio's heart. He gulped and read on in silence.

As you may or may not be aware, your father held a custodial job at a family-owned restaurant in the North end of Boston. Your father was a humble man who primarily kept to himself.

The owners of the restaurant grew quite attached to him in the three years he worked for them before his sudden death. He was a diligent worker and often offered advice on the wine served in the restaurant.

Dropping the letter to his lap, he closed his eyes and took several unsteady breaths. There was no excuse to doubt Elizabeth any longer, and no excuse to deny his mother the truth. He opened his eyes, not lifting the letter.

You will need to forgive his employer for not following his advice because Paolo did not share his background with us. He did tell us, however, his family had died many years earlier. We believed Paolo was quite alone in the world.

You may find comfort in knowing your father was not alone at the time of his death, however. Two young women acting as good Samaritans aided him.

Your father did not have much of value. I was able to salvage a few articles of his, including clothing and several books he had in his possession. I will keep these items and send them to you at your bidding. However, I have enclosed a locket your father always wore. Your family might consider it invaluable.

Please call me directly at the cemetery to discuss what arrangements you would like to make. Yours in sympathy, Mr. Antonio Gabelli

Gio's stomach clenched. Leaning forward, he banged his forehead against the steering wheel. He dropped the letter onto the floor beneath his feet. Then he struck the steering wheel with the palm of his hand repeatedly until pain forced him to stop.

"Dammit," he moaned. "Dammit." What if he

tossed the letter and locket out the window? He'd drive to the ocean and throw them in, letting them both sink to the bottom.

Would he be able put the whole nightmare behind him?

With trembling hands, he felt for the tissue-wrapped locket that had slipped between his legs. He picked the small packet up and tore off the ribbon and paper. The locket fell into his lap.

He sat still, hoping to clear his mind, not wanting to wonder how lonely his father's life must have been. He picked up the locket, fingering a chink in one chain link and noticing it was once broken but bound together with a thin wire.

The embossed cover reminded him of the one he'd hidden away in his desk drawer. Tiny dollops of grapes ornamented the dull gold. The image of a hand's frequent caress flashed in Gio's mind. He opened the pendant, careful not to snap it in two with the violent tremor of his hands. A tear dropped onto his hand, startling him. On the inside, he discovered the picture he suspected he would see. Inside the small oval frame, he found a picture of himself as a baby in his father's arms.

Chapter Eighteen

Elizabeth wiped her hands on her overalls. She looked down from her perch on the stepladder, watching Adriana adjust a cluster of grapes on the lower vines as she checked for disease or pests. She turned back to her own work and imitated what she'd observed.

She was glad Adriana agreed to show her. The work was soothing and gave Elizabeth time alone with Adriana to tell her the truth.

Her heart sped. She closed her eyes to her apprehension. "I have something to tell you." She spoke barely above a whisper.

"Hmmm? What did you say?"

She opened her eyes to see Adriana looking up at her. Paolo stood behind his wife. He offered Elizabeth a lopsided smile, straightened his dog-eared bowtie, and nodded. "Yes. Go ahead, *Bella*. It is time she learned the truth."

Elizabeth swallowed and climbed down three ladder rungs to the ground. "I have something I wanted to talk to you about."

Adriana glanced briefly over her shoulder and asked, "Ah, something serious?"

"Yes." She glanced at two workers who labored only feet away. "Shall we walk?"

"Perhaps, we could take a break for tea." Adriana's face showed reserved concern. "I can check on Marco after."

They walked the aisle in silence. Elizabeth was careful not to look directly at Gio's mother. She was about to betray him. Would he ever forgive her?

"I am not blind," Adriana said. "There is more to this visit of yours than calling on an acquaintance. It may have started this way, but I see the way my son looks at you."

Elizabeth's heart leapt into her throat. "It's not what you think."

"I suppose you are right. I have been kept in the dark, I am afraid. I have even suspected several people on this vineyard have been concealing something." They reached the end of the aisle and Adriana stopped walking. She turned to Elizabeth. "No matter what has brought you here to us, Elizabeth, you cannot deny you stay because of your feelings for my son."

Elizabeth's hands went numb, and her cheeks grew hot despite the cool air whirling around her. "I need to leave soon."

She looked back down the aisle at the shaded ground. Streaks of sun etched, leaf-shadowed lines swayed in intermittent patterns. Safety lay beneath the cover of those vines, surrounded by the hushed tones of leaves colliding with one another and the hum of busy conversation. If Paolo had returned when he was alive, he'd have found peace here, even if his family did perish. She rocked forward on the pads of her feet and turned back to Adriana.

"There's something I've wanted to tell you," Elizabeth continued. "But Gio asked me to wait. To wait until he—"

The truck rolled into its spot beside the house, and

Gio swung the door open. He hopped down, clutching something in his hand. His face was pale and drawn. Strands of his black hair hung in disarray. He gave them a curt nod and retreated in through the back kitchen door.

"Gio," Adriana called.

Elizabeth placed her hand gently on her shoulder. "Please, let me go," she said, considering her words. "I might be able to help."

A few minutes later Elizabeth stood outside of Gio's bedroom door. She closed her eyes and leaned her forehead against the solid wood. Whatever happened on his trip into town rattled him. She longed to wrap her arms around him and caress the hurt away.

Without knocking, she opened the door.

"Now who is the one sneaking?" he asked and jumped up from his bed.

"I'm sorry for barging in." She slid in and closed the door behind her. "But somehow, I didn't think you'd let me in if I asked."

"No, I don't suppose I would have. Now please leave." He pointed to the door.

"I will not," she said, feeling brave. "I think whatever has you so upset has something to do with your father."

"What if it does? It doesn't concern you."

"I beg to disagree." She glanced around the ordered room. A pair of pants on the floor looked out of place. "And didn't you say it yourself? It has everything to do with me and why I'm here." Not brave enough to leave the safety of the door, she clung to the knob and leaned back. "Besides, I'd like to go home soon. The time has come to tell your mother."

"You're leaving?" He looked away and she heard

disappointment in his voice.

Yes, we're in dreadful trouble because I don't want to leave you. Ask me to stay. Please? She dropped her hand from the doorknob and took a step forward. "Yes, I'm leaving. I don't think there is any more I can do here. But that's not why I came up. Something's upset you. What is it?"

Turning back to her, inner struggle plain on his face, he bent to retrieve a package from the edge of his bed. "I received this from Boston today."

Elizabeth crossed to him and took the parcel. "The cemetery," she read, lifting her eyebrows in question. She locked her gaze with his. "You contacted them?"

"Yes, the day after you arrived." He shifted his gaze away from hers. "I needed more than your word."

"I'd expected so." She had. She hadn't gone to the cemetery herself, though she knew Paolo's body was buried there. The owner of the restaurant he worked for had seen to it.

"You can read it if you'd like."

Her hands trembling, she opened the package and took out the letter. Easing herself down on the bed, she placed the cover beside her on the thick wool blanket.

****

Gio paced the room. His head ached as he fought the urge to sit beside her and ask if she wouldn't mind holding him. A constant, dull discomfort settled in his heart. He absently lifted his hand to rub the hurt away.

After she'd finished reading, she picked up the wrapping and peered inside. "Gio, the letter mentions a locket. Do you have it?"

Stopping in mid-pace, Gio turned toward her as he lifted out a chain from his beneath his shirt. The tarnished chain hung around his neck.

Without a word, she rose from the bed and met him where he stood. Her fingers brushed his neck, and a shiver traveled his spine. She took the locket into her hands and opened the delicate cover. "You and your father?"

His voice broke as he spoke, "Yes."

"You believe me?" Her eyes shifted from the locket to his face.

Caress my cheek, Elizabeth. Warmth enveloped him, and he whispered. "I have no choice now, do I?"

"He loved you, Gio. This proves it, doesn't it? He wore this. Never took it off."

Removing the locket from her hands, he let it drop against his chest and wrapped his arms around her. "I suppose he did." He rested his chin on the top of her head and closed his eyes. "You were one of my father's good Samaritans, weren't you?"

"Yes, my sister and I were." Her arms encircled his waist. "You'll need to plan a service. In Boston?"

"Yes, in Boston." He felt no need to discuss his father at this minute. All he wanted to do was hold her.

"I guess I'll see you there once harvest is over." She withdrew from his embrace.

Opening his eyes to look at her, he whispered, "Yes, as soon as it's over."

She turned and put space between them. "I hope you plan on telling your mother before too long."

"Yes. We should tell her together."

"I almost told her by myself before you drove up." She returned to the bed, picked up the letter, and examined it. "I meant to tell you more about him. How he worked. How he loved to read." She glanced at him.

171

"I wanted to tell you he finally opened up to people in the last years of his life, but I never found the right moment."

"You can tell me now." He took several steps toward her. She looked so pretty. The overalls she wore didn't detract from her beauty. No, they only made him want so much more to run his hands along the sleek curves they covered.

She shifted away from him and went to stand by the bureau. Picking up a thin leather strap he used to tie his hair back, she twined it around her finger. "He did nothing for years. He rode the narrow gauge in and out of Boston. On occasion he left Massachusetts, but he always returned." Untwining the strap, she turned and set it back in its place. Running her hand along the length of the bureau, she paused to pick up the ivory-handled brush he used each morning.

"Just around the time the war began, he found a job at—" She paused and turned back to look at him. "Carbone's. I've never been there myself, but they were kind to Paolo. They gave him a room to sleep in and regular meals. He rode the streetcar across to my East Boston neighborhood every day. He liked to go to the beach and stand. I think a part of him always believed he'd see your ship coming into the harbor."

She yanked the snood off her hair, tucked it in her back pocket, and ran the brush once over her riot of curls. "I saw him on the beach many, many times." Her breath hitched. She turned, set the brush down, and braced herself against the mahogany wood of the bureau. Her head rolled forward, and her shoulders slumped.

Gio approached her from behind, wrapped his arms around her waist, and pressed into her back. He didn't find relief. Instead, his pulse raced. "We can continue this later," he whispered into her hair. The scent of autumn, and of his world, rose from her curls.

"I used to go to the beach myself. For the same reason. Irrationally, I wanted to see a ship carrying my husband home." She revolved in his arms and rested her forehead on his chest.

Her hot breath bled through the fabric of his shirt and bathed his skin.

"Gio, I didn't expect coming here to be this hard. I didn't expect to find you." Tears wet the front of his shirt.

He never expected to find her either, but all he wanted to do now was to lose himself in her. He didn't want to think about tomorrow.

He looked down at her and wiped the tears away.

"Gio—"

"Shhh," he whispered. "We've talked enough. Right now, there's something else I'd rather do." Gio leaned in and kissed her, letting all his raw emotions pour through him. Elizabeth sighed and wrapped her arms around his neck.

Reluctantly he withdrew, but not because he was through. He hoisted her into his arms and carried her to the bed.

Chapter Nineteen

"Giovanni." Though muffled by the closed door, his mother's voice woke him from a dreamless sleep.

"One second." The head resting on his shoulder kept him from springing up from the bed. Warm breath caressed his cheek.

Elizabeth.

They'd fallen asleep in each other's arms after nothing more than sweet, innocent kissing. He hadn't the heart, or the courage, to do what his body yearned to do. To peel off those overalls, unbutton her shirt. He opened his eyes and eased himself from beneath her, gently laying her head back down on his pillow.

A mass of loose curls fell into her face. She was such a pure beauty. Still sleeping, she shifted onto her back.

Straightening his shoulders, Gio checked to make sure the locket was safely tucked away.

He strode to the door, opening it wide enough for his mother to see Elizabeth fully dressed.

She smiled in the bed's general direction. "I brought the groceries in from the truck after you rushed off. I ate dinner with Marco in his room when you disappeared. You and Elizabeth with you." She frowned at him. "There are plates of food warming in the oven for the two of you when you are ready."

Pushing off from the doorjamb, his mother headed down the hall but stopped to face him. "Something is going on with you. I would expect if it were information I needed to know, you would have told me by now."

Giovanni leaned into the open door, sending it bouncing into the wall. He glanced at Elizabeth, who shifted on the mattress but continued to sleep.

"You are an adult, Giovanni."

He crossed his arms over his chest and studied his mother. Her face held the esteem of a friend speaking with a friend, not a mother reprimanding a child.

"An adult with responsibilities," she continued. "There is a vineyard out there, and harvest is looming. Unless I am mistaken, these are my twilight years, and this vineyard is yours to do with as you please. I did not expect to jump back in now and manage the day-to-day duties."

"Yes, I understand what you're saying," he said. "I won't skirt my work on the vineyard any longer."

"If you need my help, fine. But my being kept in the dark, it will not do." She smiled. "Now wake Elizabeth. Feed her some polenta. We need to put meat on those bones." She spun again and approached the stairs, calling back over her shoulder, "If she is to give birth to my grandchildren, we need to fill out those hips."

He closed his eyes and mumbled, "You're a damn fool, Gio." Opening his eyes, he went to stand by the bed and stare down at Elizabeth.

Would she stay if he asked her to? Would she mother his children? Irrational ideas from a troubled, confused man. Up until a week ago, marriage and children were a distant notion in a far-off future. He wasn't one to change his mind so drastically in so short a time, but he'd never gotten this close to a woman before. Without thinking, he leaned down and kissed her, working his way down to her neck over her warm flesh. A sleepy moan escaped her lips, and she stretched awake in his arms. She opened her eyes and backed away from him.

"Gio?" she asked as her newly awakened brain struggled with recognition.

He towed her to him again and pressed his mouth to hers. He prepared himself for her resistance, but to his surprise, she pressed her body against his and threaded her hands into his hair.

She exhaled and whispered, "Oh, Giovanni."

He drew back, but she tugged him closer. Fevered energy spiked through him. Such a simple action enticed him.

Looking into his eyes, she said, "Don't get up. Not yet."

Taking his hand, she lay back on the bed and guided him to her until his head rested on her chest. He closed his eyes, breathing in her scent. He smelled the subtle scent of grapes again, and it suited her.

Elizabeth's lovely, small hands would be valuable in nurturing the grapes, but she wouldn't stay. Once he finally told his mother, Elizabeth would leave. She'd be out of his life. The idea bothered him, but was it enough to ask her to stay?

"Are you hungry?" he whispered and brushed his lips over hers.

"Hmmm," she answered. The soft, throaty sound of her voice sent a jolt of arousal surging through him. He pictured himself stripping the overalls from her and running his trembling hands over her soft, warm flesh.

He rolled away from her. Before he took such a life-affirming step, he'd better be sure he was ready to face the consequences. This wasn't a woman for *him* to share intimacies with and then let go. Not without leaving himself a changed man.

She turned her face to stare at him with her hooded eyes. Heat flushed her face, and her swollen lips parted in silent question.

He froze. Everything about Elizabeth frightened him to his core. He jumped up from the bed, held out a hand and struggled to find his voice. "My mother has plates full of polenta waiting for us."

****

Elizabeth shrugged her white nightgown off over her head and tossed it to the floor. What was the use? She couldn't sleep. The nap in Gio's arms had left her well rested and agitated, and the dinner they ate in silence two hours earlier only confused her. The man easily went from tender and affectionate to distant and cold in a matter of minutes. She sensed the true Giovanni Clemente was the man who smiled easily, took a woman's hand without hesitation, and gently caressed her cheek. The only places he seemed to sincerely be himself were the vineyard and the bedroom.

Elizabeth dressed quickly. She rummaged for her overalls, yanking them on, and didn't bother to hunt for her shirt. More of a playsuit, the overalls covered her completely. She fastened the back buttons before searching the floor in the moonlight for her cardigan sweater.

After leaving her temporary room, she tiptoed down the hall. Noticing a light coming from beneath Marco's bedroom door, she paused and placed her ear against it. There wasn't a sound. She continued down the hall and ran down the stairs on her bare feet.

177

Elizabeth exited the sleeping house through the front and took a seat on the bench. Sighing, she gazed at the waxing moon. Not even the shrill scream of a coyote floating in on a light breeze disturbed her. The muted sound of conversation traveled to her from the back of the house and piqued her interest.

She leaned her head against the bricks.

The men on the vineyard estate kept odd hours. They rose before dawn and caroused into the night. No doubt, Gio was with them, hoping to avoid her. Let him relax, and think he's safe for tonight, and then she'd go looking for him. She needed to finish what he'd started in his room. Who'd have ever judged the once shy little Elizabeth O'Brien would consider throwing herself at a man like Giovanni Clemente.

Once they told Adriana about Paolo, it didn't mean she'd have to leave at once. Wouldn't his mother want to learn all about her husband's life?

****

Gio stood outside of Marco's room and glanced toward the stairwell at the sound of the front door closing on the floor below. Then he knocked once before entering. The smell of medicine and musty sleep hit him full force.

Marco's thinning gray-haired head peeked out from a bright yellow blanket. The blanket Gio mailed from Italy. He'd taken care in picking the right one, knowing how simple Marco preferred his possessions. Gio bought it from a small shop in Foggia, both Marco's and his father's birthplace.

Gio entered the room and approached the bed quietly, careful not to wake the man. Sliding up a ladder-back chair, he sat and studied a picture of himself on the bedside table.

He stood amongst the bare vines on the original Clemente Vineyard. The vines hanging above his head twisted like ancient arthritic hands.

He didn't look too bad in his crisp sergeant uniform and closely cropped hair. He'd paid a pretty penny to have the photograph taken. A memento of his time during the war and the furloughs he'd taken to the family vineyard. The first time he'd been there since his visits as a baby and the last time he'd ever walked the soil again. Why would he ever return? The place would never mean the same thing to him again after learning his father was denied the estate.

A small pewter-framed picture stood beside the one of him. A young Paolo Clemente smiled deviously into the camera. He must have been sixteen, but he portrayed the part of a don in his trim-fitting suit and his thumb resting in his vest pocket. His brothers, Lorenzo and Michael, stood behind him, resting their hands on their older brother's shoulder. Each boy leaned in with one foot propped up on the stone bench. Their eyes showed pride and respect. They were family.

"Plan on sitting there all night without saying a word?"

Gio turned to Marco, who pushed the blanket down below his shoulders. "I didn't want to disturb you."

"Ah, so you think I am so near death you must watch over me in my sleep?" A wry grin lit his face.

"Of course not." Gio shook his head. "I hoped you'd wake soon." He looked down at his clasped hands, then lifted the locket out from beneath his shirt. "I need to show you something." He leaned in toward the bed and opened the locket for Marco to see. "This." He looked up into Marco's tired eyes. "It was my father's. A man from the Boston cemetery where he's buried sent it to me."

"It was his?" Marco asked in disbelief and extended a trembling hand. "May I?"

Gio hesitated then lifted it from around his neck and handed it to him. "It's like the one I have. Only it's been worn."

"Yes, I remember this." A tear slid down his wrinkled cheek. "Your mother had one made for each of you. Something to keep while you were to be apart."

Guilt rippled through Gio. He'd been an angry little boy, who'd grown into an angry man. He didn't have any idea of how his father cherished him.

He rubbed at the regret in his heart. "I took mine off when I was seven and haven't worn it since."

Marco studied the picture a minute longer and then thrust it back into his hand. "You'll wear this one then?"

"Yes."

"Have you shown this to your mother?"

"No." Pushing up from the chair, he went to stand at the closed window. He slid the muslin curtain open and stared blindly at the moonlit front porch roof. "But I will soon. She's concerned and thinks I'm hiding something, but she's not aware of what it is."

A person stepped from under the roof's shelter. Gio leaned his head into the glass, bringing the palms of both his hands flat against the windowpane. Elizabeth strolled around the side of the house and out of his field of vision.

"What's she doing?" he mumbled to himself before facing Marco.

Chapter Twenty

Elizabeth walked along to the side of the house. What if she did stay? Closing the door to her former life would be easy. Her family would understand, wouldn't they? She'd missed them terribly, but with Gio in her life, she'd be capable of truly opening herself to another person. She trailed her hand along the side of the stone house, wincing as a sharp pebble bit into her bare foot.

Gio would be able to hear the whole truth of how she'd met his father eventually. Wouldn't he?

One of the many reasons she'd chosen to marry Patrick was he was aware of her mother's legacy. He'd been present when people sought out Dora O'Brien to contact a deceased loved one, and he never shunned her or her family. She never hid who she was from him. Could she come clean with Giovanni Clemente as well and have more than she ever dreamed of?

"Where are you going?"

She screamed and jumped back, slipping on the dirt beneath her feet.

Gio stepped in front of her in the darkness and caught her. He helped her to her feet, then turned and led her behind him. The firelight from a nearby drum flickered over them. At the back stoop, he asked, "Should we sit?" He turned to look at her, and she nodded.

Sitting, he tugged her down beside him.

"Are you sure this is safe?" She gave an awkward laugh. Why was she so nervous? She'd slept in the man's arms, for goodness' sake. "You always seem so much nicer when you're surrounded by vines." *Or in a more intimate setting.*

"What do you want from me, Elizabeth?"

The husky tone of his voice sent a rippling wave of desire scoring through her body. She reached up and ran her fingers over the nape of his neck.

Smiling, she maneuvered his mouth down to hers. The firmness of his lips sent her into delirium. His hands encircled her waist, and she moaned. If she did what her body begged to do, she'd be lost forever. He lifted her up into his lap to face him. She straddled him.

This wasn't possible. How could she be here with this beautiful, lonely man and want him so much?

Her heart drummed in her chest, and she heard nothing but its beat. He must feel it, too. He had to sense the excitement and it humbled her. She pressed her body into his and traced her tongue over his wet lips.

Running her hands over the back of his shirt, she explored the lean, defined muscles hiding beneath the fabric. His was a strong, masculine back.

A muffled sigh passed from her lips to his. He forced the open cardigan sweater down from her shoulders. His hot hands skimmed her bare, tingling skin. Delicious tickles traveled the length of her spine.

"Damn," he whispered in a guttural voice. "You're out here half-naked."

"I was hoping to see you," Elizabeth said, brazenly. Who was this woman who'd say such a thing?

"Mmmmm," he moaned in response.

Then Elizabeth worked her hands up into his hair,

tore the black leather tie out and let it drop to the ground. Her fingers tangled through his straight locks and smoothed them over his shoulders.

"Take me to your room," she whispered.

He pulled away and lifted her off his lap. Positioned in front of him, Gio studied her with his dark eyes. "Are you sure?" he asked.

Heaven help her, but she was. She cocked her head to the side and smiling, offered him a hand. He placed his large one into her smaller one, and she stepped back, tugging him to his feet. He stood in front of her, his taut chest lifting and falling under the strain of his rapid breath.

Reaching out, she unfastened several of the buttons on his shirt. He flinched, but she gently drew him back and ran both of her hands over his hot skin. She looked up into his eyes and rested a hand over Paolo's locket. "Yes, Gio, I'm sure."

With a nod, Gio took her hand and led her in through the back door and through the quiet house. He didn't bother to turn on the lights. So, Elizabeth followed behind him, her eyes trained on his strong back as they passed through the swinging door that led from the kitchen to the hallway.

Her heart beat fast and loud to her own ears. Did Gio hear it?

They made their way to the stairs, and she carefully took each step one at a time. What am I doing? Suddenly, she wasn't sure, and her resolve seemed to evaporate into the air.

Yet, she wanted this. She wanted this man.

On silent feet, he led her to his room and then quietly closed the door behind them.

Without a thought, Elizabeth found herself standing next to the bed, staring down at the rumpled covers. Moonlit beams cast lustrous shadows on the shimmering sheets. From behind her, Gio closed the door, and she trembled.

Yes, she'd asked to come here but what was she thinking? Especially with Adriana and Marco's rooms close by. Well, she wasn't necessarily thinking with her head.

Her parents brought her up so much better than this.

Determined footfalls approached, and her shoulders stiffened. Breathing became difficult, and she closed her eyes to settle her nerves. Warmth inundated her. Gio's powerful hands encircled her waist from behind, and his warm tongue traced the edge of her ear. His breath caressed her skin. Gio leaned into her, sliding his hand to her waist.

"Are you sure you understand what you're doing?" he asked.

A taut laugh and the words, "I have absolutely no idea," fell awkwardly from her lips.

"God," he moaned. "You can't realize what you're doing to me."

She leaned her head back on his shoulder. His tongue traveled down the side of her neck, and currents of desire coiled through her.

"Mmmm. You know exactly what you're doing to me," she said. She wanted to be here, and she would stay.

He moaned into her ear and released her. Running his hands up over her stomach, Gio spun her to face him. "Undress me, Elizabeth."

She nodded and finished undoing his buttons. With self-assured motions, she opened his shirt. His lips crushed hers. His teeth scraped and tugged at her lower lip, until her mouth opened, and his tongue stole inside.

Breathlessly, she returned his kiss. Her tongue danced with his while she pushed the shirt down from his shoulders, over his arms, and let it fall to the floor. Drawing back, she ran her hands over his lightly haired chest and traced the locket's chain. He was such a beautiful man. She bit her lip, running the pads of her fingers down his hot flesh.

"You're beautiful, Elizabeth," he whispered with such emotion in his voice.

Her heart soared.

Elizabeth turned her face to hide the tears pooling behind her closed lids. The emotions rolling through her were too big to process, but being there, with him, was the most genuine thing she'd ever done.

He wiped away a tear from her cheek. "Am I scaring you?"

"No." She shook her head and caressed his whiskered chin.

"If you want me to st—"

Placing a finger to his lips, she shook her head again. "I've already made my choice, Giovanni." She leaned toward him, brushing her lips over his and then traced kisses over his face. "And I want to do this," she whispered in his ear, "with you." Wrapping her arms around his neck, she threaded her hands into his hair and drew him toward her.

Chapter Twenty-One

Gio awoke the next morning with Elizabeth enveloped in his arms. Her curly mahogany hair tickled his neck and chin. He enjoyed the look of her. Her face exuded youth. When he first saw her, he'd believed she was younger than twenty-five years old. He traced her small nose with his finger.

Still sleeping, she stretched and slid from his arms. With a sated purr, she rolled onto her stomach, the thin sheet covering them both slipped, and he ran his hand along the length of her back. He toyed with the idea of rolling onto her and waking her silently. Shaking his head, he sat up instead, swung his legs over the side of the bed, and fished his pants from the floor.

Elizabeth shifted on the bed behind him.

"Where are you going?" Her arms encircled his waist. "Won't you come back to bed?"

Gio turned to her, leaned down, and she brushed her lips over his.

She'd soon exit his life as quickly as she barged in. He stood, withdrawing from her embrace, and pulled on his pants.

Their lovemaking the night before had dislodged something deep inside and left him raw and exposed. He'd be too susceptible to hurt now, and for him, hurt led to bitterness. It was better for them both to stem the tide of emotions now.

He didn't have more to give and she couldn't stay.

He turned to face her, keeping his eyes level with hers. "A very tempting idea but I need to get to work."

She sat back on the bed with a pout. "But it's barely daylight out there."

"I need to get a head start. Yesterday was a lost cause."

Elizabeth jumped up from the bed with the sheet loosely around her. "Fine. I can help."

"Work?" His voice rose in an exaggerated surprised manner.

"Yes, you can put me to work." Her shoulders slumped, and she slid back onto the bed. "You don't want me to?"

"Well, it's very hard labor. I need to start preparing for harvest." He purposely tried to offend her, sending a small but strong wave of regret sweeping through his heart. He was falling for her, and it frightened him too much.

"I'm quite capable." She covered herself with the sheet. "But fine." She hitched her chin forward and looked away with an air of indifference, but he caught the hurt look in her eyes. "If you're blaming me for last night, remember it took two, Giovanni. I didn't force you." Elizabeth wrapped the sheet securely around her and rose.

Gio quickly pulled on a shirt and stalked to the door, opening it just as a single knock sounded on the other side.

"Gio, your *Zio* Michael is—" Adriana stood in the doorway for only a second. With reddened cheeks and a smile, she stepped out of view. "*Mi scusi*," she said. "I did not mean to intrude. When you are ready, you both might want to dress and come down for breakfast."

****

Gio lifted an empty oak barrel on its side and up into place in the rounded curve of a wooden frame. He uncorked the barrel and slammed the stopper on the worktable's clean surface.

Dammit. He took the coward's way out. In truth, he didn't like being one. He'd bypassed the kitchen, his mother, and purposely avoided Elizabeth.

Had his head been as clear as it was now, he'd have never slept with her. She deserved more than the hurt he'd eventually bring her. The same hurt his father inflicted on his mother.

Awkwardly, he rubbed his chest to chase away the constant ache. Elizabeth Reilly was simply a woman who lived on the opposite corner of the country. He'd recover from the night they shared, no matter what it cost him.

His hand rested on the locket he'd taken care to hide from his mother.

"Gio."

He turned to see Elizabeth standing in the open doorway.

Her fingers clung to the door's wooden frame. She stared at him, and unshed tears glistened in her eyes. "Your mother sent me out to get you." Her chin jutted forward like a stubborn child. "She told me to tell you the work could wait for a bit at least."

"Why would it need to wait?" he asked and bent, lifting a bucket of clean water only to set it back down.

"She thinks you need breakfast," she said softly.

"I'll eat later when the kitchen is empty." He stood, rubbing his hands on the legs of his pants, leaving behind a smear of dirt. He looked down at his pants, then his hands, and walked to the sink. "You don't mind, do you?" He vigorously scrubbed his hands under the icy water.

"When I'm not there." She sighed. "Is that what you mean?"

He glanced back at her. The hurt on her face left his entire being achingly hollow. "Since you've shown up, I've been quite distracted." Returning to stand in front of his work, he said, "There are so many things I need to do to get ready for harvest. Besides, the better prepared I am, the sooner we can get to Boston."

"We need to talk," she said.

He lifted the barrel and poured the water through its stopper hole. The chilly water splashed onto his pants, chilling him. He slammed the bucket down, picked up the plug, and pounded it into place.

"I won't let you push me out of this. I won't."

"What, Elizabeth?" Gio said and spun to face her. "So now you think you have some power over me?" Better to let her see the true Giovanni Clemente now than for her to be devastated later.

"I thought we were—" She visibly bit her tongue.

"We were what, Elizabeth?" he whispered. She looked so crestfallen. His arms burned to hold her, but it wouldn't do either of them any good.

"I guess I was wrong." Her hands fisted at her sides as scarlet rode high on her cheeks. "For me, what we did last night meant something, but apparently not you."

His heart clenched. No, he endured more emotions than he'd ever wanted to, but he was incapable of sharing them. He needed to let her go.

If he reminded himself enough, he would eventually

accept it.

She didn't deserve a hard-hearted bastard like himself. He was doing her a favor. "You've finally figured me out. Let's hope a child doesn't result from what we did."

Her face paled, and anger flared in her eyes. "God has cursed me enough. He couldn't possibly do such a thing to me."

What did she mean by God cursed her? He didn't understand. If what she told him was true, God gave her a caring family with a mother *and* a father. She was once married, and if her husband still lived, she never would have shared Gio's bed.

"Just leave, Elizabeth. You don't belong here."

"Not until we tell your mother."

"Maybe she doesn't need to know." He turned away and closed his eyes. *Dammit!* He didn't mean that. He'd tell his mother, but he harbored this unmitigated urge to torment Elizabeth.

"It's not fair of you. Your mother has a right. Paolo lived his life waiting to die so he could see the two of you again." Her shoes padded over the dirty floor towards him. "Damn you, Gio. Are you listening to me?" She grabbed his arm and yanked him to look at her.

He glanced over Elizabeth to see his mother standing in the doorway. She shook her head, but her face was peculiarly blank. With his hands trembling, he yanked his arm out of Elizabeth's grasp. His heart crashed to his feet.

"What?" Elizabeth continued with venom in her voice. "Are you going to wait until you're in Boston before you tell her you're there to see Paolo Clemente's grave?"

****

Elizabeth forgot to breathe. The gaze Gio centered on his mother held regret and fear. With his voice threaded with panic, he pleaded in Italian and rushed by Elizabeth. He chased Adriana out through the open door.

Elizabeth gulped. What had she done? Quickly, she ran through the door past elderly Sebastian and young Esteban, who both stood at the entrance watching.

She ran around to the front of the house to avoid the kitchen where Gio and Adriana would be.

A fine mist coated the air, and the dark gray clouds promised harder rain. A shiver assaulted her as she rounded the corner of the house. She was not ready to face either Gio or Adriana, but she must. She'd do what she should've done her first day on the vineyard.

She ran through the front door and up the stairs. At lightning speed, she fled into Gio's room, grabbing the letter from the cemetery off his bedside table. She paused to look at the sheets still rumpled from their lovemaking. A longing ache swelled in her heart.

Shaking her head, she dashed from the room and to the guest room. She removed the picture her sister had sketched of Paolo from the front of her walking bag. She sped back to the first floor and hovered in the kitchen doorway. Unnoticed, she watched the mother and son standing at odds.

"I asked her not to tell you. It wasn't her choice." Though his voice was low, it held the strength of conviction.

"Why would you ask her to keep it from me, Giovanni? Do you think your *madre* is too weak? Am I too decrepit to handle such news?" Adriana threw her arms in the air, speaking several words in Italian before continuing in English. "So, what did it take to convince you? Your time in bed together?"

Elizabeth's face burned.

"No, *Madre*. What we did was a mistake and meant nothing."

Elizabeth clutched the doorjamb as her heart plummeted from her chest. Hearing them now, his words hurt even more.

"You yourself told me she was a good person," he continued.

"Yes, I did." Adriana exhaled and faltered. Gio stepped towards her, pulling her into his arms.

"I didn't want to listen to her. I fought Elizabeth every inch of the way." He looked at his mother lovingly, smoothing back a loose piece of gray hair from her forehead.

Elizabeth's stomach tightened in a combination of grief and longing. She envied the affection he showed his mother.

"I see her goodness, *Madre*. She is telling the truth. She would've told you the first day, but I kept her from telling you."

The flesh on Elizabeth's forehead warmed. She imagined his fingers brushing back a loose strand of her hair.

Adriana broke from her son's arms. "You have no right to decide for me. I am not a *bambina*, but we will talk of this later." She walked to the stove, picked up the teakettle, and dropped it back down. Her head bowed, and she stood silent.

"*Madre*?"

"I am fine, Giovanni." She turned and leaned back against the stove.

Gio nodded.

Gathering her courage, Elizabeth entered the kitchen. "Excuse me?"

Both mother and son looked at her. She searched the woman's face for forgiveness but saw only unrelenting sadness. "Adriana, I am sorry for not—"

She lifted her hand to silence Elizabeth. "Gio has explained the secrecy was his idea."

Elizabeth held up the picture and letter. Her hands shook. "You might want to see these."

Adriana approached and took both from her. Slowly, the woman turned away, and her shoulders buckled under the weight of emotion. She shrank into the kitchen chair, placing the picture flat on the table in front of her. She sat in silence, blankly studying the sketched portrait. Next, she carefully opened the letter and read. She looked up at Gio. "I am having a hard time reading this. Would you?"

Gio crossed to his mother, gently took the letter from her hand, and read aloud.

When he finished, he looked at Elizabeth, but she frowned and dropped her gaze to the floor to avoid eye contact. How could he want to look at her at all after what he'd said? Making love to her was a mistake. How could he go from treating her like a harlot to telling his mother she had a good heart?

After a long silence, Adriana spoke, looking only at her son. "This is my Paolo." Cradling her head in her arms, she sobbed, her shoulders shuddering with the force of her tears. Gio knelt beside her, placing his arm around her, and whispered in Italian.

Elizabeth stood forgotten. She couldn't fathom how Adriana felt to find out such news about Paolo after so long. How'd she feel if…? No, she wouldn't allow Giovanni Clemente to be so important to her.

She turned and bumped into the chest of a thin, tall man.

"*Scusi*," the young man said in melodic Italian. "Is everything well, *Signorina*?"

Dodging back away from him, she bumped into the closed door, and it swung open. The young man gazed down at her with mirth in his eyes. He wore a black traveling suit and polished shoes. Offering her a warm smile, he glanced over her head through the kitchen door. "*Zio*," he beckoned over his shoulder, "Giovanni is in the kitchen with a woman in his arms. And I almost snared another in my own."

Another man walked up behind him, his hair peppered with gray and the soft lines beside his eyes creased with curiosity and genuine concern. "Is everything all right, *Signorina*?"

Elizabeth shook her head, unable to find her voice. She grasped the doorjamb again, holding the door open with her shoulder. There were two choices. Run past these two men or through the kitchen past Gio and Adriana.

The second was more than she could bear. She closed her eyes to gather strength and then opened them to examine the men in front of her. The younger one, with light brown hair and blunt features, she couldn't place. But the other was Gio's uncle, she was sure. His eyes were like Paolo's. The wrinkles around them held the lines of worry much like Paolo's did.

Michael had telephoned, Adriana had informed her at breakfast. He was on the way to the vineyard with his family to help prepare for harvest. Elizabeth meant to tell

Gio as well, but he'd never given her the chance to.

He stepped beside the younger man. "You do not speak Italian?"

"No, I'm sorry. I don't."

"No need to apologize. Are you a guest?"

"Yes." If a guest is what one called a human cyclone who blew in and tore their world apart. "I was going to prepare for departure, however." On wobbling legs, she walked past both men. "If you'll excuse me."

Sofia rounded the staircase and took Elizabeth gently by the arm. "I'm sorry to intrude," she whispered in Elizabeth's ear. "But I heard it all. The mistress would not want you to leave, Elizabeth. Please, give her some time." She guided Elizabeth to the stairs. "I'll draw you a bath and, perhaps, bring some soothing tea."

Elizabeth lifted her heavy legs one after the other to climb the stairs. Her head buzzed with the voices below. A woman's voice joined in. She had a definite American voice, and it was aristocratic and clipped.

"Is that Gio's uncle?" Elizabeth whispered.

"Yes, the older man is Michael Clemente and the woman his wife, Miriam." Sofia glanced over her own shoulder. "I don't recognize the other young man, but I think he is family from Italy."

Elizabeth stopped short on the stairs.

"Come." Sofia grabbed her hand and guided her forward. "We should move out of the way. More will be coming, Michael's sons, I'm sure, if they have returned home yet from the War. They come each year for Harvest, but they are earlier this year than most. I have to finish preparing the rooms."

Lord help her. Was she to be surrounded now? How many more Clementes did Elizabeth have to prove herself to? Paolo didn't prepare her for any of this.

Chapter Twenty-Two

Elizabeth walked the length of the corridor to the washroom at the back of the house. She entered the room, closed the door behind her, and turned on the clawfoot tub's faucet. She'd convinced Sofia to let her manage the bath by herself. The busy young housekeeper needed to focus on preparing the house for the influx of family.

Elizabeth stripped herself of her dress and undergarments. After letting the tub fill halfway, she dipped a toe in to check the temperature. The water was hot enough to wash away any remnants left by Giovanni Clemente. Satisfied, she climbed in and submerged her entire body, including her head. The warmth melted the tension from her joints. She let her head float up out of the water with her eyes shut and smoothed her hair back against her scalp. The door opened and closed.

"Sofia, I'm fine. No need to worry about me."

When she opened her eyes, Gio was sitting before her, leaning on the windowsill. "Oh—my—gosh." She gasped and dunked back into the water.

When she broke the surface, he was still there. Dumbfounded, Elizabeth covered her breasts with her arms and knees. "Please, leave me in privacy."

"Don't tell me you're bashful, not after last night."

"Last night was a mistake. You said so yourself." Resisting the urge to douse him with water, she tightened

197

her grip on her elbows. "I heard what you told your mother."

He stared without saying a word. His face held the look of simmering anger and feral longing.

What right did he have to be angry with her? What did she do wrong besides fall in love with the man? "Don't look at me in such a way," she said. "You make me feel dirty,"

He inhaled loudly. "I don't think what we did last night was wise."

"And standing over me while I'm naked is?" she asked. "With a house full of your family? Or would it help your cause if they think I'm a harlot?"

"There isn't much concern for either of us now. My mother and uncle are beside themselves." He stood and strode to the tub. "They're making plans to leave for Boston."

"What about harvest?" She narrowed her eyes at him, hoping he'd leave. "Will you be going to Boston, too?"

"Yes, of course. He was my father, after all." He leaned in, dipped his hand in the water, and sent it swirling around her.

She bit her lip. Lord, but he confused her. He didn't care if he made more mistakes, but she did.

"My cousins are here," he continued. "If we decide to leave soon, they will finish the harvest preparations. Marco can instruct them from bed. He won't be able to make the trip." He traced a wet finger along the bare line of her shoulder. Heat shot through her. Blast her body for betraying her.

The bath water rose dangerously close to the tub's rim. She shifted and turned the faucet off.

"Elizabeth, I was perfectly content with my life before you walked into it."

Her throat tensed, and she fought the urge to plug her ears. She didn't think she wanted to hear what he was trying to say. "Leave me in peace, please. I'd like to finish my bath. I need to pack and return home as soon as possible."

Gio bent by the tub and immersed his arms in the water, soaking his shirtsleeves. His hands grazed her hips, and a shiver ran down the length of her despite the bath's warm water.

"No, I have to say this. I don't plan to marry anyone. Not for a very long time if ever. Do you understand?"

"What's to understand, Gio? I plan to never get married again." Elizabeth blinked back tears and wiggled in a futile attempt to tug out of his grasp. "You're getting your clothes all wet."

With his hands moving up to her waist, he lifted her up to him and crushed his lips down on hers. She opened her mouth to protest, but his tongue pushed its way in, strangling the words.

An involuntary reflex, her arms encircled his neck, and tugged him down to her. Water splashed over the tub's sides.

His lips left hers. His tongue traced the line of her jaw. Her body tensed.

"Gio," she gasped. "Don't. Please don't. There's a house full of people out there." She pushed him on his shoulders, and he stood.

"You're right." He frowned at her and tugged at his dripping wet shirt, holding it away from his skin. "It'll probably be best if we keep our distance from one another."

"Fine with me." She sank into the tub, covering her breasts. "Now, please leave," she said firmly, though her throat was hoarse. Gio was one confused man and taking her right along with him. His words said one thing, while his actions said another. Well, if he didn't understand what he wanted, she was better off without him.

He closed his eyes and swiveled away from her. "My mother doesn't want you to rush off. She'd like to talk with you," he said and opened the door. Elizabeth spied Sofia approaching with her arms full.

"I'm sorry." Sofia glanced over his shoulders at Elizabeth. "I-I brought clean towels." She handed them to Gio and rushed away.

****

Adriana rose from the dinner table with an empty stomach. In fact, from the looks of the half-filled plates, most everyone lacked an appetite. She dropped her cloth napkin to her plate. "I need to bring something to our guest," she said matter-of-factly.

Michael rose with her and spoke in Italian. "You should rest, Adriana. Let Sofia prepare a tray."

"No." She shook her head and looked from one face to the next. She'd never noticed before the stark differences between Paolo's son and Michael's.

Michael's youngest son, Paolo, who sat beside him, did not resemble the uncle he'd been named after. He possessed the broadness of shoulder he inherited from the Clemente blood. His face was square and eyebrows heavy. Neither Paolo nor Giovanni were small men, but their size allowed them an aristocratic grace. Their bodies etched with sleek lines and sinewy muscles set them apart from the other Clemente men.

They all possessed the same laughing eyes, though,

passed down from their mother and grandmother, Isabella. Adriana smiled despite herself. Who was to have believed her prim and quiet mother-in-law kept such a secret? Becoming pregnant with Paolo outside of the marriage bed with a married man.

Michael looked at her, fatigue indelibly impressed in the deep lines of his face. He seemed smaller than before, his shoulders hunched under the weight of sadness and regret. He looked as if he wanted to apologize yet again for not telling her about Paolo's true father.

She wasn't angry nor did she place blame. She'd never been one to do so, and she would not start now. "Elizabeth is bound to think I am angry with her. I need to tell her otherwise."

Michael sat back wearily and rested his face in his hands. Miriam's arm rested on his shoulder.

"You need the rest, Michael," Adriana said and nodded to her sister-in-law, whose eyes silently agreed. "Go to your room. Perhaps later Elizabeth will join us for a drink before bed. She must have the chance to tell me what my son has kept her from telling. We can all thank her for bringing my Paolo home to us." She turned from the table and hurried through the door and to the kitchen.

Yes, she must thank Elizabeth and keep her from exiting their lives.

Giovanni would have her leave without a word. She'd failed as a mother. If Paolo had been with him his whole life, Gio might have learned how to love a woman. He'd have understood how to treat one with respect and cherish what Elizabeth offered him.

Adriana rushed around the kitchen, readying a tray

with a plate of aromatic food and tart chamomile tea. She doubted the *donna* would touch any of the dinner. Still, she was feeling maternal and protective toward her. Appalled at her son's boorish behavior, she recognized there were still a few hands yet to play. She'd take any advantage.

It was obvious Gio wasn't thinking clearly when he said the previous night's events was a mistake. Her son could not honestly think what he and Elizabeth shared was wrong. Had she been any other woman, Adriana might have been offended. This was Elizabeth, however, and she was not.

It wasn't any woman, but the woman who befriended her husband. Elizabeth's gift was even greater. She hadn't aided the handsome rakish younger man who left *Italia* to launch a vineyard he'd never intended to start but an old, wrinkled man with laughing yet sad eyes.

****

The hairline crack in the ceiling told Elizabeth the house was ancient and settled in its place long ago. The jagged line jutted out an inch from the wall and was so slight it might have gone unnoticed.

For hours, she'd lain spread-eagle on the bed, studying the ceiling, and in turn, frowning at the downcast sky outside the window. She watched the shadows fill the room as the cloud-covered sun slid away. She turned her head and rested her cheek on the soft feather pillow. The emotions of the day left her spent.

The house was busy. Doors opened and closed. Footsteps echoed from the hallway through the room's closed door. Voices remained low and reverent. Lord help her, she hoped the conversation had nothing to do with her brazen behavior.

Her own loneliness hovered in the air. She'd gone from pure, satisfied elation, after waking with Gio's work-roughened hand on her bare back, to this despair.

She'd packed her bags and planned to stay at the inn until she caught the next bus to San Francisco. From there, she'd take the train home. Gio would be glad to see her leave. Who wanted their mistakes hanging around?

Elizabeth ran a finger over her lips. She recalled the touch of his hands traveling the length of her body. Her blood warmed. She'd shared herself with the man, and this wasn't something to dismiss. She wouldn't let him cheapen their lovemaking, mistake or not. The man possessed a cruel streak, and he meant to hurt her with those words. He wanted to chase her away. Giovanni Clemente was acting like a coward. Tying herself to a person who pretended to be a coward was not what Patrick's ghost meant when he asked her to go on with her life. This thing with Gio wasn't living. Rather, it was torment, and a complication she didn't need.

Someone knocked three times from the other side of the door.

"Elizabeth," Adriana called. "Are you hungry? I have brought you dinner."

"Please," she said hoarsely and stood. "I'll be right there." She smoothed the front of her skirt, hurried to the door, and let Adriana in.

A radiant smile brightened the woman's tired face. She extended the tray of food for Elizabeth to see. The delicious aroma of butter and cream launched her stomach into a queasy summersault.

Adriana walked past her and set the tray on the table by the windows. "Come, you must eat." She smiled back at Elizabeth and eyed the suitcases. "You plan to leave then?" Her lips fell into a frown.

"Yes." She trained her eyes on steam rising from the food. "I originally hoped to leave today. But it's gotten so late."

"I would beseech you to stay for yet another night. I only now learned you were a friend to my husband. There are so many questions I have for you."

Elizabeth crossed her arms over her chest. "I'm not sure you should want me to stay," she murmured. "My behavior hasn't been the most proper." She looked up into Adriana's tear-swollen eyes. "And I should have told you the minute we met."

"I will not hold this against you, *cara mia*. My son has explained the circumstances to me," she said. "You were only doing as he bid. And though I do not necessarily agree, I understand why he chose to wait." Adriana smiled warmly. "Now with this business behind us, will you stay?"

Elizabeth winced, surprised the woman could look at her. Gathering her courage and her voice, Elizabeth said, "I need to apologize for my behavior with your son. I'm not ashamed." She shook her head. "Because I care for Gio, but I haven't used the best judgment since I've been here."

"Shush, shush." Adriana opened her arms and Elizabeth rushed into them. The embrace was a haven of friendship and motherly love.

Adriana patted her back. "No one here needs to be aware of what transpired between you and my son. If Sofia or any of the staff did see, I assure you they will be quite discreet." She loosened the embrace, and Elizabeth stepped back. "However, I will talk with my son about planning a wedding once we have time to adjust to all of this." She smiled.

A wedding? Elizabeth shuddered. She and Gio already agreed they didn't have a future together. Adriana would learn they didn't soon enough.

"Now when you are up to it," Adriana said as she patted Elizabeth's shoulder. "I would like you to meet Paolo's brother properly. Michael is as interested as I about where my husband has been all these years."

Chapter Twenty-Three

Raw nerves sent Elizabeth speeding into the kitchen. She wasn't in any rush to face the family, but she'd now settled into a constant state of anxiousness.

"Elizabeth." Adriana stood to greet her. "We are glad to have you join us."

She fidgeted, conscious of their eyes on her. She braved a smile and glanced around the room.

Paolo leaned against the window. The expression on his face bordered between sadness and elation. His hair was untidy and dull. A snug, dog-eared bowtie rested neatly at the neck of his tattered shirt. If she weren't acquainted with the man, she'd have seen him as a pauper or a thug, if not for his kind, soulful eyes.

Elizabeth took a deep breath and centered herself to keep the ghost's emotions from crashing in on her or she'd never survive the introductions. Offering him a brief smile, she turned her gaze away.

The younger man she'd collided with earlier stood by himself at the back of the room. He tapped his hand against his thigh to an imaginary tune. With his shoulders held erect, he seemed to brace himself for a weight to fall on him.

The room was too quiet. She'd interrupted them like an intruder. Always the stranger looking in.

On the side of the table facing her was a shocked Michael Clemente. He was dressed impeccably in an expensive black tailored suit covering a large framed, well-toned body. His distinguished looks left hints that in his youth he'd been stunning. His olive skin glowed in contrast to his salt-and-pepper hair.

A younger man stood behind him. His son, to be sure, for their resemblance was too close to be mistaken for less.

Michael's wife sat beside him and caressed the hand he rested on the table. Tears occasionally strayed down his cheeks and she lifted her hand to swipe them away. Her features were more striking than beautiful, with sharp defined lines from cheekbones to nose. Her hair, ashen blonde with streaks of gray, sat on her head in a tight bun accentuating her thin face.

"Come, have a seat." Adriana held her arms open to Elizabeth. "We were discussing memorial service arrangements, but first you must meet everyone."

Elizabeth sat in an empty seat at the table and nodded to each of Paolo's family as they reached out to take her hand during the introductions.

After she'd met everyone, Elizabeth said, "Whatever help you need with the arrangements, please let me know."

"You've done so much already, *Signora* Reilly." Michael spoke. "You are a wonderful woman to have befriended my brother."

"Thank you, but he helped me, really. I needed his friendship as much as he needed mine." She nodded and looked around the room again. Gio wasn't there.

Michael leaned in toward her. "Please, then, could you tell us what happened to Paolo? Why did he think us dead?"

She gulped. Paolo had never told her the details.

She'd taken him on his word. His family needed more. She saw it in their eyes. They needed an explanation. She looked toward the apparition. The moonlight shimmered around him, and for a moment, he appeared translucent.

Paolo, I'll need your help. She hoped he'd hear her silent plea. He nodded and approached her.

Elizabeth took another deep breath and pressed her back into the chair's solid wood. Closing her eyes, she concentrated on Paolo and opened herself to his emotions. Cool air hovered over her. Paolo rested his hand on her shoulder.

If only her mother were there to guide her. This was Dora's medium. She spoke to the dead at a living person's request. Dora summoned her spirits and Elizabeth had witnessed her do it repeatedly with ease. However, her mother was never challenged to perform the task while trying to make it look like she wasn't.

Elizabeth popped one eye open to see the entire roomful of people looking at her, puzzled concern on their faces.

Michael Clemente cleared his throat. "If this is too hard for—"

"No," she said, opening both of her lids. "I'm trying to remember the whole story. I don't want to leave anything out."

Paolo squeezed her shoulder. "Just relax, *Bella*," he whispered in a hoarse voice.

Her heart sped. *Okay, compose yourself, Elizabeth. This is Paolo whom you trust implicitly, not his son.* She trained her gaze on a new but empty vase on the kitchen counter. It displayed roses, painted light pink, poised between golden-etched leaves.

"Relax," Paolo's voice soothed her again as a

warmth settled in her mind.

Paolo, show me your memories.

I had a long wait at the harbor. Hours upon hours. Paolo's memories echoed through her. She swallowed hard and resisted the urge to close her eyes. Forgetting Adriana, Michael, and everyone else in the room, she spoke, relaying the images flowing unfettered from Paolo to her.

"Paolo crossed the harbor to East Boston by ferry before sunrise. He was anxious for you to arrive. He waited in the cold, not wanting to miss sight of your ship coming in. But he grew impatient despite all he learned about patience growing up on the vineyard in Italy."

****

Another hour lapsed with no sign of the ship. Less than a half dozen cargo vessels docked on the rocking waters under the gray, rain-filled clouds. Paolo watched with little interest as weathered seamen unloaded crates of varying sizes.

His patience ebbing, he entered the building for warmth. Several people stood in line at the front desk. First in line was a young Russian family.

"If you'll give me a minute," the man working the desk said haughtily.

The mother spoke through her tears. "Please if something has happened you must tell me. I am waiting for Mikhail, my husband. Please."

Paolo ignored the line and stepped up beside the crying woman and her children. "Yes. Can you tell us of the arrival of the passenger ships today?"

"Sir, there is a line. Please wait your turn," the officious man ordered, pushing his wire-rimmed glasses up on the bridge of his nose.

"I would like to, but you see, I have been waiting all day for my family to arrive. Many of these people here I have seen waiting, too. We would all like to understand."

"Sir, if you'd wait your turn, someone will be able to talk with you."

"No, I would like you to tell me now."

"Sir, all I can tell you is the weather is causing problems. The passenger ships were forced to change course, causing delays."

Paolo leaned in to look at a wrinkled paper on the clerk's counter. "How long for these delays?" He extended his hand toward the missive.

The clerk snatched the paper up before Paolo was able grasp it. "That is not your property, sir. Take your place in line *now*." He set the paper down, smoothing it flat with his thin hands.

"It is my family on one of those ships. How long for this delay?" Paolo fought to keep his voice calm and under control.

"I don't have all the information. The information I do have is one ship is delayed and the other lost," he said, pursing his lips and averting his eyes. "I-I cannot say anymore."

The young mother gathered both children to her and asked, "Which ship was lost?"

"Ma'am, I'm not at liberty to say at the moment."

"Yes, tell us which ship," Paolo said coolly, despite the rapid beat of his heart.

"Sir, if you'd just—"

He reached across the desk and grabbed the man's white tailored shirt by the collar. "I am Paolo Giovanni Clemente, and I demand you tell me which ship."

Flustered, the middle-aged clerk wrenched his collar

from Paolo's grasp and leafed through the papers in front of him. Looking down he spoke the words angrily. "If you must know, it is…" he narrowed his eyes, reading before saying, "the *Elijah*." The clerk jabbed his pointer finger into the desk as if punctuating his words.

The air around Paolo grew arid. He shook his head. No, not the *Elijah*. Adriana, Giovanni, and his brother, Michael, were on the way to him in *that* ship. He'd prepared a home for all of them. He would not accept this pompous man's words.

"Thank God!" the woman beside him cried in relief. "Thank God," she bent down, enveloping both children in her arms. "Your poppa is safe."

All feeling bled from Paolo's limbs as he stared down into the little girl's wide eyes.

"Read it again." He faced the man again and grabbed him. "*Si sbaglia*," he said and released the clerk.

With an indignant air, the man straightened his shirt and stepped to the side, out of Paolo's reach. "Sir, I don't understand you. You must speak English."

"You are wrong," he snarled.

"I am not." The clerk slammed his unsteady fist into the paper on the desk. "The information I have here tells me a ship sank late yesterday evening, and there aren't any survivors."

Paolo backed away from the desk. "*Si sbaglia*." You are wrong. He turned and ran through the building as the cry of a grieving woman rang out behind him. He reached the front doors and burst through them into the bone-numbing winter air.

Paolo walked the streets of East Boston well into the night. He dodged the mix of motor vehicles and horse-drawn carriages while drinking brandy from his flask until it was dry. His hands and feet swelled from the cold, but the brandy dulled the pain inside and out.

He damned himself. If his pride hadn't been more important than his wife's wishes, they would all be alive and still in *Italia*. The pain of losing his family far exceeded the loss of the family vineyard.

He continued his aimless journey until he arrived at a small pub. Music and drunken laughter spilled out its doors. He pushed numbly into the dark bar and through the men who stood shoulder to shoulder. He shoved an arm, next a back out of his way, ignoring the complaints of those he affronted.

It took all his concentration to keep walking. *Would it not be easier to sink to the floor and give up?* The hum of voices and muted laughter melded into one steady din and assaulted his ears. Some still found the world amusing. He did not care. He would go anywhere to get warm and have a drink.

Paolo barreled up to the bar. "*Vino*," he called and grimaced at the proprietor who turned to face him.

"Vino?"

"Yes, wine, please." His hands shook as he reached into his pocket and pulled out a roll of money. He threw three bills onto the counter. "Two bottles."

The bartender placed one bottle and a glass on the bar. Someone standing beside him snickered. He glanced to the left. A sour-faced man glared at him with his beady eyes and swiveled away to whisper in another man's ear.

Paolo scowled at him, grabbed the single bottle, and left the glass. He turned and weaved his way through the crowd to the back of the room. There he fell into an empty seat and lifted the bottle to his lips. Third-rate table wine, but such an occasion did not call for the best.

After Paolo drained the bottle, he rose on unsteady feet and pushed away from the table. He lumbered through the crowd.

"More wine," he whispered and knocked into a table, nearly capsizing it. Ignoring the complaints of faceless patrons, he stood and continued to the bar.

"*Piu vino*," he slurred at the proprietor's back. "*Piu vino!*" he shouted, too numb and exhausted to use English. He pounded his fists on the smooth wooden bar.

"Hold on a minute there." The man swung around, sloshing beer from two mugs onto the floor.

Paolo yelled in his face. "Wine!"

"It seems to me you've drank enough."

"I demand it!" He took money from the inner pocket of his coat, staggered backwards, and dropped it to the ground. "*Vino!*" He bent to pick the money up and fell face-first onto the rancid, lager-soaked floor.

"Get that dirty guinea out of here!" The proprietor yelled from above him.

Someone tugged at Paolo's jacket and lifted him from the grimy floor. He possessed no strength to fight the person. Paolo's jacket tore under his weight but did not give way. Tottering on his feet, his head flopped to the right, and dull pain shot through his neck. He sneered when a short, pug-faced man stepped up beside him and yanked his arm back. The person behind him grabbed Paolo's left arm and released the grip on his jacket collar.

They propelled him forward. Paolo closed his eyes and moaned each time his slack, heavy limbs rammed into an unseen object in their path.

"Nooo," he sputtered and opened his eyes in time to see the door swing open in front of him. The rush of freezing air stole his breath. He choked and fended off a

213

wave of nausea rising in his throat.

Letting his head roll forward, mind-numbing sleep beckoned, and he gave in. He regained his senses as his body collided with the slush-covered ground. His mouth hit hard. Coughing, he thrust up on his hands, threw his head back, and gave a muffled yelp. Warm blood ran down his chin.

Hard-soled shoes forced him down from behind, followed by a man's frantic whisper, "Don't let him get up."

Kicks struck him from all angles. Sobbing, he prayed for death. "*Per favore. Per favore.*"

He heard the sickening sound of the bone in his arm snapping. Fresh pain seared from wrist to shoulder. He was unable to stop the scream building from the depths of him and pushed past his lips. He drew in short, shallow breaths.

Rough hands rolled him over and pressed his body into his broken arm, and he screamed.

"Jesus, shut him up," was the last thing he heard before a foot flattened his nose.

****

Elizabeth gasped, and a wave of nausea ran through her as Paolo withdrew. She clamped her lips tightly and glanced at the stricken faces surrounding her.

With a deep shaky breath, she made sense of the final remnants of his thoughts, then spoke. "He awoke the next day to children poking a stick in his side. He rolled over, and they ran screeching from the alley. He rose from the ground and trudged to the open street in his stocking feet. The men who beat him must have taken his shoes and his overcoat, too."

Elizabeth took a breath. "They'd bloodied him

beyond recognition, broken his nose, and bruised his jaw. Paolo decided at once he didn't have a place to return to. This vineyard meant nothing without all of you. He'd wished he'd never woken in the alley. He knew Marco would either keep the vineyard or sell it and return to *Italia*."

Adriana spoke first, her voice raspy with tears, "My poor husband. What happened for this man, this clerk, to say such a thing? And those ruffians to beat him so. I cannot bear it." Her voice broke, and with a pale face, she looked to Michael, who spoke next.

"Was a ship lost in Boston at the time, *Signora*?"

"I'm not aware," Elizabeth said. She didn't have the information. Paolo hadn't told her the whole story until now. Why didn't she ask more of the ghost? Where was the ghost? She shot up from the chair and stumbled forward, bumping the table. The locking of minds drained her, and Paolo, too, she was sure. He'd need to recoup his energy before appearing again. He might not have a chance to say goodbye to his family before she left.

She straightened and smoothed out her skirt. Smiling uncertainly, she turned and rushed out through the swinging kitchen door.

On tenuous legs, she staggered to the front entry and made her way out to find rest on the porch bench. She only imagined how the Clementes viewed her now.

"Elizabeth, *Cara*, is everything all right?" Adriana asked as she exited the house.

"Oh, I'm fine." She leaned her head against the brick exterior. "Just been a very draining day."

"*Si*, it has been a hard one for us all." Adriana sat beside her. The woman glanced quickly at Elizabeth and away. "Michael and his son, Paolo, will drive you into San Francisco to catch a train for home if you would like."

"Yes. Yes, I'd appreciate the ride. Tell them thank you."

Adriana turned to her, grasping her hand. "There is something I must ask you." She blinked, her face ashen and concerned.

Elizabeth gulped and nodded.

"When you told us my husband's story, it was almost as if—" She shook her head and stood. "I am such a foolish woman. Foolish, tired, and sad."

Wishing her legs were not still rubbery, Elizabeth rested her hands on her knees, and leaned into them in lieu of standing. "Adriana, please ask. I'll answer if I can."

"Was Paolo with you?

Shocked electricity shot through Elizabeth's system, leaving her more spent than minutes before. "What?" she murmured.

"I told you it was foolish. At times when you spoke, your words and inflections reminded me of how Paolo would speak to me."

"That's not foolish, Adriana. Not foolish at all," she whispered.

Adriana nodded and rejoined her on the bench.

Elizabeth waited for the woman to say more, to ask more, but she didn't. Instead she said, "So, *Cara*, tell me more, *per favore*. What kind of man did my Paolo grow into?"

Elizabeth let out a raspy breath, yearning to tell Adriana how she and Paolo really met. To tell her, yes, Paolo was truly with them all in the room. However, the woman had experienced too much pain for one day.

Instead, she smiled solemnly and told Adriana about the man, not the ghost.

Chapter Twenty-Four

The next morning, the sound of glass breaking reverberated around the room. Gio shot up from his reclined spot on the wooden floor and glanced down at the large, shattered pieces. In his sleep, he'd knocked over the jar he drank from the night before. The chestnut-colored liquor branched out into fingers, crawling along the hardwood surface.

He wiped a sleep-numbed hand over a spot of brandy he'd dripped on his pant leg. What a mess. With a thrumming head, he turned to Marco, who leaned back on his pillow staring wide-eyed up at him.

"Drinking in my room all the night?" Marco shook his head. "They'll think this broken man is lying in bed with a broken hip getting drunk."

Gio rubbed at the fierce headache rising behind his temples. "We can tell them it was medicinal." He rolled his dry tongue over the inside of his cheek. He needed water to wash the stale taste away.

"Ah, yes, medicine for your heart." Marco shifted to a sitting position. "But I warn, do not use the brandy to hide away those feelings. It could become too much a habit."

Scowling, Gio snatched up the glass fragments and empty bottle from against the wall. Nothing about this time in his life would become a habit. Everything about him was in peculiar disarray. He'd always lived a

218

fastidious life and tended to things as needed. Since Elizabeth's arrival, he based every action on futile emotion. He glanced at Marco again. "It isn't even dawn yet. Go back to sleep, old man."

"Who is it you are hiding from? Is it Michael or your mother?" His bright but tired eyes assessed Gio. He shook his head. "Ah. It is Elizabeth. How long do you expect to hide in my room? She does stop by on occasion to speak with me." Marco grinned. "And then you will be caught."

"I'm not hiding." Who was he fooling? He'd succumbed to low expectations of himself and gotten all-out drunk. He'd passed out before giving in to the urge to visit Elizabeth in bed. He'd avoided the chance to make love to her—though she wouldn't have allowed him to touch her—in trade for a head too heavy to hold on his shoulders. His stomach rolled. He wouldn't eat anytime soon, but there'd also be no daring himself to touch her. "There's no need to hide from her. We both agreed to keep our distance from one another."

"Until when, my boy?"

"Until…" His hollow heart dropped. "I have no idea." He crossed the room and deposited the broken glass and brandy bottle in Marco's wastebasket.

"Do you not care for the *donna*?"

Gio sighed and grasped at the locket resting against his chest. Yes, he cared, but his sentiments toward her were irrelevant. "I'll come back with a bucket to clean this up." He pointed at the wet floor without looking at the man. "You should sleep."

He left the room and quietly closed the door. The sleeping inhabitants of the house would stir before long. He needed to wash away all evidence of his night of drunken debauchery before he greeted anyone.

Thanks to Elizabeth Reilly, now debauchery meant cowering on the floor of an injured man's room. She'd made him pathetic.

Stop with the self-pity, Gio. It's your own actions that make you pathetic.

Elizabeth offered him the truth, her friendship, and love.

He traveled down the hall, halting at the sound of Elizabeth's voice from behind the guest room door. He leaned his head into the solid wood.

"Where are you, Paolo?" she said. "I don't want to feel guilty about you not seeing them one more time before we go."

Paolo? Why the hell would his cousin be in her room? Without thinking, he grabbed the handle and forced the door open, and it slammed into the wall.

She flinched and spun to face him with one hand covering her mouth, the other twisting in her skirt.

She was alone. Who was she talking to, then?

Anger flared in her eyes, but she remained silent. Fully dressed, the back of her hair hid beneath a black snood, and her lips shone with rose paint. She'd outfitted herself for an escape.

He scrutinized the suitcase standing ready against the wall. "Are you leaving?"

"Yes. Michael and your cousin, Paolo, have promised to take me into San Francisco." She took a deep breath and jutted her chin forward. "I'm boarding a train for home today."

Michael and Paolo. Was she practicing what she was going to say to his cousin then? The muscle in his jaw ticked. This sudden jealousy was idiotic. And for what?

Thinking he heard her say the name *Paolo*?

After his mother had told him the story about what happened to his father, he'd shared a jar of brandy with his cousin. And the man didn't express any interest in Elizabeth. He was too young for her, for one. Nothing happened between his cousin and Elizabeth.

Pitiful, Giovanni. Stop being so irrational.

Elizabeth smoothed her skirt, grabbed her coat from the bed, and draped it over her arm. Glancing out the window, she said, "It's raining. Do you get much work done when it rains?" She faced him again. "You don't look like you'll get much done today anyway. You look exhausted, Gio, and smell as if you bathed in a tub of brandy."

He squirmed on his heavy feet. "There is always work to be done and I'll do it no matter my condition."

A lump rose in his throat, but he swallowed it back. Yes, work would save him. Sweat would wash away any remnants of her. He glanced around the room. "Who were you talking to?"

She closed her eyes and mumbled under her breath. Opening them, she set her lips in a determined frown. "A ghost," she answered and locked her gaze on his.

Pain radiated behind his eyes. "What kind of nonsense is that, Elizabeth?"

"It's not nonsense at all." Averting her eyes to the ground, she put on her coat. "But I don't expect you to believe me."

"Good. Because I don't." He approached her.

Despite the aches and pains from the night on the cold, hard floor, his body warmed as he drew nearer to her.

Poor sweet Elizabeth.

221

He gently swept a stray curl out her eyes. He should have been more respectful. She'd lost a husband and a friend. The strain must have been too much for her. She'd suffered a breakdown. Why'd her family let her travel alone? What would they think of him for taking advantage of her in this altered state?

"Elizabeth, it might be wise if we keep what happened between us to ourselves." Unable to resist, he wrapped his hands around her tiny waist. "I'll speak with my mother. Make her understand what we did wasn't wise and put it all behind us." His voice broke when he realized he didn't want what his words were suggesting, but at least he'd give himself this, "And be friends. I could use a friend right now."

She stiffened and thrust him away from her with a quick shove on his chest. Her face looked pinched in anger, and she visibly shook. "Don't worry, Giovanni, I've already forgotten my mistake." She pushed past him and headed toward the door. "Don't bother with my bag," she said. "I'll ask someone else to come up and get it."

A shiver flooded his spine at the sound of the door opening and closing. He closed his eyes. *Fool*. He'd made a mistake, but which of his many actions were the actual mistake? He'd never been so unsure of himself in his life.

****

Twenty minutes later, Gio pulled on a crisp white shirt, buttoned it quickly, and tied his wet hair back with a thin leather sash. He glanced in the mirror above his bureau. Even with his eyes tinged red and his face a bit pale, he was presentable enough to say goodbye. If Gio was able to count on anything, his mother wouldn't let

Elizabeth leave until after she sat down to a hearty breakfast.

He left the room and descended the stairs two at a time. He couldn't let her leave angry. He'd meant what he said about being friends. They should have begun as friends, and she might have gotten to see him in his element, not as the brooding man he was around her.

The scent of garlic and thyme hung heavy in the air. The clink of silver on stoneware echoed from behind the closed door. With a deep breath, he pushed the door open. Aunt Miriam sat beside his young cousin, Vincenzo, from Italy. Gio's mother sat at the head of the table with Sofia seated shyly beside her.

"Where's Elizabeth?" he asked and heard the disappointment in his own voice.

His mother looked up at him. "She is on her way to San Francisco."

"She didn't stay for breakfast?" He leaned against the doorjamb.

"No. She graciously said she was not hungry and was anxious to leave. She did not want to miss her train."

Chapter Twenty-Five

In East Boston, Elizabeth pushed off the porch with her foot and set the swing in motion. She was home. She'd been home for one entire day and still her mind wouldn't quiet.

It was a haven away from Giovanni Clemente. She was no longer his mistake. He was free to wrap his arms around anyone he pleased. Still, she hurt each time she pictured him touching some faceless woman. She shuddered with jealousy. Would he tell this stranger what a beautiful woman she was? Elizabeth hoped he only said those words to her. Lord, she was a fool. If she'd stayed, she would've given herself to him if he asked. She loved him, and her body ached to show him how much.

She closed her sweater over her chest to fend off the New England chill. She missed Paolo. If the ghost were lurking in the house, she'd neither seen nor heard him. She'd gotten no bursts of energy, no whispers of air, no brushes on the shoulder from an unseen hand, nothing.

Was he angry with her for taking him away?

She glanced at the darkening sky and sighed. She'd closed her mind off again when she prayed to God to take the gift away the entire train ride home. There was no world where both her ability and Gio co-existed. The man treated her like a child when she suggested she'd been talking to a ghost. His eyes told her he considered

224

her mad.

Gio asked her to deny anything ever happened between the two of them. He only needed her to be his friend. As if they could be friends after they'd made love. There was so much more between them and there was no sense in ignoring it.

Elizabeth leaned her head back on the wooden swing and studied the slats of the porch ceiling. She was home. The Clementes would soon descend upon Boston. They'd say goodbye to Paolo, and he'd depart. She'd have her own life back, as Paolo wanted.

The front door opened with a creak. Elizabeth sat straight and offered her mother a half-hearted smile.

Dora frowned and approached her. "Beth, are you going to sit out here all night?"

"Not all night but for a while yet." She scooted nearer to the swing's arm to make room for her mother.

"You haven't eaten a thing all day. It's not healthy." The swing teetered under her mother's slight figure.

"I've eaten enough. More than my share on the trip back." She lied. Adriana packed her a basket full of meals which now sat in her room still untouched. Later, she'd go in and dispose of the spoilt food. For now, her heart was too hollow to do much of anything.

"Honey," Dora said and brushed her hand over Elizabeth's cheek. "I wish you'd tell me what's on your mind."

Elizabeth closed her eyes and rested her cheek against her mother's hand. "I'm not sure I can."

Dora hugged her. "I hate to see you hurting this way. This trip to California was supposed to help you begin to heal. Instead, you're sadder than ever."

Tears welled up behind her eyes. If she let them fall,

225

she'd lose control.

"We all miss Patrick," Dora continued. "He was part of our family. But I can't sit back and watch you close yourself off. Patrick would want more for you, Beth."

"You're right and he told me so himself." She bit her lip. "Because he visited me." A single tear escaped the corner of Elizabeth's eye. "He said goodbye to me, Mother. A week before we received the telegram about his death."

"You saw Patrick," she said with a mixture of concern and sadness coloring her face. "And now you're receiving the dead again." Her mother shook her head.

"Yes, I opened myself up, hoping he'd come. He did, and others followed."

Dora sat erect. "The spirit in the house, around your room, do you know who he is?"

Her arms numb, Elizabeth rose and went to the porch railing. Paolo was there. She did not feel him. "Yes." She frowned, sad over abandoning her friend. He needed her. "His name's Paolo Clemente."

"Clemente? So, your trip to Clemente Vineyard was for him."

"Yes." She let her shoulders roll forward, free from the weight she'd dropped. She looked into her mother's eyes, grateful to be able to tell someone the truth. "I intended to tell his family about his death."

Dora shifted in her seat. "He was the man you and Anna helped," she said more to herself. "I should have known this trip of yours meant more than you told us." Dora said. "Beth, why didn't you tell me this sooner? Were you afraid I'd stop you?"

"No, I wasn't." She spun to look out at the dark street. "I think I knew there'd be more involved." More than what? She'd hoped for change when she set out on the trip, and her life had transformed in so many ways.

"What is it? I'd be a hypocrite if I scolded you for trying to help a lost soul. I've spent my whole life doing the same thing. Our gift isn't one to take lightly."

The swing's wood groaned, and Elizabeth listened to her mother's footfalls on the wooden porch floor. Dora now stood beside her.

"But you helped me turn it off," Elizabeth said.

Dora sighed. "Yes, only because you were so young. I remember what a frightening thing it was for me. Of course, I was there to teach you how to use it, where I had no one. It was wrong of me."

"No, Mother, don't say such a thing. Please." She grabbed her mother's hand. "I wasn't ready back then. And to be honest, I'm not sure if I'm any more ready now. I'm not as strong as you are. I think this gift was wasted on me."

"Absolutely not," Dora scolded. "You are a very special woman, Beth. I'm not saying this because you're my daughter. Your potential to love is so great. You'd never turn your back on a soul who needed your help."

Elizabeth shook her head. "My potential to love is so great." She half-laughed. "Now, this is my curse, isn't it?"

"What do you mean?"

"It's my own entire fault. I left for California without a real plan. I thought I'd be taken at my word without needing to do too much convincing. Of course, I took him by surprise. I was a stranger. Why wouldn't he have doubted me?" Elizabeth closed her eyes to chase away the guilt. The words tumbled forth, and she gave no regard to the lack of sense they made. "He didn't ask me to fall in love with him. Regardless, it's all over now." She leaned her head on her mother's shoulder.

"Who, Beth? What are you talking about?" Dora placed her arm around Elizabeth's shoulder and embraced her. "Who are you in love with?"

"Giovanni Clemente." The minute she spoke his name and admitted her feelings aloud, acquiescent relief washed through her. "The ghost's son."

Dora grabbed both of her shoulders and turned her, so they faced one another. "I think you need to tell me everything, starting from the beginning."

****

The obstinacy he inherited from his *padre*.

At the vineyard, Adriana sipped her steaming hot tea at the kitchen table. Through the bay window, she watched Giovanni. Soaked from head to toe, he stomped through the rain.

The weather took a turn, and an autumn chill seeped into the valley along with the mist. She wasn't close enough to see her son shiver, but she was sure he did. Unless his temper still heated him from the inside out.

The door bordering the hallway swung open and admitted Vincenzo, her nephew by marriage.

"Aunt Adriana," he said in Italian. "What is he doing out there?"

"Autumn in this part of California brings cold air. A thing you battle rarely in Foggia. It challenges the grapes and means harvest will need to start. He is making the preparations."

Vincenzo slid out a chair across from her but kept his dark eyes trained on the scene outside. "He looks to be doing nothing more than pacing in the rain."

"Ah, so you see right through your cousin, too." Her

lips curved into a smile despite herself. Giovanni paced like a man in combat. What he fought against did not deserve a battle. Elizabeth offered him happiness.

As his mother, Adriana wished to knock some sense into him. Sometimes, being born a man would have been much easier. A father was better suited to thrusting his will on a mulish son. "Yes, he fools himself he is working, but, in truth, he is walking off his frustration."

The young Clemente faced her. "Is it the woman then?"

"Yes, the woman and the news she brought with her. In all truth, though, my Giovanni has always been a lonely soul. You can see it now, can you not? The way he walks about."

He nodded.

"He suffered more than I from your Uncle Paolo's absence. And I did suffer more than enough for two lifetimes." She set her teacup down in its saucer. "My son was a troubled man before Elizabeth Reilly arrived." She looked away as the heat simmered in her cheeks. Yes, she had grown foolish in her dotage. She hoped the young woman would make Gio's rich laugh a commonplace thing.

Vincenzo looked at her with curious concern.

She shook her head. "It is not important now." She patted his hand. "You have been here for days now, and I have not welcomed you to our vineyard. I am glad your father was able to spare your hands."

"Yes, he had no other choice but to spare them." His voice held a tone of disdain. "My father hoped for me to stay for a time. To observe." He glanced back towards the window. "Giovanni is gone now."

"Yes, he walks into the wine house every so often,

but he'll be back out."

She expected to see him cross in front of the window and disappear into the vineyard aisle. If only he were her young child again and she could promise him the world. She couldn't. Nor could she force Giovanni to follow Elizabeth. If anything were ever to become of their feelings for one another, they both needed to stop being muleheaded and decide for themselves. While this was not her affair, she was his mother, and she could supply gentle prodding from time to time.

The rain fell harder now and battered the glass.

"My father hoped I could learn what has made Giovanni's vineyard a success," Vincenzo said and rose from the chair. "Our vineyard has fallen to disrepair."

Adriana nodded. "I receive letters from home telling me the pain the war has caused for so many."

"The war is not to blame for our circumstances. We have never achieved what you have here." He swept his hand around the room. "Our fruit reaps nothing more than pungent table wine. The Clemente name does not hold the same meaning it did when my father was a boy."

He walked to the window and spoke, with his back to her. "My father wants the vineyard to be what it could have been if Uncle Paolo had stayed."

Chapter Twenty-Six

A month later, the first snow blanketed the East Boston streets. The November air seeped under the Obriens' front door as Elizabeth closed it behind her. The house was warm and welcoming. The only place she wished to be.

She draped her coat on the standing rack beside the door and yawned. How many more sleepless nights would she have to spend consoling herself? She missed Patrick. Not as the husband but as the friend she'd climbed trees with as a child. She'd passed through the house, half-expecting to turn a corner and see him standing there.

There was, also, the aching need of heart and body when Gio barged into her mind. Her mother and sister always seemed to know and distracted her with conversation. She'd told them both the truth down to the details of what she and Gio's relationship became and how it ended.

When Adriana wrote to say they decided to wait until after harvest before coming to Boston, she'd been relieved. Marco would've healed enough to make the trip. It would be soon, however, and her time to tell Paolo was running out. She needed to speak with him.

She turned and passed through the parlor doorway.

"There you are, *Bella*. At last, you have called me."

Startled, she stumbled back against the propped

open door. Closing her eyes to gain composure, she spoke, "Paolo, I wasn't sure if you'd come to me again."

When she opened her eyes, she joined him on the sofa.

He smiled, and his crooked nose twitched. "I have been here, but you did not listen to me."

Her heart lurched into the pit of her stomach. Lord, she'd been selfish, thinking only of herself, and blocked him out. "Paolo, I couldn't hear you. I'm sorry."

"Beth?" Dora entered the room. "He's here, isn't he?"

Paolo shot up from the sofa, and Elizabeth rose beside him. She nodded to her mother.

"I see." Dora grasped her upper arms. "I almost forgot why I came in here. Adriana Clemente is on the telephone for you."

Elizabeth caught her breath and grasped Paolo's hand.

"I'll stay with him." Her mother glanced in the direction where Paolo's ethereal form stood. Like all her encounters with spirits, Dora could feel Paolo but not hear or see him. "Taking this call may finally help him find peace."

"Elizabeth?" he questioned. "She cannot see me, can she?"

She shook her head. "My mother can only feel you. She might be able to sense what you're feeling or hear you in her mind. And she has a lot more practice than I do."

Elizabeth smiled, hoping to calm him. Nothing, however, would ease her own nerves. The call must mean only one thing. Gio and his family would soon be on their way to Boston.

****

A week later, Elizabeth's boots sank into the snow. Her whole body shivered, but it wasn't due to the biting cold. Yes, the frigid air stung her eyes and cheeks, but the disquieted spirits all around caused the chill climbing her spine. The multitude of ghosts, the saying of goodbye to Paolo, and the risk to her heart in seeing his son all set her ill at ease. She clung to her mother's gloved hand and was glad for her sister's grasp on her opposite elbow. They'd be her strength.

A handful of people assembled at Paolo's gravesite. How they could find the spot under all the snow was a mystery.

She scanned the group and tightened her grip on her mother's hand. An ache squeezed her heart. Gio was not there. Surely, he attended. Even Marco was there. His wicker wheelchair stood half-hidden by snow, and a yellow blanket adorned his legs.

"Beth," Dora asked. "Are you okay?"

"He's not here." She scanned the faces again. "Gio isn't with them," she whispered into her mother's ear. She gulped to wash down a sudden rush of panic. She hadn't looked forward to seeing him, but she wanted—no, needed to. A small imprudent piece of her hoped he'd eventually love her, and he'd accept her for who she was.

Their feet crunched forward through the snow. The air smelled cold and muted. An aura of sadness emanated from the mourners who'd come to say goodbye to Paolo's aching soul. Still, his son wasn't there.

"His father's not doing well," Dora whispered.

Her mother's link with Paolo was strong. Their connection was a blessing since they had only a week to prepare him for his chance to say goodbye. When this was over, he needed to let go of all the things which might have been.

Michael Clemente was the first to notice their approach. He trudged to them over unblemished snow, leaving deep footprints behind.

Gio's uncle was kind to her. They had shared a comfortable drive into San Francisco and struck up an instant friendship. Michael, however, was more serious by nature than his brother, Paolo, and commanded authority. Still, his serious nature didn't hold the intensity his nephew's did. He kept no bitterness locked up inside, and no regrets.

"Elizabeth, we are glad you are here." He nodded to the three of them.

"Thank you." She released the grip on her mother's hand. "This is Michael Clemente. *Signore* Clemente, this is my mother, Dora O'Brien." She turned toward her sister, who hung several paces behind. "And this is my younger sister, Anna O'Brien." She smiled at the ruddy-cheeked Anna. "She is the one who sketched the picture of Paolo."

He greeted each woman in turn and stopped to take Anna's hand in his. "You have great talent, *Signorina*. If it would not be an imposition, would you be able to draw yet another picture of my brother for me?"

Anna smiled with confidence. "I already have a picture for you. I found him a remarkably interesting subject."

"Excellent. Perhaps you might show them to me tonight at our dinner?"

"Of course," Anna answered. "I'd love to."

He bowed his head and turned, taking Elizabeth by the elbow.

She took a deep breath and allowed him to lead her toward a patch of snow someone had cleared and packed earlier in the day. In the spring, there'd be a gravestone to mark Paolo's place.

Paolo's family stood there with a priest in front of them who'd prepare his release from his earthly bindings.

Michael led her to stand beside Adriana. A black lace veil shrouded the woman's face. Still Elizabeth felt the warmth of her eyes and the gratitude of the woman's grasp on her hand. Out of the corner of her eye, Elizabeth saw both father and son.

Gio approached. He dragged his feet through the snow like a small boy. Her heart sped, and her hands trembled. She used all her self-control to keep from running to him and flinging herself into his arms. He stopped yards away and stood off to the side. He meant to keep a good distance from his family and from her.

Paolo stood beside him. Did Gio feel him there?

She turned her head and offered them both a smile. Paolo nodded in response, but his son looked away.

So, this is how it's going to be.

Chapter Twenty-Seven

After sunset, Gio stood outside the house. He willed himself to go up, knock on the door, and enter Elizabeth's world. He'd promised his mother he'd take this crucial step. She saw a future between him and Elizabeth where there was none.

The morning Elizabeth left, she'd tried to push him away. Her story about talking to a ghost at the vineyard was no more than a fabrication to chase him away. An elaborate scheme she worked on during her entire stay. But why? The woman he'd come to care about didn't seem the type. No, she would have said exactly what was on her mind.

Bright lights illuminated the front of the house. Through the open curtains of a large bay window, he saw strangers—her family. His mother told him the two women who accompanied Elizabeth to the funeral were her mother and sister. Not staying to meet them had been rude, yes, but there was truly little gallantry left in him.

The attractive redhead from the cemetery sat beside his mother and flipped through pages in a large tablet.

A man resembling Elizabeth stood in the background. He was taller and broader of shoulder, but Gio would wager he was her brother. People from his life and hers sat or shifted about the room, engaged in conversation.

Together.

Elizabeth entered the room. She was alluring in a slim-fitting, shoulder-baring red dress. Her hair, gathered atop her head, displayed a long, graceful neck. He imagined pressing his lips to her warm delicious flesh. Unwanted heat crept up through him.

She stood behind a high-back armchair occupied by a gray-haired man. He was most unlike her with his fair complexion and presence. Still, Gio guessed him to be her father. Elizabeth took after her mother, the woman who'd also attended his father's funeral.

All at once, the entire roomful of people rose and left. Elizabeth lingered behind. She approached the window but stopped when his Uncle Michael entered the room and led her out. The two of them had become fast friends.

Envy spiked within him. What did he need to do to be her friend?

Gio had promised his mother he'd attend dinner, but he couldn't go in. The hair rose on his arms beneath the layers of clothing as a breeze passed over him. Where did the breeze come from? The air stirred, yet the naked trees were still. A voice echoed in his head. *Go to her, Giovanni. Do not be the fool I was.*

He closed his eyes to steady his breath. He wasn't ready to go to her. Not yet. To force himself would only bring disaster. He'd allow himself time to find out who he was. He might even discover who his father was. Perhaps he'd also discover why he and Elizabeth were meant to be together.

Gathering his coat around him, he hurried away.

****

After dinner, the O'Briens and the Clementes retired to the parlor. Elizabeth's father poured snifters of brandy for the men and sherry for the ladies.

She excused herself from the parlor activities, grabbed her long winter wrap, and snuck out the front door. She sat on the snow-cleared front stoop.

Adriana had promised Gio would come. Elizabeth should be glad he didn't, but all she wanted to do was sink her face into her pillow and sob. She owed herself an all-out cry. Such things were mind cleansing and, after, she might just see things more clearly.

Paolo's scent cut through the frigid night air.

"He was here, *Bella*. Gio," the ghost said.

Rising, she approached the swing where he sat. "He wasn't." She stood in front of him and shook her head.

"Yes. He stood out there on the walkway." He pointed. "I spoke to him. I tried to urge him to go in."

The swing rocked under her weight when she sat.

"I do not know, but I think heard me," Paolo continued. "But he left without coming to you. I did try to follow but speaking to one who does not hear the dead drained me. I lost myself and simply faded away."

"What did you say to him?" She leaned back and rested her head on the rigid wood.

"I told him to go to you. I told him not to be the fool I was."

"Your son is being a fool, Paolo. Because I love him." She studied her friend whose once solid body glistened like fluid. He'd be leaving her soon. Reaching out, she touched his cold face. She gasped, afraid if she pressed too hard, her hand might slide through his velvety, thin skin.

"I think this will be our last time," he said with a breathless whisper. "I can already feel myself being drawn away. I was not sure if I would be able to come to you tonight."

"And earlier I didn't think my heart could feel any worse." Tears pooled in her eyes. "How about you? How are you feeling?"

"Would you doubt me if I told you I was happy?"

"Is that how you feel?"

"Oddly, *si*. I am happy my wife is content." His eyes held a faraway look, and his lips a wistful smile. "Adriana and Marco fulfilled my dream and have now handed it down to Giovanni. I am happy my Adriana still loves me. She does not regret waiting for me."

She bit her lip. "What about Gio?"

"My son is a strong, stubborn man, but eventually he will find his way."

"Can you see the future, Paolo?"

"No, I cannot," he said. "However, I do feel it in my heart."

She needed guidance. Perhaps the heavens might grant him some sight before he left her behind. Should she let her heart shatter now or hold onto any threads of hope Giovanni Clemente might ever love her? She pushed up from her seat. "Have you tried to talk with Adriana?"

"No." He shook his head. "No, my heart cannot bear it."

"Come." She held out her hand. "Don't be a fool and let this chance pass you by. At least come and be near her."

Together, they walked in through the front door, into the parlor and around to the edge of the sofa where his wife sat beside Dora. He stood beside Adriana, his eyes transfixed on her face.

Elizabeth pressed back against the bookshelf-lined

wall. From where she stood, she watched. Paolo's lovestruck eyes centered on Adriana. His trembling hand grazed his wife's hair. Adriana's back stiffened, and she glanced to where he stood.

Elizabeth held her breath and glanced at her mother, whose eyes also focused in his direction. Did Adriana see him?

"*Ti amo*, Adriana, *per tutto il eternità*," Paolo whispered and faded away.

Adriana shoulders relaxed, and she leaned back into the padded sofa.

Dora rested a hand on the woman's shoulder and leaned in to whisper in her ear. Several moments passed before both Adriana and Dora rose and left the room.

Elizabeth followed them out on tired, heavy legs. For a moment, she feared her heart would swell under the mixture of joy and pain. The love passing between Gio's parents was awe-inspiring in its power. Warmth flooded her and her eyes filled with tears. Would she ever have a love like they did?

The two women's voices carried to her from the kitchen. Another friendship bloomed. Each action interlocked her life more to Gio's and it would help no one.

She turned and ran to the stairs and up. Her mother would explain what happened and judge how much Adriana was ready to hear.

Once in her room, she shed her wrap and dropped it to the ground. She unfastened the front of her dress but caught sight of one of Anna's drawing tablets on the edge of the bed. She picked the sketches up and flipped through several pages. They were of Paolo as the older man. Yes, her sister found him an interesting subject, indeed. She must have filled at least two books with pictures of him. The one she'd shown the Clemente family still rested on the sofa table in the parlor.

Here she'd sketched him standing on the beach, staring out at the barren ocean horizon.

Elizabeth sank down to the bed and studied several more pages. Smiling, she turned to a picture of a young Paolo leaning against a ferry's rail. She recognized the harbor, how it would have looked when her Grandfather O'Brien's clipper ships carried wares in and out of the docks.

Anna captured images she could never have seen except in visions through the family gift.

Elizabeth turned to a picture of Paolo as he looked in his wedding picture, young and handsome, like his son. She gasped. For he sat on the streetcar with his tattered coat sleeve pressed against his forehead like she'd watched him do on the day of his death.

She turned to yet another. In this one, she knelt on the Boston street, holding a youthful Paolo Clemente in her lap before he died.

Anna never claimed to have the gift, but she did. Elizabeth's sister assumed herself to be immune to it, but wasn't and seized the images in her art. She told their stories, revealing their pasts through her drawings.

Chapter Twenty-Eight

Gio walked through the quiet house. There was work to do before he left on his trip. Vinny would capably oversee the vineyard. He'd done well so far under Gio's tutelage. Still, Gio never let go of things easily, be it beliefs or emotions—or women who snuck into his heart.

He hadn't seen her in three months, but at times, he still turned a corner half expecting to see her. She wasn't on the vineyard long, but damn, he'd experienced memories enough to last him a lifetime.

He ran his hands through his newly short-cropped hair, still wet from his bath as he pushed into the kitchen through the swinging door. Moonlight streamed in, with dawn still hours away. He grabbed an apple from the icebox and headed out the back to stand on the stoop's top stair.

He bit into the apple, wiped away its juice from his chin, and yawned. His body and mind still hummed with dreams he only remembered bits and pieces of. Disjointed images of Elizabeth made him toss and turn in his bed throughout the sleepless night. He recalled the look on her face when she'd confronted him in the wine house. The hurt in her expressive brown eyes when he'd told her to hope their lovemaking hadn't produced a child. *God has cursed me enough. He couldn't possibly do such a thing to me.* In his cruelness, he forced her to say those words.

"Dammit," he moaned and leapt down the three stairs to walk off his frustration.

Why was she on the forefront of his mind when the trip to visit his estranged relatives should have been all he focused on? Here he was about to travel to New York and meet his father's other family, the d'Amato half of his family. Marco once met Paolo's real father, and Gio's mother had been acquainted with the family during her childhood, growing up in Rome.

The d'Amatos were silk merchants. Fidelio d'Amato amassed a fortune in the trade and part of his fortune made its way to Gio by way of the vineyard. Unfortunately, with a name meaning fidelity, Fidelio didn't live up to it. He'd been infamous in his lifetime as a man who amassed women as easily as he did his fortune.

With the wealth of information, Gio tracked one of his half-aunts to New York. With no idea what the trip would really accomplish, he needed to explore this link to his and his father's past.

He walked toward the wine house but stopped when he heard the rattling of the leaves. Odd. There wasn't a breeze. Rubbing a chill away with his empty hand, he headed to the vines.

Static electricity shot through him as he entered. For a moment, he contemplated turning back. He shook his head. When had he ever been afraid to walk the vines in the dark? Not even as a small boy. In fact, he always found a spiritual peace in the shadows of the vineyard.

To his right, more leaves rustled. His steps faltered. A vine rattled to the left. How would an animal have time to travel between the two spots so quickly?

He dropped the apple, and it rolled inches away. He backed up and stepped two aisles over, through breaks in the vines, to wait for a coyote or gopher to claim the fruit.

Something hit his head. His heart jumped in his chest, and he swallowed a groan as he ran his hands over his hair in one frantic motion. Damn, he was as skittish as a small girl afraid of the dark. He'd tramped through the cold mud during the war with less trepidation. He turned, and something else skimmed his face and fell to the ground. He scooped up the item. A broken twig.

Were birds creating the ruckus?

He fought a cold surge of anxiety as he checked over his shoulder. Nothing touched the apple.

Do not let Elizabeth slip away. It will only bring regret.

What the hell? "Who said that?" he whispered and checked over both of his shoulders. There was no one there. He was the only one out at this hour.

He pressed his fingers to his temples. The woman was tormenting him from clear across the country. How long before he got her out of his system? He needed to see her again to figure out the answer.

If you truly love her, Giovanni, it is worth the risk. You have lost your heart already.

He hurried to pick up the apple and headed back toward the house. What was wrong with him? Of course, a man needed rest to think clearly, and he'd spent too many troubled nights over the last few months thinking about Elizabeth.

The time away from her hadn't lessened his desire for her but rather strengthened it with the thought of what if. What if they met under different circumstances? He may have been able to give his heart freely. Or he'd have no remorse in a passing affair. No remorse? What kind of man let a woman like Elizabeth in and out of his life so easily? With trembling hands, he opened the back door.

The strong aroma of coffee filtered into the air, and his stomach growled in response to fresh barley boiling in a pot on the stove. The overhead light illuminated his mother standing at the stove. She'd dressed in her work clothes, overalls for maneuverability, and her hair rested at the nape of her neck in the usual chignon. She glanced over her shoulder and smiled at him.

"Have a seat. You need breakfast before your trip, and some coffee, it appears. Did you not sleep well last night?"

He shook his head and slumped into a seat at the kitchen table. With a sigh, he closed his eyes.

What kind of man turned away from a precious woman like Elizabeth Reilly? A slack-witted one. Gio wasn't about to let anyone think of him as a fool.

It wouldn't take him too much out of his way to drive to Boston to see her after he'd spent time in New York. This was something to consider at least.

****

Adriana strolled down the aisle, gazing at the trimmed, fruitless vines. Heat warmed her head where her husband's hand touched three months earlier. Dora O'Brien confirmed Paolo had been there.

He whispered the words, "*I love you, Adriana, for all eternity.*"

She'd long forgotten his voice, but she'd not forget again. She rested her hand against her heart as it swelled with elation. *My love, I, too, will love you forever.*

"*Madre,*" Gio called from behind her.

She turned, her lips twitching into a smile. Gio ran his hands through his hair. He looked daringly handsome and healthy. The early spring sun kissed his cheeks with a ruddy glow.

"I'm ready to go," he said and extended a hand to her. "Would you care to see me off?"

"Of course." She met him and placed her hand in his.

They walked in silence to the new sedan he'd purchased for his trip to New York. He was making a pilgrimage to find himself and his father's roots.

"Will you stop in Boston?" she asked as he ducked into the driver's seat and shut the door.

"Yes, I'll check on the gravestone."

She sighed. Though his demeanor softened, the stubborn streak stayed firm.

"You know as well as I why I am asking," Adriana said.

His lips twitched into a crooked smile.

"Will you visit Elizabeth?" she asked.

He started the engine. "I'm considering it."

She nodded. "You must also consider the regrets you will have if you do not."

He looked over his shoulder, preparing to back out into the driveway.

"Giovanni." Adriana reached in through the open window, staying his hand on the wheel. "Do you not think your father regretted not returning to the vineyard?"

He frowned at her. "He died thinking we were dead."

She longed to tell him his father now knew the truth. If she told him, she feared he'd never search out

Elizabeth. He'd grown up in modern-day America where the superstitions of old-world *Italia* were more fallacy than fact.

Squeezing his hand before stepping away, she said, "Regrets may not end once our lives have. Remember this, *per favore*."

Chapter Twenty-Nine

A month later, Gio walked the streets of East Boston on foot. Moonlight shone on the triple-decker houses and brick apartment buildings standing sentry on either side.

Children yelled and laughed with one another in his native Italian tongue. Old world women smiled at him from their lighted stoops and called, "*Buonasera!*"

A burst of balmy early spring weather caused the neighborhood to hum with energy. There was warmth and amiable friendship, yet Elizabeth claimed to have been lonely here.

For my brother, sister, and me it was small. My parents kept us close. The kids in our neighborhood were a little fearful of us. We were different from them.

He shook his head but was unable to clear the memories of her. They continually invaded his mind. Why should he? Why not enjoy the look of her in his mind's eye? He saw her as she'd looked the first day. Their first walk through the vineyard. Her full lips set with both caution and determination. Her soulful brown eyes held affection each time she spoke of his father.

She'd done a brave and noble thing. She'd persevered even though he challenged her every step of the way. This fact alone was enough to cause him to love her.

There'd been their one fiery night together. His footsteps quickened with the rushing of his blood.

Nothing good could come from him showing up at her family's door aching with need.

Four months and six nights had passed since last he stood outside Elizabeth's house, too much of a coward to enter. And the need crushed him so often at many inopportune moments.

Making love to her may have been a mistake, but not for the reason he once considered it to be. He should have courted her, treated her like the lady she was. He hoped to have time now to rectify his mistake. Unless she tossed him out on his ear.

He rounded the corner to her street, beautifully set under a canopy of sparsely budded trees on either side.

So close now.

Blood rushed to his ears, and his palms sweated like a pubescent boy's. She'd be angry with him, but he couldn't leave without a promise from her. If she agreed to come to California, it would be a start.

Come to California with me, Elizabeth. Give us a chance to start fresh. He'd promise to ebb his desires until she married him. Staunch determination would get him through.

He arrived. The white house stood tall behind a large spreading oak tree, the one Elizabeth must have climbed as a child with her sister and brother. He took the stairs, setting his feet firmly down on each one and remembered the words he'd heard when last he was there.

Go to her, Giovanni. Do not be the fool I was.

****

Gio sat on the sofa. He twirled his hat in his hands and perspired in the coat he'd refused to relinquish to Elizabeth's mother. An asinine and juvenile action, maybe, but her look of disdain when she realized who he was had floored him. She appeared to know more about him than he'd expected a mother to be aware of.

Where his mother would have embarrassed him with words, Dora O'Brien shriveled him with silence.

"Will you be in Massachusetts long, Mr. Clemente?" she asked with a frown.

He opened his mouth to remind her his name was Giovanni but realized Elizabeth's mother was not at all happy he was there, and she did not want to call him Giovanni.

"Possibly," he answered.

"Hmmm. Would that be for business?"

Before he answered, she spoke again. "It appears Elizabeth will be later than I expected. May I take your coat? You look awfully hot." She rose.

"No, I think—" He froze at the sound of the front door opening.

"We're home," Elizabeth called from the hallway. There was an undertone of joy in her voice.

Dora O'Brien looked first at him and back at the open doorway where Elizabeth stood.

"Oh. Gio," she said. "You're here." Crimson rode high on Elizabeth's neck and cheeks. Her chest rose under her rapid breath, and she wavered on her feet.

He stood, dropping his hat absently to the floor. He opened his mouth and shut it without saying a word.

Dora looked at her daughter. "I'm sure the two of you have some catching up to do." She crossed to the door, stopping beside Elizabeth. "Should I bring in tea?"

Elizabeth shook her head. "I don't think *Signore* Clemente will be staying long."

So the woman held grudges. Why not? He had a lengthy list of offenses. Calling her a mistake, repeatedly asking her to leave, and not to mention visiting her while she was naked in the bath when the house was full of people. Worst of all, not admitting having a child with her would have been a blessing.

He swallowed his pride as Dora rose to leave. "Actually," he said, clearing his throat. "I'd love some tea."

Dora nodded in his direction and left as the sound of the front door opening and closing reverberated from the hall.

"Beth," a young woman said from the hallway. "Why are you standing there?"

The woman, Elizabeth's sister, Anna, reared up behind Elizabeth and peeked around her shoulder. "Oh," she murmured. "Is he?"

Elizabeth glanced at her sideways and nodded her head so slightly Gio might have missed it if he wasn't so aware of her every gesture. The soft tapping of her foot on the wooden floor, her hands bunched in tight fists at her side, and the lower lip she bit nervously.

"What are you two doing?" A man's voice echoed in behind them now.

Elizabeth sighed. "I have a visitor."

Her older brother strode by, risking a quick glance, and whispered, "Is he?"

"*Signore* Clemente," she said through clenched teeth, and she stepped out into the hall, escorting her siblings away.

Only seconds later, she hurried into the room and closed the door behind her. "We should have a few minutes of privacy," she said. Avoiding his gaze, she sat on the far end of the sofa.

He itched to scoot over the green velvet upholstery

until his thigh pressed against hers but suspected she'd take offense.

Neither of them spoke. He studied her. She fidgeted, running her finger back and forth along the cushion seam. Next, she tugged at a lock of her mahogany hair, which had grown and now hung to her backbone. If she noticed his hair, she didn't let on.

Let me, he wanted to say. He longed to run his own fingers through her silky curls. She darted her gaze to his face and blushed. With a muffled groan, she leapt from the couch.

His thoughts must have shown on his face.

She scooted to the parlor window with her back to him.

He rose and approached her. "Elizabeth," he whispered. "I'm sorry." He extended his hands.

"Don't," she said harshly, seconds before his grasp met her waist. "Did you expect I'd fall into your arms? Do a jig because you think you want me at the moment?" She spun to face him, determination set on her beautiful face. "Well, I won't."

Gio stood his ground. Her breath brushed his face. Heat shimmered up through him. "No, I didn't expect you to." He swallowed and dared to run a finger down her cheek.

Her breath caught, and she backpedaled against the glass. "Gio, please."

"When you first saw me, you said, 'You're here.' Why?"

Embarrassment flitted across her features before she quickly composed herself. "Your mother wrote to me about your trip. She said you were off to find yourself."

"Oh, I see." So the wicked woman he called *Madre*

252

had no doubt he'd show up at Elizabeth's door.

"Did you find what you were looking for?"

"In part." He flexed his hand to keep from touching her again.

She bit her lip. "If any of your trip has something to do with me, you might as well consider it lost and go home."

"Why?" His voice caught.

"Because there's nothing between us, Gio." She pointed to him. "Not like what I'm seeing in your eyes."

Damn, the woman would make him beg. Before this, he'd never begged for anything. "I'd like to see if I can change your mind."

"To what end?" she asked.

"I'm not sure exactly. Perhaps we have a future together."

She sighed and bowed her shoulders. "Now you say so. I'm fine with my life the way it is."

"Don't you feel like you're missing something?" *Me, perhaps*?

"Maybe. I don't know. There are things about me you don't understand."

"It would be a pleasure to find them out." When he stepped toward her, she dodged to the side, rushed around him, and fled to safety behind a high-back armchair.

He smiled despite himself and quickly frowned as her expression grew dour. He'd waited too long. He'd been too cruel while she was in his near grasp. No matter when he'd come, it would have been too late. This was a sad day when a man realized he'd jeopardized his own chances at true happiness. He'd been a fool.

Gio turned his attention to the room. A cluttered

ensemble with tables and shelves filled with vases, books, and framed photographs. An open book lay half beneath a tall armchair. The room emanated warmth and a cozy sort of joy—like Elizabeth—and it suited her. She belonged here.

He spotted a photograph of her, a wedding picture.

Gio paced to the shelf and studied the picture with his nervous hands clenched behind his back. Elizabeth's wedding day. She hadn't changed much, though her face was thinner now. He longed to see Elizabeth's youthful beauty mature. Her large oval eyes sparkled in the black-and-white image. A lace dress graced her form, and loose ringlets hung down from the hair piled atop her head, accentuating her long neck. Without hesitation, he unclenched his hands and picked up the wooden frame.

She looked happy in the photo, but he wanted to make her shine.

The man beside her looked elated. Dark curls lay neatly on his head, and he stood over Elizabeth, but wasn't as tall as Gio himself. He supposed women found Patrick attractive. At least the kind-hearted nature drawn on his face would charm more than his fair share.

Elizabeth's husband and he were as different as night and day. He turned to face her. "He knew everything about you, didn't he?"

"Yes." Her voice caught, and she clung to the chair's top.

"And he loved you. Give me the chance to show you I can, too." His voice rumbled in his chest. This was the closest he'd ever come to admitting feelings of that magnitude to anyone.

With an abrupt laugh, she bowed her head and avoided looking at him.

Heat rose in his face. This was a major event in his life. One he'd never thought he'd reach. Yet the woman laughed.

"It's not an amusing matter." He fought to keep his voice steady and his ire at bay.

"No." She cleared her throat and hid her face. "You're right and I apologize," she said through the fingers covering her mouth. "You are so set in your ways, Giovanni. You'll never accept me for what I am."

"Tell me." He dashed to her side, not allowing her time to react, and wrapped her in his arms. "Give me a chance to show you I'm a changed man."

"No," she whispered and rested her forehead on his chest. "I can't risk it again."

She shifted to step away, but he tightened his hold. There was no way he'd let her slip away again. If he'd decided to change his life's plan for this one woman, she was sure as hell going to— What? She owed him nothing.

"Elizabeth, I apologize for not telling you I was coming. It was—"

"Pigheaded," she whispered.

He fought hard not to smile. "Inconsiderate was the word I was looking for."

She sighed. "At least your mother had the foresight to tell me you were."

He and his *madre* would have a talk when he returned to Cana. "I'm planning on being in Boston for a few days at least," he said. "And my sole purpose is to see you."

She stepped back, and he relinquished his hold. Frowning, she cocked her head to the side and said, "And I'm not supposed to be wary come two days from now you'll have rethought this great need to spend time with me?"

She was making this hard, and he deserved it.

"At least," she continued, "you can't tell me to leave this time."

"You're right. Nor can I insist you see me." He lifted his hand and caressed her cheek. She flinched, and her breath sped, but she didn't step away. Her skin was warm, smooth, and luxurious like satin. He longed to drape her over him. *Enough.* The current circumstances required patience even if it drove him mad.

Tense heat simmered within him along with fear he might have lost any chance with her. He'd bide his time and hope. "I'll be waiting at the Grandview Hotel if you wish to call. If you don't, I won't blame you for not wanting to," he said. "But please trust me when I say I truly regret how I treated you."

He stepped away, scooped up his hat, and left.

Chapter Thirty

The rain pelted Elizabeth's head and ran down her forehead to drip off her nose. She'd left the house without an umbrella despite the gray, closed-in sky.

The cemetery stood deserted of the living, but the energy of the dead vibrated in her bones. She was surprised at finding comfort in their presence. At least, the ghosts were a constant in her life.

She still hadn't recovered from seeing Gio the night before. In truth, even though Adriana wrote to say his trip would bring him to Boston soon, she didn't believe it until she found him standing in her house.

The branches hanging over the road were ripe with buds, and the grass beside the road was already a vibrant green. She inhaled, content the walk was diminishing her anxiety, even if the downpour drenched her to the skin. She gathered her boy-cut, knee-length coat around her, but in its wet state, it did nothing to combat the chill. The cold swirled through her, and her stomach churned. The last fourteen hours were like a battering ram to the emotions she'd kept so deeply guarded.

How could Gio show up and say all those things to her?

Elizabeth had counted on him being the ass she'd come to recognize. If he stuck to his routine, she wouldn't be torn to shreds. She would have felt right refusing him. Instead, she required all her willpower to keep from grappling on to him and not letting him leave. At least, thank the Lord, she'd been able to keep her composure and hide her inner turmoil from him.

Do not be afraid, Bella. Paolo's voice echoed in her mind, and she fought back a shiver, shocked Paolo still spoke to her.

He is his father's son.

"Where are you, Paolo?" She glanced around but didn't see him. Didn't he move on?

She jerked to a stop as she rounded the corner and Paolo's gravesite came into view. Gio crouched down, an umbrella held overhead, in front of a brand-new headstone marking Paolo's final resting place.

"Oh no," she whispered. He wasn't waiting at the hotel for her call as he said he'd be. Feeling the heaviness of her drenched shoes, she continued her march forward, dragging her feet through the brown, shriveled leaves now turned to liquid pulp.

Should she turn back the way she'd come?

"No," she said to herself. Curiosity wouldn't let her. There was something sweet and heart-warming about seeing him there talking with his father. Had he forgiven Paolo?

Unless, of course, Gio was there to curse him for all the ills of the past. No, the man who visited her the night before wouldn't berate his father. He seemed different. What did he say? *Give me a chance to show you I'm a changed man.*

Elizabeth swiped a drenched strand of hair out of her face.

"I think you'd have liked Cousin Angelina," Gio said as she approached him from behind. "Very boisterous. She is the daughter of your oldest sister,

Loretta. Angelina's nearing fifty and has a large family. She accepted me without question and said I was *famiglia*."

Elizabeth stopped in front of an oak tree a few feet behind him and propped herself against it. She closed her eyes and listened to the melodic tone of his deep, masculine voice. Reckless love simmered through her.

"I saw pictures of your father. I was surprised, but you didn't look much like him at all. Your mother's blood was strong. Though Angelina said I looked like the son of our third cousin, Tony, who also lives in Brooklyn." He laughed as he stood up from the ground. "But I suppose, I should be getting back. I'm hoping Elizabeth will see me today. I told her I'd be waiting at the hotel."

She opened her eyes in time to see him turn from the grave. Ducking behind the tree, she snagged her pants on the bark and bit back an unladylike curse.

"Elizabeth?" Gio laughed. "I can see you behind the tree. How long have you been there?"

Mortified, she stepped out, avoided eye contact, and murmured, "Not long."

"You're soaked. Come and stand under this umbrella." He pointed to her, and his lips turned up into a crooked smile. "Were you sneaking up on me? I recall you weren't too keen on people creeping about."

He walked towards her, a crooked smile illuminating his handsome face even without any sunlight overhead.

She exhaled the breath she didn't know she was holding. "Fine," she said. "I suppose I was eavesdropping, but I didn't want to disturb you. You were having such a nice conversation with him."

"What did you hear?" He stopped in front of her, the umbrella scratching the tree's surface.

She leaned back against the uneven bark. "Something about the son of your third cousin, Tony."

"Yes. I traveled to see relatives. Cousins through my grandfather. My real grandfather."

"That's what I thought you were talking about. You found out who he was?"

"Yes, once I was ready to listen, Marco was able to tell me enough about the family for me to trace them. My father had four sisters and two more brothers. They were from Rome. After corresponding with the family in Italy, I found relatives here in America.

"Two of his sisters immigrated to America with their husbands. As it turns out, I have quite a large family in New York."

"Your mother didn't mention what you were doing exactly, Gio. All I can say is I'm impressed. He matters to you."

"Yes, he does." He toyed with her chin. "And so do you."

She closed her eyes, urging her legs not to give out.

"You've let your hair grow," he said, wrapping a wet strand around his finger.

"Yes, I like it better long." She opened her eyes and looked up into his penetrating gaze. Without thinking, she lifted her hand and ran her fingers through his black hair. "And you cut yours."

"Do you like it?" he asked as he brushed his lips over her forehead. His hot breath warmed her skin.

"Yes," she whispered. Without the hair, the sleek lines of his face stood out and carried with it an aristocratic handsomeness she definitely appreciated.

"Gio?"

He kissed her nose.

"What are you doing?"

"Should I stop?" he breathed into her ear. "Should I move away?"

She bit her lip. Her legs weakened more, and she fought the mad desire to drag him against her. "Maybe," she murmured. "But maybe not." She wrapped her arms around his waist.

He leaned into her and nuzzled her neck.

Lord, she missed him. She moaned. "You have the umbrella."

"Yes, I do."

Her stomach turned to liquid. "Someone will see us," she rasped. If they did, she wasn't sure she cared.

"There's no one around." His mouth now found its way to hers, and he gently sucked her lower lip between his teeth.

With her body a quivering mass, she opened her mouth to take in a breath, and his tongue found its way inside.

This wasn't supposed to be happening. If he'd come to see her, she'd planned to turn him away like she'd done the night before. What a weak, weak woman she was. No self-control whatsoever.

"God, Elizabeth, I've missed you," he murmured and peppered kisses over her face. He dropped the umbrella and cupped her face in both hands, letting his lips stroke hers. Raindrops poured unfettered between the branches above and washed over them both.

Elizabeth's mind was a blur. Perchance, she'd enjoy this time with him while he was in Boston. There wasn't a future for them, and he'd realize soon enough, but it didn't mean she couldn't measure out a fraction of happiness now.

Gio withdrew from her, his eyes clouded with desire, and his voice raspy. "What do you say? Should we get out of the rain?"

She nodded. He retrieved the umbrella, took her hand, and led her to a black sedan parked on the cemetery road.

****

Towel drying his hair and wearing fresh clothing, Gio exited the washroom. He glanced at the woman sitting on the edge of the hotel bed wearing his red-checkered flannel robe. She bit her lip and nervously traced the colorless floral pattern on the cotton spread, not bothering to look at him.

Being near him seemed to make her uncomfortable. He'd never intended to bring her here, but she'd insisted. With the rain beating a steady tattoo on the shaded window, he crossed the room to the radiator where Elizabeth had draped her clothing to dry. He ran his finger over a tear in the rain-soaked, cotton slacks. They would take an eternity to dry. He turned to face her and smiled. She looked so pretty with her hair drying into tight ringlet curls and her cheeks ruddy.

Now she was there, he had no idea what to do with her. Of course, he did have *ideas*. He'd been lonely and aching in the unfamiliar full-sized bed the night before. The ache magnified by the fact she lived across the harbor. And the loneliness increased tenfold with the realization he'd most likely lost her.

He refused to bed her, no matter what images passed before his mind's eye. Scenes of tugging her to her feet, untying the sash, and pushing the material down over her smooth bare shoulders stirred his blood. He swallowed hard and gazed at the undergarments she'd also laid out to dry. He stiffened with desire. The woman was nearly naked.

He cleared his throat and said, "Elizabeth, I didn't bring you here intending to seduce you." *Idiot*. She hadn't implied he did.

"No?" She laughed, and her voice wavered. "Well, I did." She stood.

Her uninhibited words hit him with a jolt. "Elizabeth, I'm not sure," he whispered and supported himself on the hard wall.

"Don't worry," she murmured as she approached him. She tugged at the buttons on the shirt he'd only just donned. He'd intended to be a gentleman with her. He lifted his hands to stop her, but instead opened his eyes, and drew her in, not quite touching. This was torture.

She stretched up on her toes and brushed her lips over his. "I'm very sure," she said.

"Dammit," he muttered and lifted her into his arms.

Chapter Thirty-One

Elizabeth closed the door behind her and Gio as voices carried in from the kitchen at the back of the house. She shifted in her damp clothing, eager to dress in dry ones.

"I'll change and be right back down," she whispered but before she stepped away, Gio wrapped his arms around her and stole her breath away with a kiss.

"Beth?" her mother queried from down the hall.

Elizabeth withdrew from his arms and, with heated cheeks, turned to face Dora.

"Mother," she said. "I stopped home to change out of these wet things. I got caught in the rain."

"Good evening, Mrs. O'Brien." Gio nodded and slipped out of his coat.

"Good evening to you," she said with a frown. "Have the two of you had dinner?"

"No. We're dining out," Elizabeth said.

"Oh. Well, your father and I are just starting if you'd rather join us."

Elizabeth shook her head, but Gio answered, "Why, I'd love to. What do you think, *Cara*?" He rested his hand on her waist and grinned down at her.

She wrinkled her nose at him as she lifted his hand and pressed it to his side. "Be good," she said under her breath and continued with a sigh of resignation. "Fine. I'll be right down to eat."

She ascended the stairs and rushed to her room. She dressed quickly in a pinafore dress. She glanced in the bureau mirror at her hair. A riot of curls covered her head. What a mess. She sighed at her reflection and ran her suddenly trembling fingers through it, untangling the strands and tying it back with a ribbon.

What was Gio thinking, saying they'd stay for dinner? She wanted to spend time with him, to enjoy him. Still, this didn't mean she wanted him insinuating himself into her family. Things would be difficult enough once she told him the truth about what she was. With a deep breath, she left the room and joined everyone in the kitchen.

Gio looked up and offered her a warm smile as she sat in the chair next to him at the small, square table. Her parents preferred to eat in the kitchen when it was just a few of them home.

Bella glanced at Gio's profile. He looked at home with his plate full of helpings of boiled potatoes, cabbage, and bits of pork.

"Gio was telling us his new Reserve wine will be coming out this summer." Her father nodded at Gio, a strand of his gray hair falling on to his forehead. "He's promised to send me a case." Neil O'Brien's eyes sparkled with instant like for Gio.

"Isn't that nice of him." She looked at Gio with growing irritation. Lord, but she wasn't sure why. Trying to hide the trembling in her hands, she served her own plate, then simply shifted the food around with her fork. Her stomach turned somersaults, making the idea of eating difficult. Maybe her parents wouldn't notice she wasn't eating.

Her father inundated Gio with questions about the

vineyard. Gio smiled and glanced at her. "Elizabeth learned a thing or two about making brandy while she was in California."

"Really, Beth?" Neil O'Brien asked.

"Yes, I suppose." She half-smiled at her father and kicked Gio under the table. Now he was sharing cozy, private little jokes with her. Like they were a couple.

He certainly fit right in. What happened to the quiet, reserved man she met last autumn? If he'd remained the same, she could cope. Seeing this new and improved Giovanni Clemente would cause her to hurt even more when he rejected her again. Forgetting herself, she looked up. Her mother's eyes met hers and Elizabeth set her fork down, no longer pretending to eat.

"Mrs. O'Brien, thank you for the delicious dinner," Gio said, placing his cloth napkin on his plate. "I think I'll pass up dessert for a drive. How about you, Elizabeth?" He grabbed her hand under the table. "She's promised to show me Boston."

Even though she didn't respond, he excused himself and stood, guiding her up with him. "I'll have her back early," he said and led her to the front door.

Without speaking, he helped her into her slightly stiff but dry coat. After she'd buttoned it, he shrugged into his own and he took her hand to usher her outside. "The rain has stopped. Should we walk?"

She sighed. "Why not?"

"You're worrying me, Elizabeth," he said softly. "What's happening here?" He lifted his hand to stop her from talking. "No, maybe I don't want to know."

They passed through the gate and walked down the cobblestone path.

"Gio, I—"

He squeezed her hand. "How far is the ocean from here?"

"It's quite a walk, and I have something to tell you."

"We have time," he murmured. "Do you remember telling me about the time my father spent at the ocean?" He stopped and drew her to him.

"Gio," she whispered as she braced herself against him, fighting off the weakness creeping into her entire body. "Please, listen," she pleaded. "Let me talk."

The crown of her head warmed from the kiss he planted there. Shivers ran up her spine from where his fingers caressed circles into her lower back. Tears pooled in her eyes. If she didn't speak now, she'd follow him back to California and live a lie.

"Gio," she whispered and looked up into his shadowed face. "I need to tell you the truth about how I met your father."

"The truth?" He brushed his mouth over hers. "You already did."

"No." She broke free of his embrace and spun to avoid seeing his face when she told him. "I didn't tell you everything. Not the whole story."

His arms encircled her, and she rested against his hard body for one last bit of comfort.

"I'll repeat myself. You're worrying me, Elizabeth." His voice caught.

Biting her lip, she warded off the tears. *Lord, give me the strength.* "I hadn't spoken to your father before the day he died except just once. And it was just to say, 'thank you.' It wasn't until after—"

"Don't. I don't want to hear this." He tightened his embrace.

She clasped her hands over his and pressed them

firmer into her abdomen. "But I have to tell you."

Gio's breathing increased and he stiffened behind her, but he didn't step away.

Light drops of rain fell around them.

"I did help your father as he died, but we didn't become friends until later, when he sought me out, after."

"Dammit, Elizabeth." His voice sounded sad, not angry. He withdrew, and cold enveloped her without his body pressed into hers.

Despair washed through her, and she hugged her chest. *Lord, if there's any way to keep this from happening, please let me know.* She spun to face him.

"I'll take you back to the house." He turned, grabbed her elbow, and propelled her forward.

It was right to tell him, wasn't it?

She should have lied and told him she didn't love him.

No, Gio would never accept the falsehood. She shook her head. Somehow, the stubborn man had decided he wanted her. Lord, she wanted him right back, but not if it meant pretending her gift didn't exist.

"Giovanni." She stumbled on the rain-slicked stones and jerked back on his arm to stop him before he entered her front gate. "Gio, please." She drew in a lungful of air and exhaled. "Please hear me out."

"I don't need to hear anymore, Elizabeth." He caressed her cheek. "Whatever help you need, I'll make sure you get it."

"No," she moaned.

"Yes." He twined his fingers with hers, kissed the back of her hand. "I love you. And there's no way I'm turning my back on you because of these delusions."

She groaned and snatched her hand from his grasp.

"I don't need psychiatric help. I understand what I'm saying is impossible to accept." She clung to the wrought iron fence in front of her home for support. Her heart burned, and she gulped back a sob. There'd be no tears. None. "I love you, too, Gio. I do. But I can't be with you unless you accept me for what I am."

"I do." His voice broke as he spoke. "I'll accept everything about you, Elizabeth. I want you to be my wife," he whispered.

"Living with me you'd see things that don't make sense. You'd think I'm normal at times because weeks would pass, even months, without a visit. When a spirit appeared again, it wouldn't always be at a convenient moment. And they're not always pleasant. Sometimes they scare me. You'd have to accept I communicate with them. Or eventually you'd think I'm too mad to ignore it any longer."

"No," he said more harshly than she thought he intended to. He opened the front gate, leaving it to swing open and approached the front door. "I think I need to speak with your parents. They can help me talk you into getting medical care."

She dashed after him, passed him by, and faced him, barring his entrance. "Don't. They'll only tell you it's true." A chill spread through her like a crack in an ice-covered pond.

The rain fell harder now, bombarding the roof above them, and dripped steadily onto the porch rail.

Gio stopped in front of her, his hands flexed into fists at his side. His chest rose and fell under labored breaths. "Fine, you don't want me to talk to them. But dammit, you have to help me out here. What do you expect me to do?"

Yellow light from the bay window bathed his face, showing a brow creased with concern.

Lord, this hurts. He truly does love me. I only wish things were different.

"I can live with this." He nodded as if to convince himself. "If you need to believe you have this power, whatever it is, well, then, I can live with it. If you promise you'll come back to California with me."

She shook her head. "You asked me if Patrick knew everything about me, remember? I told you he did. He never once doubted me or my gift." Her voice broke along with her heart as the tears bled down her cheeks. "The only way I can marry you is if you accept it and accept me for what I am."

"Do you want me to lie?" He sounded almost hopeful.

"No. I don't want lies. There's been too many surrounding us all along." She stretched up on her toes, brushing her lips over his. "I'm sorry," she whispered and pressed her heels to the wooden porch floor. "It's over, Gio. So please forget about me."

She walked away from him, her heart collapsing from the dejected look shadowing his face. "I think you should go," she sobbed, fumbling with the door behind her, and escaped into the house.

Resting her head against the inside of the door, she cried, careful to be quiet and not alert her parents. Lord, what she wouldn't give to make things different, but she wasn't able to close off the dead again. She'd tried.

Minutes, five, maybe ten, passed before she heard his vehicle drive away.

Chapter Thirty-Two

Her body rocked in long, choppy jolts along with the floor beneath her. Reaching out, she called, "Momma! Momma!" filled with childish fear. A woman's skirt appeared in front of her, and she burrowed into the damp fabric.

"Hush, little Gio. You must not be frightened. We will be with your poppa soon."

The roar of the ocean rushed the walls around her. The smell of salt and sickness overwhelmed her senses. She wanted to go home. Go back to Nonna and to Italy.

Eyes closed, Elizabeth woke with a whimper. Gio's small, childish whimper and the act of it made her feel so much a part of the boy—and the man. She opened her eyes to the dark room.

Lord, forgetting the man wasn't possible when he haunted her dreams so often. But never like this before, never like one of her visions.

Suddenly, an unbearable cold filled the room. Shivering, Elizabeth gathered the bed's blankets to her chin. She fought hard to control her chattering teeth.

She glanced toward the half-open window.

"Lord," she moaned. "Why did I leave that up?" Sitting up, she twisted the key switch to illuminate the red crystal lamp sitting on her bedside table. Outside was still dark with no hint of the sun.

Throwing back the covers, she dashed to close out

the frigid air, but as she lifted her hands to shut the window, a humid breeze accosted her. This was August, not December, and the chill had nothing to do with the weather. The hairs rose on her arms, and a current traveled her spine. Something, or rather someone, was in the room and she didn't think she felt comfortable with whoever it was.

She turned from the window. An apparition stood between her and the bedroom door. His lips were blue. His skin was gray and swollen like a body too long in the water.

"C-can I help you?" she whispered.

"Yes," he said with a thick Russian accent. He took off his cap and bowed. "I need to find my family. My wife and children. They are lost to me."

Oh, no. Not again. She fisted her hands in the skirt of her nightgown. "W-where are they? Your family?"

"They were to be waiting on the dock." He twisted his tattered hat in his large hands and water dripped to the floor. "My letter told them to wait on the dock in Boston Harbor where the ship would set anchor."

Breathe, Elizabeth. Slow breaths. One. Two. Three. Her gaze fell to the water pooling in front of him. "And they weren't there when you arrived?"

"No," he said in exasperation. His face contorted in his anger and sadness.

Elizabeth dared not look away. Energy shot from him and rode over her in waves. A damp cold settled in her and she trembled uncontrollably from the unbearable chill.

"No," he said again. "I have walked there for so long. Yet they do not come."

"How long?" she murmured. She edged left along

the wall.

"I do not know!" He stopped short. "I remember the ship I was on, the *Canopus*, coming to America."

Elizabeth gasped and let her eyes fall closed. Her stomach lurched with the floor beneath, and she was sick. The ghost's memories filled her mind.

He had been sick for days with the relentless rocking of the ship. This all would be worth it if the Godforsaken vessel got him safely to America, to his sweet Kalia and his babies. He plucked at his eternally wet jacket. In it, he sweated like a pig despite the cold clothes.

Mikhail grasped his legs to his chest and muffled a moan when the swollen wood against his ear creaked and shuddered. Terrified screams echoed around the cramped cabin as water seeped up from below. Mikhail rose on unsteady legs and slumped back to the slanting floor. The pleas for help from those too weak to make it above deck bombarded the boards. Until the saltwater rose high enough to surround him and extinguish the voices.

Elizabeth coughed and gasped for breath. Shaken, she braced herself against the wall and opened her eyes. The ghost, Mikhail, stood crestfallen, gazing down at the puddle about his feet. The poor man. For all she knew, he only needed her to hear his story.

Sometimes all the dead needed was someone to listen to them and to understand.

"You died in the water," she whispered.

"Yes, I died in the water." He lumbered toward her, and Elizabeth's heart dropped. Though she sympathized with him, he still frightened her.

He reined up in front of her and bowed his head. "Did my wife, my Kalia, get my letter? Did she know I was coming? Did she wait for me?"

****

A few nights later, Elizabeth knocked on her sister's bedroom door with one hand and clutched a stack of handwritten notes in the other. Her hands shook with the excitement of the news she'd discovered earlier in the day. She'd found the last puzzle piece explaining why Paolo never returned to the vineyard. The ghost Mikhail's appearance had led her right to the answer. Something told her his visit was more than a coincidence. *It must be.*

When her sister didn't answer, she edged the heavy oak door open. A shaft of moonlight sliced through the dark room and washed over her sister's sleeping form, hidden beneath the thin cotton sheet.

"Anna," she whispered, not wanting to wake her parents, who slept in their room down the hall. She pressed the light switch beside the door, turning on the overhead light. "Anna," she said again, raising her voice.

Lord, her sister always slept soundly. Even hurricane-strength winds didn't wake her. Elizabeth walked over to the bed and snatched the covers off her sister's nightgown-clad body. Anna rolled over onto her back with her auburn curls covering her face. Reaching for the covers, she groaned through her clenched teeth, "Go away."

Elizabeth grabbed the cotton sheet before her sister had a chance to grab it and sat on the edge of the mattress. "No, Anna, I need to talk to you."

Her sister glared up at her but remained silent.

"It's very important. Please, will you listen?" she pleaded.

"Oh, all right." Anna sat up and rested her back

against the oval, walnut-paneled backboard. Sighing, she brushed a wild curl out of her eyes. "But what is so important you had to wake me?" She glanced at a small wooden tabletop clock on her bedside table. "At two a.m., for goodness' sake?"

Elizabeth wrinkled her nose and glanced at the papers she held. "I need you to come to California with me."

"What?" Anna leaned towards her. "Why? To chase down Giovanni Clemente?"

Did she want to see Gio again? She loathed admitting so out loud, but yes. Elizabeth shook her head. "No." She handed Anna her notes and stood. "I need to tell the Clementes about what I've written there."

Her sister crisscrossed her legs and spread the papers out on her bed. As she read, she shifted them around.

Elizabeth paced the room and nervously tugged on the bodice of her thin cotton nightdress. Her whole body hummed, down to her bare feet, with apprehension and excitement at seeing the vineyard again. The chance to see Gio again. She didn't have any misguided expectations he might now accept what she was and what she saw. However, she did harbor a glimmer of hope they might someday be friends.

His family expected her to continue to be a part of their lives. To clear any bad blood between her and Gio would make things easier for everyone.

"Beth, what does this all mean?" Anna looked up at her.

Elizabeth hopped on the foot of the bed and gathered her knees to her chest. She picked up a page of her notes. "This means a ship did go down back in nineteen-twelve.

However, it wasn't the Clementes' ship. The *Canopus* was due on the same day as the *Elijah*, and it was the one lost at sea."

"Okay, makes sense. Paolo was mistaken about which ship. But what does that have to do with any of it? You've already convinced his family."

She bit her lip. "It's the final piece to the puzzle. They deserve to know." Besides, Michael Clemente had asked her if another ship had been lost. Now she figured out the answer.

"You can't write them or telephone them with your findings?"

"True." She rose to her knees and collected her materials into a neat pile. "But they're friends now, Anna. I owe it to them to deliver this news firsthand."

"And it has nothing to do with seeing Giovanni?"

"Fine. Yes, it does. Only it's not for the reason you're thinking. Gio and I can't have a future together."

Anna jumped from the bed. "See, now I don't understand, Beth. You told me yourself the man professed his love to you."

Elizabeth's heart dropped. Anna repeatedly questioned the sense of refusing Gio's proposal over the last four months.

"The point is I can't commit my life to a man who doesn't accept me for what I am."

"You aren't the gift, Beth. You're much, much more."

"Am I?" She sighed. "It's hard for you to understand."

"No." Anna shook her head. "I have the gift, too, you know."

Elizabeth saw from the look on her sister's face she

offended her. She didn't mean to, but they received the gift differently, just as their mother did. "But for you it's purely visual. You see their faces and purge them in your drawings. I, on the other hand, meet them face-to-face. With some, I share their memories. I don't forget them once they've gone. It's like they become part of my own life."

Anna strode to the window. "If you love Gio, Beth, why don't you try?" She turned to face her sister again. "I mean, do you have to tell him everything?" She shrugged and continued, "When I fall in love, I don't intend to tell the guy my latest drawing is of a man who died by hanging two hundred years ago. He will think I'm insane."

"Exactly!" Elizabeth pounded the mattress to punctuate her point. "And when a spirit leans over me when I'm sleeping in Gio's arms and scares me senseless, what will he think?" She stood from the bed, her notes grasped to her chest. "No, he has to trust me. Like father does with mother."

Like Patrick trusted in her. Yes, she'd been blocking the visits out when she'd been married to him, but she was never able to shut them out completely. She'd still experienced the tingling in her blood or the images and sensations she chose to ignore.

"How about trusting in him, Beth?" Anna asked. "If he's worth it, put the gift aside. Block it out like you used to."

Elizabeth's grip tightened on the paper clutched in her hand. "Don't say it like that—if he's worth it." She swallowed. Hadn't she asked herself the same thing repeatedly? "Don't you think it was worth it when I helped his father? I'd never have met Gio if I hadn't received Paolo. With my intervention, the whole family found peace. Gio, too.

"And now the man who died on the *Canopus* visited me. I can help him." Was she only trying to convince Anna? How many nights did she lie awake considering the possibility of choosing between Giovanni Clemente and the gift?

She lifted the heel of her hand to her heat-flushed cheeks. "Why do I have to slice out a piece of me? Why can't he set aside his preconceived notions and at least attempt to have faith in me? Is that too much to ask?"

"If I go to California with you, will you ask him?" Anna stood firm, her hands folded across her chest and a look of stubbornness written on her face.

Elizabeth nodded. When did her little sister become so smart? "Yes," she mumbled. "If you come to the vineyard with me."

"Fine," she said with a smile. "We've solved all your dilemmas, now please take your detective work and let me sleep?" She dashed to her bed and quickly buried her head in her pillow.

Feeling dismissed, Elizabeth left the room and retreated to her own. Closing the door quietly behind her, she laid her notes on her bureau and climbed into bed.

Anna obviously has never been in love. If she had, she'd have understood Elizabeth's need to have Gio accept everything about her. This was essential.

She quieted her mind, preparing to summon the Russian ghost, Mikhail.

His wife, Kalia, had been in both Mikhail *and* Paolo's memories. She'd been at the counter the day Paolo received the devastating news. The woman with tired brown eyes and sandy blonde hair hidden beneath a crudely made black kerchief. Kalia was the woman who enveloped her children in her arms and cried in relief, "Thank God! Thank God. Your poppa is safe."

****

Gio raked the dead weeds into a pile in the vineyard aisle, his skin slick beneath his cotton shirt with sweat from hard labor and the hot sun. He stopped and swiped his arm across his moist brow. A figure passed through a space between the leaf-laden vines, but he didn't see who. Vincenzo tended the vines several aisles over and it must have been him. He shrugged and returned to work.

Each day he worked himself into exhaustion until he fell into bed. His mother, frustrated with his brooding, kept her concern to herself.

On occasion, she'd mention news she received in letters from Boston, but he quickly found excuses not to hear any of it. If there was no work left to do on the vineyard, he'd jump into his automobile and drive. When he'd return, his mother often glared at him. He was sure she'd concluded he fled to see Zola or another woman, but he didn't. He only drove.

Sometimes, when his tires skimmed over the dirt or concrete roads, he'd allow himself to think about Elizabeth. How she'd hurt him. *It's over, Gio*, she'd told him. *So please forget about me.*

He did deserve it, but he'd never expected to be the one left wanting. The damn woman was under his skin, and he wasn't able to shake any bit of her. He was likely to go mad. Maybe he'd even go as mad as she pretended to be.

He collected the weeds in one of his gloved hands. With the rake in the other, he retreated to the aisle opening.

Other than her story of speaking with the dead, Elizabeth didn't act like a woman with delusions. There had to be a good reason or two. Either to find a cruel excuse to turn him away, or she really did see what she told him.

He'd been over the same argument a hundred times at least. The only sane conclusion was she'd made the whole tale up to scare him off. The whole thing gave him a headache.

Dammit—that must be the reason, because he'd offered to love her.

"Ahhh," he groaned and threw the rake and weeds to the graveled ground. All she asked him to do was to accept what she told him, and he hadn't even tried.

He tore off his cloth gloves, stalked to the back door, and trudged into the kitchen. There was only one person he trusted to help him make any sense of his dilemma. She stood at the white porcelain sink rinsing potatoes. Marco sat eating a favorite family treat, *café orzo,* at the table, the cane Gio gifted him resting on the back of his chair.

Better yet, the two people he most admired would help him figure out the mess.

He tossed the dirty gloves on the kitchen counter. His mother shot him a scolding look, and he retrieved them, tucking them in his back pocket. He pulled up a seat.

Gio cleared his throat before saying, "Elizabeth told me she didn't become friends with my *padre* until after he died."

Marco choked on his food and set his spoon down in the bowl with a clink.

Adriana turned off the faucet, set the potatoes down, and turned to face him. She dried her hands on her waist apron and nodded.

"You believe that, don't you?" he asked his mother.

"Yes. Yes, I do."

"But how?" He shook his head, leaned his elbows on the table, and cradled his face in his hands. This was supposed to be the voice of reason. After rubbing his temples, he glanced at her again. "Please, tell me how."

Adriana looked from Marco to him and sighed. She untied her apron and approached the table. "I do because, Giovanni, your *padre* spoke to me the night of his memorial service. He touched me." She caressed the crown of her head. "Here. And he told me he would love me forever." She sat. "I heard his words, not with my ears, but in my mind."

"What?" Gio threw his hand in the air and jerked back into his chair. A voice echoed in his head the same night. *Go to her, Giovanni. Do not be the fool that I was.*

Remembering the chill that caused his hair to stand on end, he shot up and sent the chair scooting several inches back.

He paced the floor. He recalled the strange events in the vineyard, the twig falling in his face before he left for New York and the words he'd assumed were his own. *If you truly love her, Giovanni, it's worth the risk. You have already lost your heart.*

Had his father's ghost manipulated him?

"It is hard to accept, Gio, I understand. I did not see him. Yet, he was there." She pressed her hands to her heart. "I sensed it down to my soul."

Gio looked at Marco. "Do you believe this thing she says?"

The man's wrinkled face paled, but he answered, "I have no cause to doubt her, Giovanni. She has never told me a falsehood in all the years I have known her." He nodded. "And if you will excuse me, I will leave you alone to talk some sense into the *figlio*, Adriana." He grabbed his cane and, placing his weight on it, lifted himself from the chair. With another curt nod and a reassuring smile, he slowly retreated to his new bedroom off to the right of the kitchen, where young Sofia used to sleep. She'd taken quarters in a cottage near the vineyard workers.

As Marco firmly shut his door, Adriana asked, "Do you believe me?"

"I guess you've never told me a falsehood in all the years I've known you, either." He laughed nervously, threading his fingers through his short hair. "Elizabeth told me she couldn't marry me unless I accepted her for what she was. And if it wasn't enough, I needed to believe her, too."

"You never told me this, Giovanni."

"No." He stopped, mid-step, and faced her. "I didn't want you to know she'd rejected me. I didn't want anyone to. I took the chance and failed."

"Oh, my *figlio*, you did not fail." She rose and met him, wrapping her arms around his shoulders. "Do you think you could find it in your heart to accept it to be true?" she asked.

"I don't know," he replied but reminded himself his *madre* was the most levelheaded person in his life. "I'll try. God, I must truly be going mad."

Smiling, she hugged him, stepped back, and patted his back. "You should talk to Seb," she said. "Esmerelda had the gift, you know. He could help you to see the truth of it."

Chapter Thirty-Three

A warm summer breeze blew through the driver's side window, and Frances Langford crooned over the car radio about a *Kiss in the Dark*. Gio had attended a show featuring her and Bob Hope once. On a USO tour when they entertained the troops. She was a petite brunette, even shorter than Elizabeth. Her songs didn't mean much to him at the time, but now every sugary word reminded him of Elizabeth. He truly was a lovesick fool. He turned the music off. He didn't need any sentimental songs taunting him.

He had no idea how Elizabeth would receive his letter, nor if he genuinely believed what she said about seeing the dead. His mother, Sebastian, and more than half the people on the vineyard believed the dead could walk the earth.

Who knew? Maybe, too many bombs exploded near him during the war, or—he ran his finger along his faded facial scar—the shrapnel that cut his cheek must have imbedded in his brain. Or perhaps he wasn't hearing people correctly? Maybe he was suffering from delusions.

Once he'd started asking, trying to get opinions if many people believed in such things, he'd gotten an earful. Seb's wife had heard things she claimed were messages from angels. When she was ten years old, she'd fallen, hitting her head on train tracks on the outskirts of the Mexican village she'd grown up in. After her injury, she began talking of her aural gift. Gio trusted old Seb as much as he trusted his mother. He saw no other choice but to consider the possibility.

Other people reminded him of the story about a woman who ran the road leading from town to the vineyard. The woman was said to be a kitchen maid who worked for the previous estate. Rumors said she disappeared after her love affair with the estate's owner ended badly. Not long after the woman's disappearance, the man himself died of a broken heart, or so the story went. His death left the vineyard in the inept hands of his widow. The land fell into disrepair until Gio's father bought it.

It was all romantic hogwash as far as Gio was concerned, but the local people put merit in the story. He shook his head. He'd traveled this road hundreds of times in the dead of night and never saw the woman.

He scanned the leaf-laden trees along the roadside. No one dashed out, scaring the living daylights out of him.

Wait, hadn't Elizabeth been frightened on this very road her first day with him?

A quarter mile down the road, a vehicle stood off to the side, its nose pointing in the direction of the trees. Gio leaned in near his windshield, trying to make out the stocky man who trudged down the road toward him away from the stalled car. He squinted and caught sight of his young cousin, Paolo.

"I'll be damned." He whistled through his teeth. He didn't expect him or his father until harvest. And he'd hoped before they set out, they'd pick up Elizabeth from the train station and bring her with them. Well, if she accepted the invitation he was on his way to send.

He rolled up beside Paolo, leaned toward the passenger door, and rolled down the window.

Paolo looked toward him, startled. "Giovanni." A tentative smile brightened his unusually pale face. "I didn't realize that was you." He knocked on the steel door. "New automobile?"

"Yes." Gio laughed. "Now what are you doing out here walking?"

He glanced over his shoulder. "We were on the way to the vineyard when—" He swallowed. "Well, when something frightened Elizabeth, and my father ran us off the road." He looked at Gio and dropped his gaze. The look on his face spoke of his own fright. "We blew two tires, and we only have one spare. So I was on the way to you for help."

Gio shook his head, and all blood drained from his face. "Did you say Elizabeth? As in Elizabeth Reilly?" He hadn't even gotten a chance to mail the damn letter. Of course, she would show up unexpectedly and not let him be the first to make peace.

"Yeah. She and her sister, Anna, arrived in San Francisco yesterday. We picked them up and headed out this morning."

"What is she doing here?" He trained his eyes on the small figure sitting on the ground on the side of the road. Anna and his uncle, Michael, hovered near, but he only focused on her. Elizabeth braced her head against her bent knees.

Not only did his blood now drain from his body, but his heart also pulsed in rapid succession. As he ran his tongue along the inside of his dry mouth, he realized he'd never been so nervous in his life.

"I. Uh." His cousin fidgeted on his feet. "It's unbelievable really. I think I'll let her tell you." He glanced over his shoulder at the vehicle down the road. "Do you mind if I get in?"

"Of course. Of course." Gio grabbed the cool handle and pushed the door open. "Hop in." Only then did Gio notice blood marring the skin above his cousin's left ear. The man had barely closed the door when Gio screeched to a start and sped down the road.

****

At the sound of squealing tires, Elizabeth lifted her head. The wave of nausea still rippled through her body, and pain pounded behind her eyes. Never had she suffered anything as intense as the poor woman's memories. Never had she experienced such a violent death. Lord, was this a memory she'd have to live with for the rest of her life? Suddenly, the gift didn't seem so important, rather it seemed like a dire curse.

Gio's black sedan parked behind Michael's automobile. Swallowing her pride, Elizabeth struggled to her feet but fell back to the ground.

"Beth." Anna knelt in the dirt beside her. "Don't try to move again. One of the men will lift you. Understand?"

Unable to talk, Elizabeth nodded and closed her eyes, ashamed and too frightened to look at Gio. If his cousin informed him about what happened, Gio would pity her for her lunacy.

I can't bear his pity.

"Does she need a doctor?" Gio asked, his voice raw and laced with worry.

"No," Anna murmured. "She needs some rest. When a spirit takes control without a person's permission, it drains them completely."

"What?" His voice caught. "Can someone please tell me what happened here?"

Strong arms lifted Elizabeth into the air, and she let her limbs go lax. *Gio.* She'd recognize his sensual, burnt-wood smell anywhere. He pressed her head to his chest, and her ear rested over his erratically beating heart. She wanted to open her eyes to see the handsome yet stubborn set of his jaw, but feared doing so would break the closeness. His warm breath washed over her, and she knew he was watching her as his boots crunched over the gravel.

A door squeaked open and, too soon, her back pressed into the warm cloth of the vehicle's seat. Gio's work-roughened hands caressed her forehead, her cheeks, and he pulled away. If she were able to find her voice now, she would say, "*No, Gio, don't move away. Don't ever leave me again.*"

Instead, she leaned over, resting her cheek against the scratchy upholstered seat, and listened to the conversation taking place outside.

"She's as cold as death," Gio whispered. "I'm taking her back to the house. Now. Then calling the doctor."

"She doesn't need a doctor," Anna said. "When my mother acts as a vessel—though it's never been exactly like this—she rests and, in a day or less, she's back to normal."

"Please, don't start with the delusional talk." His tone was even, but Elizabeth heard an undertone of trepidation.

"Yes, that's right. Our whole family is insane. Certifiable." Anna's voice traveled to the side of the vehicle and stopped at the window above Elizabeth's head. "Now I finally understand why Elizabeth turned you away, Mr. Clemente. I was terribly wrong to ask her to give you another chance. Now, please take us to your vineyard so my sister can recuperate. We'll be out of your hair as soon as she can travel." The door opened, and Anna slid onto the seat, and she gently lifted Elizabeth's head into her lap.

No, Anna, you weren't wrong. I was. I should have never chosen this curse over him. The images of the poor woman's death—Moira's death—threatened to reappear. The excruciating pain and the fear. Moira's screams as she fell, and out of corner of her eye, she'd seen a boy.

Elizabeth clenched her fists tightly in her gabardine skirt and steadied her breathing. She pushed the vision from her mind. She refused to ever experience this kind of terror. She'd block out the visits whatever it took. Moira would never have a chance to contact her again, because she didn't have any idea of how to help the woman's lost soul.

The sound of the automobile trunks opening and closing carried on the air. The vehicle bounced under the weight of the men, and they slammed the doors shut.

"I'm sorry, Anna." Gio's voice was deferential. "I didn't mean to insult you or your family," he said and turned on the engine.

What exactly did his apology mean? Was he trying to understand? Elizabeth shifted in the seat as he swung the car back toward the vineyard.

Chapter Thirty-Four

The next day, Gio paced the front porch.

The yellow sun hung high in the sky, telling him it was past noon. A chilling hush permeated the whole estate. If he hadn't seen a person or two, he'd have guessed every individual on the vineyard was still sleeping.

Except for Anna O'Brien.

Elizabeth's stubbornness was tame next the cinnamon-haired pixie called Anna. The young woman guarded her sister with ferocious possessiveness. After one day, Gio had yet to step foot in his own room.

He hadn't stopped to contemplate why he'd carried Elizabeth to his room until now. It had been his way of marking his territory. Once she recovered from the shock Dr. Whitmore said she'd suffered, he would not let her leave.

The front door opened, and Gio turned to face his uncle. A purplish bruise covered his cheek, and a mean, stitched gash rode high on his forehead.

"Giovanni," Michael said as he sat on the wooden bench. "We need to talk."

"Hmmm," Gio grunted in response. The turn of events over the last twenty-four hours caused him to brood as never before. He continued to pace.

"Something unnatural happened yesterday." Michael shook his head, his face weary. "I still—" He took a deep breath before continuing. "The voice

Elizabeth spoke with was not her own."

"Ah." Gio waved his hand in dismissal.

"I am not finished yet, Giovanni. You will listen."

Unbelievable. They were all losing their minds. Michael, Marco, his mother, and from all indications, the entire O'Brien family descended into madness years ago.

"When she spoke," his uncle continued, "she had the voice of an Irish woman. Like someone new to this county, *figlio*. Such fear I have never heard in a voice."

"Michael, I don't want to hear—"

"Then walk away, *Signore*, because I am still talking." He stood. His broad chest and shoulders rose under his deep breaths.

Numb and crestfallen, Gio leaned against the porch beam. "Fine, go on."

"This *fantasma* begged us not to kill her until Elizabeth fainted. It was not something I wish to experience again."

"What's your point?"

"I do not know." Michael shook his head. "I care very much for Elizabeth. She befriended *mio fratello*, but…"

"You don't want her in your life and don't think I should either." Gio crossed his arms over his chest. He didn't intend to listen to his uncle's advice. "You don't think I should ask her to marry me, do you?"

"No, Giovanni, I do not think you should. Imagine if your children are born with this power. Would you want your children so afflicted?"

"No, I don't want these ghosts terrifying my children. What man would purposely wish such a thing, but—"

"Ah, you do see." Michael spoke, not letting him

291

finish. "I am only concerned for you, Giovanni. You and your *madre*. It would not be wise to marry a woman such as Elizabeth."

The sound of feet on gravel attracted Gio's attention to the side of the house. He glanced first to one side than the other, but no one appeared. He held up his hand to signal his uncle not to speak and called out, "Who's over there?"

When no one answered, he turned back to Michael. "If I choose to marry and have children with her, it's not your concern."

****

Gio didn't want children with her. Not that it should have come as a surprise. Hadn't he once said he hoped children didn't result from their night together? This time he said, *"No, I don't want these ghosts terrifying my children. What man would purposely wish such a thing?"*

Elizabeth walked away, bracing her hand along the house's stone exterior. Her heart was numb from Gio and Michael's words. After his family experienced the shock of her gift, they turned away from her as she feared they would.

Adriana accepted the truth. Would the woman's wish alone be enough to keep them all from turning her out of their lives?

Elizabeth rounded the corner of the house and stumbled her way to the back kitchen door. Tears welled in her eyes. Michael spoke as if any child she bore would be an abomination. As if she was one.

She needed to find Anna and tell her they'd leave in the morning. No one, not her sister nor Adriana, and most of all not Gio, needed to be aware of what she overheard.

****

Later in the night, Elizabeth stretched her legs out on the back stoop. Too restless to sleep and too afraid of what her dreams might bring, she opted for fresh air. No matter how irrational, her body ached to be back in Gio's bed. She'd slept there without him, but his scent surrounded her, and she imagined his arms around her.

Elizabeth moved to a guest room that evening before dinner. She'd hoped being out of his room would ease her aching heart.

It would take more than separating herself from Giovanni Clemente to ease the pain. She loved him even though he didn't want her. She couldn't shut off her feelings. Blocking out the dead was easier to do.

A light summer breeze played with her hair and cooled her warm face. Anna agreed they should leave in the morning, and Adriana would take them to San Francisco. Elizabeth was sad to leave the vineyard. She feared she'd never visit again.

The back screen door bumped her back.

"Elizabeth?"

She turned to see Gio staring down at her. She scooted to the side to let him by.

"What are you doing out here?" he asked softly.

"Couldn't sleep." Her throat raw, and her heart too hollow to say more.

He sat beside her. "Hmmm, me either."

She glanced at him and away. Her cheeks grew warmer. Their bodies didn't touch, but she heated from their closeness. He seemed restless, running his hands through his hair, and grinding his bare feet into the ground. She heard his breathing as his hand hovered near hers.

"We need to talk," he said.

"No." She shook her head, not daring to look at him. "I don't think there's much more for us to say that we haven't said before."

He brushed her hair off her shoulder, smoothing it against the length of her back.

She shivered. "Gio, please."

His hand stilled and rested on the small of her back. "I love you, Elizabeth," he whispered.

Air rushed from her throat. If she hadn't already been sitting, she might have collapsed. "What?"

"I love you," he said louder.

She gulped. "No. You can't. Why else would you have—" She bit her lip.

"Why else would I have what? Left Boston, you mean?" he asked.

It was time to crawl away. This was not a confrontation she was willing to have.

He sighed, his fingers now rubbing circles on her back. She stiffened but did not want him to stop.

"I left because you told me to and because I'm an idiot. I never should have doubted you," he said. "You can't blame me completely, though. It isn't every day the woman you love admits to not only seeing ghosts but talking to them and traveling across the country for them."

What was he saying? This didn't correlate with what she heard him discussing with Michael.

She turned towards him. "Gio—"

"Shhh, let me finish first. Please?" He encircled her waist with both arms.

Gulping back tears, she buried her face against the

warm skin his open shirt exposed. She smoothed her cheek over the downy curls peppering his chest. Her blasted body betrayed her.

"I'm not always the most easygoing man."

She smiled and was glad he didn't notice.

"But there are times I can admit my mistakes." He gently touched her chin and guided her face up to look in his eyes where tears welled. "I should've told you I'd at least try to accept your story about my father. It took me awhile to figure that out."

"I don't understand. You told Michael," Elizabeth whispered and hid her face in her hands. Lord, had she gone and jumped to conclusions? Now all the questioning smiles Gio sent her way during dinner made sense.

"What do you mean? Damn," he groaned. "You were on the side of the house when I was talking to him, weren't you?"

Gazing up at him again, she nodded.

"Oh, *Cara*." He lifted her into his lap and kissed her forehead.

Her skin there tingled.

"I'm sorry you overheard that," he said. "Now at least you see my pigheaded behavior is deeply inbred." He brushed his lips over her temple. "I told Michael either he accepted I intended to marry you, or he leave. I'm sorry to tell you this, *Cara*, but he decided to leave. That's why I had him and Paolo taken into town to wait until the garage repaired his vehicle. He's afraid and doesn't understand."

She'd lost the friends she'd found in Gio's uncle and cousin, and it hurt. If Gio at least understood, she'd bear the disappointment. She shifted in his lap to study the shadowed lines of his attractive face. His strong, stubborn jaw, the perfect straight nose, and the lips made for kissing her.

"And you do?" she asked.

"I'm not frightened of you." His voice was husky. "I'll stand by you no matter what comes our way," he said. "Even visits in the night."

Was she really hearing this? Gio believed her and accepted her gift? Whether she allowed the dead in any longer was another matter, but he understood. Her heart swelled with sweet adulation. With a trembling voice, she asked, "And children, our children—if they inherit this from me?"

"Their wonderful mother, and Grandmother O'Brien, will teach them how to live with it."

"Oh, Giovanni." Her voice caught in her throat. "Lord, I love you." Throwing her arms about his neck, she peppered kisses along his stubbled jaw.

He lifted her hips, so she straddled him. He tugged her lower lips between his teeth and splayed his hand on her bottom. Moist heat slammed into her.

This was not what she expected when she stepped out for air. She sighed into his mouth and brushed her tongue over his. This was what she needed—Gio—mind, body, and soul.

He needed her in the same way. He showed his love by the way his arms tightened around her and the sweet sounds he didn't stop from rising in his throat.

She wasn't in this alone.

Chapter Thirty-Five

Three months later, Elizabeth Clemente lay in bed, watching her husband stroll about their bedroom, naked as a jaybird. The newly awakened sun cast eerie shadows about the room.

By her former standards, the hour was too early to rise, but she'd undergone vigorous training the past couple of months. Gio was teaching her about vineyard work. She was his partner in all things, he told her. He didn't wait long to show her the entire process of winemaking. He explained the procedures to her once, he reminded her, though he doubted she remembered since she was shamefully drunk.

He was a magnificent-looking man. Gio had long muscular legs and arms and a strong chest smooth enough to sleep upon throughout the night. And a backside she could look at for hours if he'd ever stay still long enough.

"Come back to bed, *Signore* Clemente." She threw off the cotton sheet covering her own naked body and patted the mattress beside her.

He turned to her, a broad smile lighting his face. "A very tempting offer, *Signora* Clemente, but we've work to do." He grabbed a dress out of the bureau and tossed it at her. "Up and at 'em, lazy bones." The gown missed the mark and dropped to the floor.

"I'm not lazy, *Signore*." She crawled, smooth as a

297

jungle cat, to the end of the bed. "Just aching for my husband." She smiled. From the looks of it, she'd set him aching as well.

He groaned and dropped his shirt to the wooden floor. "You're a wicked woman, Elizabeth Clemente."

He took two steps toward her when a loud crash sounded from the floor below. Adriana's voice followed. "Giovanni!" she called. "Elizabeth!"

Elizabeth lunged from the bed and fumbled for her robe on the floor and slipped it on.

Gio quickly dressed in a pair of pants and dashed from the room, shirtless. He descended the stairs two at a time, and she followed at his heels until they entered the kitchen.

With her heart pounding, Elizabeth stepped to Gio's side and saw the translucent form of his father, Paolo, standing at the window. His soul bordered this world and the next. "Gio." She looked up at her husband. "Your father."

****

"Yes," he murmured. "I see him."

Giovanni held tight to his wife's hand. His heart hammered his chest, but he only imagined what his mother felt. She leaned against the kitchen counter. A shattered clay bowl lay at her feet, and batter covered the front of her apron and dress.

"*Madre?*"

"I am fine, Giovanni."

Marco braced himself against the doorjamb of his bedroom, his eyes closed.

The door leading from the hall swung open, and Gio turned to see Vinny entering the kitchen. He glanced about the room, but nothing registered on his face. "*Zia*

Adriana, are you ill?" he asked.

"She's fine, Vinny. Elizabeth and I will help her," he said. "Please go."

His cousin nodded and left the room.

Gio faced the man at the window. "*Padre*?" His voice caught in his throat. "Have you come home?"

Paolo turned. By appearance, he was younger than Gio.

"Am I here to stay, do you mean?" He shook his head. "No, I am not. I came to say goodbye. To tell you I love you." He smiled at Elizabeth. "And to say how happy I am for the both of you. She is a precious *donna*, Giovanni. Cherish her always."

Gio swallowed. "I will." He wrapped his arm around Elizabeth's small waist.

Paolo crossed the floor to stand in front of his own wife. "Adriana, I am sorry I was not here for you during my life. Had I known, I would have come here to you. I wanted nothing more in all those years than to be with you." He lifted her hand to his lips and lingered there. "I love you, *Cara mia*. Please live your life and be happy, *si*?"

Tears welled in her eyes as she nodded. For a split second, Gio swore he saw his mother as a young woman. Beautiful, plaited waist-length hair. Vibrant in her youth, her face wore the longing of unadulterated love.

A lump rose in his throat, and he squeezed Elizabeth's hand, grateful for her strength. She squeezed back.

His father dropped his mother's hand, turned to leave, but stopped and rested his gaze on Marco. "And you, old man, thank you for watching over my *famiglia*. To you I owe so much."

Marco heaved a sigh and nodded. "You are welcome, Paolo. You are welcome."

His father—Paolo—bowed and faded away.

Gio tugged his wife to his bare chest and embraced her tightly. Kissing the crown of her head, he said, "Elizabeth."

She glanced up at him, her eyes swimming with tears. "Yes?"

He'd found a love like his parents once had—*still* had. "I want nothing more than to be with you, *Cara mia.*"

Smiling, she nodded and lifted on her toes to brush her lips across his. "Thank you," she whispered.

Holding hands, they walked to his mother and gathered her into their embrace.

Epilogue

Elizabeth sat in the parlor with her swollen ankles propped on the ottoman. Her gracious husband gave up his favorite chair to her. He now lay sprawled on the couch with their three-year-old son, Thomas, sleeping on his chest and five-year-old Bella sitting beside them on the floor.

Their new television stood against the wall, but no one watched the pictures flitting across the screen.

Gio nodded every so often in response to their daughter's constant questions. Her large brown eyes never left her father's face.

Lord, was Gio aware he promised to drive the girl to the ocean after the new baby was born?

With a sigh, Elizabeth rested her hands on her round belly. The child there finally slept. This one she feared was going to be tireless and stubborn like Gio.

The hardheaded man blossomed as a father. She was proud to give him the family he never knew he needed. Even now, Gio tousled Thomas's thick curls and planted a kiss on the boy's head.

Each day he worked hard to instill his knowledge and pride in the vineyard in both children. With Bella, though, Elizabeth didn't know how much the girl absorbed. When Bella wasn't talking, the child's mind was often somewhere else.

Gio locked gazes with Elizabeth and offered her a

lopsided grin. She smiled in return. She'd never realized how deep her love could go for the man, but her affection was boundless. She was happy and utterly normal. Since Paolo's visit, she'd tuned out the gift. Of course, the feelings lingered at times, a niggling distraction on the outskirts of her mind or a stiff chill climbing her spine, but that was all.

"Is it bedtime for little boys?" Adriana asked as she entered the room, wiping her hands on her apron. She lifted Thomas from Gio's chest.

The boy shifted in her arms. "Mommy," he moaned.

"Shhh," Adriana cooed. "It is *Nonna*. Should we go to bed?"

"A story, *Nonna*?"

"*Si, bambino*, a story," she answered and stopped by Elizabeth's chair for her to plant a kiss on his sweet head. Thomas nestled against Adriana as she carried him from the room.

"You look exhausted, *Cara*," Gio offered.

"I am." Elizabeth yawned but was content to stay where she was.

"I better put Bella to bed." He winked. "Then come back for you."

The man found her pregnant body very arousing, and she didn't mind at all.

Cool air suddenly wafted over her, and dull energy tickled her mind. Someone was trying to get in, but she clamped her mind tight.

Just as Gio was helping the little girl to her feet, the raven-haired Bella asked, "Who are you, please?"

"Do you like to hear yourself talk?" Gio teased. "You know who I am."

"No, Poppy, I was talking to that person there." She

302

pointed to the empty space by the stone fireplace.

Elizabeth's heart slammed into her chest, and the child in her womb stirred.

Bella inherited the gift.

As Elizabeth struggled to push herself up from the chair, Gio dropped to his knees beside the little girl. "Who do you see?" he whispered. "It's not a woman, is it?" Gio knew Elizabeth feared the woman from the road and would be the first thing she'd suspect.

"No, this is a man, Poppy. He says Mommy will not talk to him, but maybe I will."

Elizabeth reached Bella's side and grabbed her little hand. "Do you see others?" she asked, trying to calm her own breath.

Bella nodded.

"How long have you seen them?"

"Not long, Mommy." Her eyes grew wider.

"I'm sorry, baby, I don't mean to frighten you, but I need to know." She gathered her daughter snug against her hip. "I saw them, too, when I was little like you. Tell me, does a woman visit you?"

Bella nodded again. "Only by the road."

"Why didn't you tell me or Poppa, Sweetie?"

"She told me not to tell you, Mommy. She says she scared you once." She buried her forehead in Elizabeth's belly. "But she doesn't frighten me. She hides her face from me. And says she needs a friend 'cuz she's so lonely." Bella backpedaled and looked up. "Am I in trouble, Mommy?"

Elizabeth eyes sought Gio's. He rose and scooped Bella into his arms. "No, you aren't in trouble." He nuzzled her hair. "You need to tell your mommy and me when you have visits. Understand?"

She nodded.

Elizabeth sighed and caressed the girl's soft cheek. "We can talk more later, Sweetie. You should go to sleep now."

"How'd you like to sleep in Mommy and Daddy's bed tonight?" Gio swung her out of the room, pausing in the doorway. "Are you coming, *Cara*?"

"In a minute."

"Are you sure?" Gio asked, not bothering to mask the concern on his face.

"I'll be fine, Gio. I can feel he isn't a threat."

Elizabeth flexed her hands before rubbing the small of her back. Heaven help her, her baby girl had the gift. Before she'd be able teach Bella how to live with it, she needed to remember how to do so herself.

Turning to the fireplace, she closed her eyes and whispered, "Show me who you are."

A word about the author...

Minnesota-based author, Joie Lesin is a life-long fiction writer and the author of *The Passenger*. She has long been fascinated by anything otherworldly including ghosts. She loves to write a good ghost story—especially when it includes a touch of romance.

Originally from Massachusetts, at six years old, Joie moved to her mother's birthplace, Minnesota. By eight, Joie lost her New England accent, however, it's gradually returning as the years go by. She grew up in Minneapolis but now resides in St. Paul with her husband and their blended family—which includes a rambunctious grand-corgi.

Joie misses the ocean, but she often finds herself walking by one of Minnesota's many lakes and travels to one of the coasts as often as she can. In fact, she considers California her home away from home. When she's not writing, reading, or walking, you can find her listening to music. She absolutely loves music—especially live—and songs have sparked most of her story ideas.

Joie also loves connecting with readers. Visit her blog at jlesin.com/blog.

www.jlesin.com